Dave

Glad to know
we're all from
the same family.
Please enjoy this —

Cousin

Frank

A Birthday to Die For

Frank Atchley

A Birthday to Die For
Frank Atchley
Copyright © 2010
All Rights Reserved

This book is protected under copyright laws of the United States of America. No part of this book may be reproduced or transmitted in any form or by any means, electronic or mechanical, including photocopying, recording, or by an information storage or retrieval system, without permission from the author or publisher except for review purposes.

For information about the contents of this book, or permission for reproducing portions of this book, please contact the publisher at www.mysticpublishers.com or the author at [website/email].

Library of Congress Control Number: pending
ISBN: 978–1–934051–48–1

Published in the United States of America by:

Mystic Publishers

Henderson Nevada
www.mysticpublishers.com

Dedication

A Birthday to Die For is dedicated to the memory of Jerry Riggs, a man who lived by the Marine Corps ethics. His loyalty to our nation and his family was what guided him through his last days. He treated every person he met with kindness and respect. He treated people fairly and expected them to do the same with him. His pride in family was always apparent in the way he treated his wife Toby and the manner in which he spoke about the accomplishments of his sons. He was a man anyone would be proud to call a friend.

Acknowledgement

During my thirty–three years in law enforcement, I've had the occasion to investigate a wide variety of crimes. As a result I blended many of the different investigations together to create this fictional story. Along the way I've worked with and received the support of and encouragement from many of my friends, fellow officers, and family. I would like to thank each and every one of them for their help as the story progressed.

Delores Atchley, Frankie Masterjohn, Micky and Max Osborn, Barbara and George Pope, Robert and Robin La Moria, Joyce Reese, Janice and Larry Kent, John and Lorie Goldsmith, John Decker, Ron Ryals, Stephanie Knowles, Trishca Masterjohn, Tailor Masterjohn, Glenda and Robert Sandberg, Pat Mohon, and the Riggs family.

A special thanks to Carol (von Raesfeld) Zimmerman [The von Raesfeld Agency, Henderson, NV.] It was through her professionalism, dedication, and persistence in assisting me with my manuscript that this novel finally made it to print.

My appreciation for the guidance and sometimes critical comments offered by Carol Zimmerman, my family, friends, and fellow officers goes beyond any written or spoken word.

A Birthday to Die For

Chapter 1

"They're going to kill me!"

The terror in her patient's voice slammed Dr. Paula Mitchell back in her chair, her own breath wedged in her throat. She stared into the terrified eyes of Kae Carlson. For the first time since she'd been treating Kae, they were making real progress. The young woman was opening up to her.

Two weeks before, Kae had entered the office, obviously afraid of something, grabbing glances over her shoulder, her eyes darting around the room as if looking for a place to hide. Although it was cold and raining outside, she'd worn no coat. She was sopping wet, her clothes soaked through, exposing the outline of her bra, her nipples rigid against the fabric. She looked fragile standing there in the dim light of Paula's office, swiping errant strands of light brown hair out of her eyes with a trembling hand.

"Who's going to kill you?"

Poised on the edge of Paula's brown leather

couch, Kae's body was rigid. She nervously traced the inseam of her light blue jeans, but didn't respond to the question. Occasionally she'd glance in Paula's direction, then quickly return her gaze to the floor. It had become a routine. Kae had showed up for six sessions so far, but still hadn't offered any explanation for her fears. Paula felt no closer to having the answers.

"Kae, you know I can't help you unless you tell me what you're afraid of and why? Do you understand?" Despite her frustration, Paula tried to sound calm and reassuring.

Dr. Paula Mitchell, a clinical psychologist, specialized in patients with sleep disorders, some with violent or erratic behavior, but she'd never encountered a situation as perplexing as Kae's. All of her studies and research at the University of Washington as a post–grad before opening her own practice could not have prepared her for a case quite like this one.

During their first session, Kae withdrew into herself, then became silently aggressive, obviously suffering from a "Dissociative Identity Disorder," often referred to as "Multiple Personalities." She stopped talking in the first person. Thereafter, communication was conducted through different personalities, all of whom seemed to be in conflict with one another most of the time.

Suddenly, Kae's body started to shake. Tears streamed down her cheeks. She started to rise as if to leave, then fell back on the couch. She snatched up a pillow and buried her face in it,

A Birthday to Die For

sobbing and moaning.

Paula sat watching this emotional outburst, wondering how best to deal with it. She had witnessed similar displays with other patients and each time she'd sat silently waiting for it to subside. This time her first impulse was to wrap her arms around Kae and console her, but knew it could be counter–productive in their doctor–patient relationship. *She's trying to escape something which explains the multiple personalities, but why is she so convinced that someone is going to kill her?*

Paula poured a cup of tea and set it on the coffee table in front of Kae. Knowing Kae desperately needed comfort and stability in her life, she reached over and touched her shoulder. The crying stopped immediately. Kae lifted her face to meet Paula's gaze, but the expression was that of anger as the personality of Connie appeared. She seemed to be the primary spokesperson. "I told you, they're going to *kill* me!"

Paula blanched, but trying to keep the surprise out of her voice, repeated the question. "Who is going to kill you?"

"The Devil," Connie said, her tone matter–of–fact as she grabbed several tissues from the box sitting next to the untouched cup of tea and wiped her face. "That bitch can't even cry with style," she mumbled under her breath.

The off–handed use of an obscenity was a rare display of emotion from Kae. Paula knew she had to keep her talking. "Why the Devil?"

3

Connie glared at her as if she were completely stupid. "Because she didn't give him a baby."

Although puzzled, Paula felt she was onto something. This was the first time Kae had offered any information to explain her fears, even though it was through the personality of Connie.

"What do you mean, Connie? Tell me why you didn't give him a baby?" Paula had learned early in their first session that if one of the hidden personalities came forward, she had to acknowledge them by name. If she didn't, they'd all stop talking...deny that they even knew Kae and the opportunity to gain information would be lost.

"When I was thirteen, I was raped by a man who told me he was the High Priest for the Devil. He told me the Devil would protect me forever if I gave him a baby. He told me the Devil was my father."

"Did you believe him?" asked Paula, realizing the enormity of the abuse that Connie was suggesting.

"No, but he held me down and tore my clothes off. Other people helped him force my legs apart, then he laid on top of me and raped me."

Excitement raced through Paula's mind. *At last, some progress.* "You said others helped. What do you mean?"

"There were other people wearing red robes. They held my arms and legs while he raped me." Connie's answer had come slowly, as if she was re–living the horrible experience as she spoke.

A Birthday to Die For

"The man who raped you, was he also wearing a red robe?" Paula asked, wanting to learn as much as possible while Connie was willing to talk.

"Yes, but he didn't have any clothes on under the robe."

"Could you see his face or the faces of the other people?" Paula pressed on.

"No, they all were wearing hoods that covered their faces. I really couldn't see anything."

"While they were holding you down, did anything else happen?"

"They were all chanting and they poured red stuff all over me. I think it was blood."

"Did they ever tell you why they poured blood on you?"

"No!" Connie said. "I begged them to stop, but they kept doing it until they were through."

"What happened next, Connie?"

Kae's body stiffened, but Connie gained control again.

"They dried me off with a white towel, then they made me stand up and they put a long white robe on me."

"Then what happened?"

Connie cut her off. "I don't want to talk about it anymore!" She folded her arms across her chest and glared at the floor, pouting like a petulant child.

It was hard for Paula to believe what she'd just heard, yet a picture was forming in her mind about the horrors Kae had endured. A devil–

worshipping cult was something totally foreign to Paula. She'd grown up in a small town on the Oregon coast, never traveling far from home until she entered Oregon State University in Corvallis. Had she not chosen psychology as her major, she might never have imagined that something like this existed, much less that it might possibly be true. Other than a brief mention during a course on deviant behavior, she'd had no firsthand knowledge about devil worship or satanic rituals.

"You're doing good, Connie. Did anything else happen after the man raped you?"

Paula watched as Connie stood up, unbuttoned her blouse, then turned around to expose a large scar resembling a pentagram on her back. "He did this right after he raped me," she said.

Paula's skin prickled at the sight of it. *The depravity of one human inflicting such atrocities on another human is appalling.* "Why, Connie? Why would he do that to you?"

"He said it showed that I was a member of the family and under the protection of our father, the Devil," she explained. "He told me if I delivered a baby to the Father that I'd be protected for the rest of my life."

"Did you deliver a baby?" Paula asked, fearing what she might hear next. Just thinking about what degenerates like that might do to a baby aroused her own sense of anger.

"No. That's why they're going to kill me," Connie responded.

A Birthday to Die For

"Are they looking for you right now?"

"I don't know if they are at this very moment, but I know they plan to kill me on my twenty–sixth birthday. They poured blood on my car windshield and drew a pentagram in it, just like the one on my back. They wrote my birth date too. I've been getting phone calls. When I answer, you can tell that someone's there, but they don't say anything...and I think I'm being followed."

"How long have these things been happening?" Paula asked, trying to determine if these acts were significant or only a figment of Kae's imagination.

"The blood on my windshield with the pentagram and my birth date happened about six weeks ago. I know they'll do something else, but I don't know what or when," Connie said, a look of desperation masking her face.

"When's your birthday?" Paula asked.

"The twenty–second of May."

"That's only three weeks away," said Paula.

Kae grimaced. "Yes."

"What's the significance of the pentagram on your windshield?" Paula asked.

Kae shook her head sadly. "In my case, it's a warning. It was a circle around a five–pointed star pointing down."

"Before you came to me, did you tell anyone else about the blood and the drawings on your windshield?"

"No. I didn't think anyone would believe me."

"How about the phone calls and being followed?"

7

Paula asked, now beginning to understand Kae's fears.

"No. You're the first person I've told and I'm not sure you believe me."

Ignoring Kae's comment, Paula continued. "Tell me a little more about the person you think is following you."

"What do you mean?"

"What do they look like? What type of clothing were they wearing?"

"I think he's a white man, but I'm not sure. It looked like he had a full beard and mustache, but I couldn't really tell because he had on a dark–colored jacket with the collar pulled up around his neck … and he was wearing a hat."

"What else? What did the hat look like?"

"Everything he wore was dark–colored, even the hat. It was a knit hat, the kind that can be pulled down over your ears."

"Okay, Connie, that's good information, but what makes you think he's following you?"

"It was the way he kept looking at me. Every time I caught him looking, he would turn away and whenever I started to walk, he'd follow."

"Did he ever attempt to approach you or talk to you?"

"No! I escaped by going into a book store. I could see him waiting outside, so I stayed in the store until he left."

While Connie's answer was ambiguous at best, Paula chose to believe these acts were indeed warnings or reminders to Kae of the ritual

A Birthday to Die For

to be held on her birthday, when she was to be sacrificed to appease Satan.

"Connie, you said you were thirteen years old when this happened. How did you even get involved with the High Priest and the other people in the red robes?"

Connie's eyes flashed with anger. "My foster mother."

Paula immediately picked up on what sounded like hatred in Connie's voice. "What do you mean?"

"Rebecca Shelby—she's my foster mother. She knew one of the men in the red robes."

"The man you were told to go with, what did he look like?"

"I don't know. I never saw his face. He was wearing a red robe and sitting in a car. My foster mother told me to get into the car and do whatever the man told me to do. I never saw his face."

"Did your foster mother ever go to any of these meetings or rituals with you? Are you still in touch with her?"

Connie could no longer contain the hostility she felt towards her foster mother. "Hell no, the bitch is one of them. She's the reason this happened to me. I'm going to die because of her."

In disbelief, Paula weighed the chilling information she had just received with the question of what to do about it. If what Connie said was true, she would be killed in three weeks. *I've got to do something, but what?* She was ethically required to uphold the doctor–patient privilege and tell no one of the danger, but if she did that, Kae and her make–believe personalities would probably be killed. The realization that she could do nothing to prevent that from happening was overwhelming.

While Paula mulled over her options, Maxine, another of Kae's personalities, interrupted. "She's a liar!"

Paula immediately recognized Maxine's voice. "Hello Maxine. Why is she a liar?"

"Because there's no cult and she isn't going to die on her birthday."

Paula tried to relax. Such dramatic progress all at once had given her hope, but what if all these ramblings about cults were just that— incoherent nightmarish imaginings of a very disturbed mind trying to make sense of reality? "How do you know it isn't true?"

"I just know!"

Paula considered Maxine to be a troublemaker, but also a personality that could not be ignored. She watched as Maxine moved herself to the front edge of the couch trying to get face–to–face with her in order to dominate the conversation. The domination and control displayed by Maxine confused the issue at best, but by asking right questions, she could possibly offer some clarity about what she'd learned from Connie.

A moment earlier, Paula had come to the conclusion that she needed to get the police involved in order to prevent Kae's death, but Maxine's accusation renewed her doubt. The

A Birthday to Die For

revelation that Kae's foster mother was involved seemed unbelievable. *What if I'm wrong? What if it turns out there was no threat?* It would be a major embarrassment, but on the other hand, if the threat was real and she didn't bring the police in, Kae would die. *Patient confidentiality ... what can I do?*

"Maxine, I need to talk to Connie. Is that okay with you?" Paula asked, expecting a barrage of insults to be thrown at Connie, something Maxine seemed to enjoy doing. But she knew it was Connie who spoke for Kae and was the most reasonable personality to deal with.

"Sure you can, but you know she'll lie to you. She's weak. She'll tell you anything you want to hear. If you really want to know anything, I'm the one you should talk to," Maxine replied. The grin on her face carried a threat, as if she was trying to intimidate Paula.

"Connie, may I talk to you?" Paula asked, maintaining a soft tone and waiting for a response.

The delay was only a second, but for Paula it felt longer. She knew what she had to do, but patient confidentiality was something she didn't want to violate if there was any way to avoid it. She had to take the risk or lose the opportunity to help Kae, maybe to save her life.

"What do you want to talk to me about?" Connie asked.

"Connie, I need your help to decide what we should do to make sure nothing bad happens to you," said Paula, watching for a reaction.

Connie studied Paula's face for several seconds. "What do you want me to do? That's why I came to you—for help."

"I know you did, but what if I need someone else's help to make sure you're safe? Would it be okay if I asked someone I trust to help us?"

Connie seemed so innocent, yet her eyes were filled with sadness. "Are you sure you can trust them?" she asked, shrinking back into the couch again, clutching the pillow against her chest.

"Yes, I'm sure," Paula responded confidently, even though she knew it might be difficult to convince the police, but she had nowhere else to turn.

"Who is this person you trust?" Connie asked.

The moment of truth had arrived. *What if Connie rebels when I tell her I want to involve the police?* "It's a police officer. Someone who'll protect you and won't be afraid."

Paula held her breath as Connie sat perfectly still, her gaze locked on Paula eyes. She was prepared for the worst when Connie said, "If you're positive we can trust them, then it's okay with me."

The answer was a surprise. It felt like a tremendous weight had been lifted off her chest. The confidentiality issue was resolved and she could now move forward.

* * *

A Birthday to Die For

Paula waited for Kae to leave before calling the police. She picked up the phone and dialed 9–1–1, but hung up before the connection was completed. *They won't believe me. They'll think I'm some kind of professional nut case and I can't really blame them. I have a patient telling me a bizarre story, but she'll only talk to me through different personalities.*

Paula closed her eyes, resting her head against the back of the chair, feeling her fear for Kae's life increase with every passing minute. She knew she needed to involve the police, but what should she say or do to convince them that Kae's life was in jeopardy and she needed their protection? *Maybe the tape recordings of the sessions will convince them.* Today's session revealed enough to persuade them to help. She picked up the phone and dialed 9–1–1.

Chapter 2

Her shift was nearly over when the telephone rang on Sandra Reed's desk in the King County Sheriff's Department Communications Center. She picked it up, hoping the call didn't involve a crime in progress. She'd never make it to the day care center on time if the call kept her late. They'd called earlier to tell her that her two–year old had a fever, but they'd manage until time to pick up both kids. The last thing she needed tonight was overtime.

"King County Sheriff's Office. Is this an emergency?"

There was a momentary pause at the other end of the line as the caller took a deep breath. "Yes, it is. I am Dr. Paula Mitchell. I'm a clinical psychologist and I believe one of my patients is going to be killed."

The worry in Dr. Mitchell's voice got Sandra's attention. "When is this supposed to happen?"

"In three weeks."

Sandra blanched and stared at the phone.

Was this a prank call? "Why in three weeks?"

This was the question Paula dreaded most. The story she was about to tell was so far–fetched that even she had a hard time believing it might be true. *She's going to think I've gone off my rocker and hang up on me, but what else can I do?*

"Dr. Mitchell, are you still there?"

"Yes, sorry. What I'm about to tell you is going to sound weird, but please hear me out."

Sandra glanced at the wall clock. Only ten minutes to go before she was off duty, but the anxiety in the caller's voice convinced her that this matter was serious or she wouldn't have called in the first place. "Okay, Doctor, tell me your weird story. I can handle it."

It took Paula nearly fifteen minutes to tell Sandra why she believed Kae would be killed in three weeks. She described Kae's panic, the carvings on her back, the High Priest and his assistants all dressed in red, hooded robes, and the actions of the foster mother. When she'd finished, she held her breath, listening to the silence on the other end of the line, waiting for Sandra Reed to tell her she was crazy.

"I'm sorry, it's a lot of information to process, but from what you've told me, I'm convinced that there's a strong likelihood your patient's life may be in danger. I'm going to forward your call to Detective Jerry Riggs. Please tell him what you just told me. He should be able to help you. Good luck!"

Paula was surprised at how easy it seemed to

A Birthday to Die For

convince Sandra that she was not a prankster or a loon and that Kae really did need help. *If only it will be that easy to convince Detective Riggs.*

Jerry Riggs picked up the phone on the second ring. "Homicide, Riggs."

"Riggs, this is Sandra in the Communications Center. I'm transferring a call to you—Dr. Paula Mitchell. I believe what she told me. I told her you can help her."

Jerry cocked an eyebrow. "What's she going to tell me?"

"It's better that you hear it directly from her. It's hard to believe, but I think it's for real. Line four."

He punched the button. "This is Detective Riggs, how can I help you?"

"Detective, my name is Paula Mitchell. I'm a Clinical Psychologist. I have a patient by the name of Kae Carlson who came to my office about two months ago. She's twenty–five years old. She claims she was raped by a satanic priest when she was thirteen. Today, I discovered the reason why she came to see me. She claims she will be killed on her twenty–sixth birthday, which is three weeks away. I cannot save her on my own. I need your help."

A frown narrowed Riggs' vision. *This has to be a joke.* He glanced around the squad room. No one was paying the least bit of attention to him. *Okay, I'll play along, but paybacks are a bitch.* "Doctor, why don't you start from the beginning and tell me everything you can remember that makes you believe she's going to be killed."

"Okay, I'll do my best."

Riggs listened carefully as the doctor told a bizarre story of a thirteen year–old virgin impregnated by the High Priest of a satanic cult. The girl had had a miscarriage and failed to deliver a baby to be sacrificed to Satan. Her failure had placed her own life in jeopardy as she was now expected to take the place of her dead baby and be sacrificed on her twenty–sixth birthday to appease Satan.

The story was ridiculous, impossible to believe, especially when the doctor explained that the young woman suffered with multiple personalities, one of which had compelled her to see Dr. Mitchell.

"Connie speaks in the first person, as if everything that has happened to Kae happened to her. Maxine, the combative one, accuses Connie of lying and won't admit that Kae even exists. Then, as if two personalities aren't enough, there's a third—Cathleen, the protector and peacemaker."

Riggs interrupted. "Do you really believe what you've just told me?"

She was surprised by the interruption, but not the question. "Yes, I do."

Her tone of voice told Riggs that she was sincere in her belief that her patient had been raped, had had a miscarriage, and now her life is in danger. He could hear the plea for help, something he couldn't ignore.

A Birthday to Die For

"Dr. Mitchell, I must admit I'm not as convinced as you obviously are, but I'm going to honor your expertise in this matter and give you whatever help I can."

There was discernible relief in her voice. "Thank you, Detective. I really appreciate this. Where do we start?"

"Well, the first thing I'd like to do is watch the tape recordings of your sessions. I want to listen to what Kae Carlson has to say and see how she acts while saying it. Maybe I can see or hear something you don't. It may just convince me that her story is for real and give us a starting point."

"When would you like to do this?"

Riggs checked his calendar. "Tomorrow morning, nine a.m., your office—if that's convenient for you."

"That's perfect. I'm looking forward to meeting you face–to–face, Detective."

"Same here! I'll need any names you have regarding your patient—her family, friends, neighbors, work associates, as well as their addresses, phone numbers, dates of birth, and places of employment."

"I only have her address and phone number, but I'll try to get more information before you get here."

He hung up the phone, wondering what the hell he'd just gotten himself into. He'd never handled an investigation involving devil worshippers or anyone with multiple personalities. He knew he was probably crazy for getting involved, but this investigation would be challenging and certainly intriguing with its possibilities.

Chapter 3

The evening hour was still early when Riggs sat down to dinner with his family. He remained deep in thought, mulling over the information Dr. Mitchell had given him. As always, Toby and the boys, Todd, Shane, and Trent, sat there watching his every move, waiting for him to say something. They'd seen him like this before and knew it had something to do with one of his investigations.

Toby could only imagine the depth and seriousness of it. She wanted to ask questions, to be of some help to him, but he wouldn't hear of it. He'd explained the risks involved if he shared any information with her. "If I told you anything, you might become a witness, maybe have to testify in court and the bad guys will do anything to keep that from happening." She knew he was simply protecting her and the boys.

Several minutes passed before Riggs brought his attention back to his family and the meal Toby had prepared. "Sorry, I was thinking about a new case I'm working on," he said, embarrassed that they'd caught him again.

"We know, Dad," said Todd, the eldest.

"What kind of case is it, Dad?" asked Shane, knowing his dad always refused to discuss any of his cases.

"Shane, I know you want to know everything that's going on, but I won't discuss it now. I'll tell you all about it when it's over."

Riggs looked at his youngest son, Trent, waiting for his usual "But Dad" comment that didn't come. It must've been the way he looked at Trent that stopped further inquiry.

"Okay boys, finish your dinner and go do your homework," Toby instructed.

What little he knew about satanic cults was frightening. Not only were victims like Kae in jeopardy, but also anyone involved in the investigation of the cult and its activities, including him and his family as well. He'd been down this road before on other investigations, so he made it a rule to keep everything to himself.

He'd never forget the case involving a Mafia don who'd put a contract out on him. The threat was real and the risk to his family was obvious. Officers staked out his house to protect him, Toby, and the boys, but he said nothing to Toby until several months later.

"When I took this job, I knew there would be risks involved, but I promise I'll do whatever's necessary to protect you and the boys, even if it means keeping the facts of my investigations to myself."

A Birthday to Die For

Over the fifteen years they'd been married, Toby had developed a sixth sense about Jerry and she could always tell when something was bothering him. She knew he was serious about his work, but when it came to her husband, she knew what she had to do to help him keep things in perspective, which had earned her a reputation as a prankster.

Her pranks started shortly after they were married, when Jerry was in the Marine Corps, stationed at the Cherry Point Marine Base in North Carolina. She wrote him a love letter on a roll of toilet paper. He shared a good laugh with his comrades as he read it. His fellow Marines enjoyed her pranks almost as much as he did. They teased him unmercifully the time she wrote him a love letter on a paper plate, watching him turn it around and around to read what she'd written.

Not long after his promotion to Homicide Detective, he took her in his arms and kissed her. "Toby, I just want to say thank you for all the things you do for me. Because of you, I'm better able to handle stressful situations, which helps me more than you know. I love you!"

Toby could tell that Jerry was preoccupied with the new case he'd mentioned earlier and decided it was time to put her plan into action. She poured two glasses of wine and took them upstairs and set them on the nightstand. She tucked the boys into bed and called down to Jerry to kiss them goodnight, then she slipped into the bathroom to change into a sexy nightgown. When she emerged he was sitting on the bed. She stopped in the doorway and flicked the lights on and off to get his attention. Her maneuver produced the response she was hoping for when he turned and gave a low whistle. She gave him a suggestive, slow–eyed wink, knowing that the new investigation would be far from his thoughts tonight.

Chapter 4

The weather was cold and dreary when Riggs arrived at the office of Dr. Paula Mitchell half an hour early. She wasn't there yet, so he remained in his car, sipping hot coffee and remembering last night with Toby. While he waited he kept the engine running and the defroster on to keep the windows from steaming up so he could see the doctor when she arrived. The outside temperature was hovering just above freezing. Inside the car he could see his breath when he leaned his head against the cold glass away from the defroster.

He'd been waiting less than ten minutes when he saw a woman approaching his car. She was quite agile as she navigated around the patches of thin ice on the sidewalk. She wore a light–colored trench coat with its belt drawn tight, accentuating her slim figure. It was obvious that she took good care of herself. The turned–up collar and the way she carried her umbrella hinted that she was a professional. As he peered at her through his windshield, he surmised she was about five feet four inches tall, maybe one hundred and twenty pounds at the most. She walked with purpose—back straight, head up, and eyes forward. There was no doubt in his mind that this woman possessed a lot of self–confidence.

She leaned over and asked through the open window, "Are you Detective Riggs?"

"Yes, I am. You're Dr. Mitchell?"

"One and the same. Come inside. I'll make a pot of coffee and we can get down to business."

"Sounds good to me, Doc."

He followed her inside, stopping in the small reception area as she disappeared around a corner. Paula wasn't used to being referred to as "Doc," but she didn't feel insulted by the way Riggs said it. In fact, she felt the tone was friendly. He was clean–shaven with neatly trimmed hair. She guessed that he was about 5'11" with a muscular build. He wore a wedding band on his left hand.

Judging from their conversation the previous evening, she believed Riggs to be a man of sincere beliefs, who took great pride in doing his job well. Although he had a friendly manner, her first impression was that he was not someone to challenge or to flee from. There was no doubt in her mind he was a man used to being in charge and not afraid to use whatever means available to accomplish his goals.

"The coffee's on," she said, hanging her coat in a small closet. "We can start in my office while it's perking, if that's okay with you, Detective?"

"That's fine with me. I had a cup while I was

A Birthday to Die For

waiting for you. By the way, you can call me Jerry. It sounds like we're going to be working together on what might be a pretty intense investigation, so let's not be so formal."

She grinned. "Okay, Jerry...and you can call me Paula."

"Doc sounds good to me," he replied with a twinkle in his eye. They both knew he'd continue to call her Doc whether they worked together or not.

"Doc, how much do you know about devil worship and satanic cults?"

Her brow furrowed. "Not much, to tell you the truth. I've attended lectures and, of course, read some books on the subject. Academically, the subject has been covered extensively, but not so much so scientifically. From what I've learned, they are extremely dangerous and will do just about anything to protect their anonymity."

"It's about the same with me. I've read a little about cults, but other than that, I really don't know anything about them. When you think of something like devil worship, you hope it isn't true, but deep down you know it is, don't you?" Riggs said, watching Paula's face for a reaction.

Paula nodded, "Unfortunately, I have a feeling that what Kae has told me is the absolute truth. Where would you like to start? I can give you a few more details."

"I'd like to look at the videotapes of your sessions with Kae first, then I want to do a little research on cults and compare what we see and hear in the videos with what my research reveals."

"It sounds like you have a plan," she said. "Kae signed all the releases via the personality of Connie, so there's no violation of doctor–patient confidentiality—unless it goes further than your office."

Jerry smiled. "Not really, let's just say we're collecting information so we can develop a plan."

The videos were stored individually in paper envelopes with Kae Carlson's name printed on the outside, along with the date and time of each session. Riggs started with the very first video, watching it from beginning to end with Doctor Mitchell watching him for any reaction or question he might have.

The first video showed Kae as she was seated on the brown leather couch positioned against the west wall. Dr. Mitchell was seated in a high–back leather chair of the same color as the couch, about five feet from Kae. Kae was dressed in a light blue jogging outfit and sat with her legs folded under her. She held a large blue–colored stuffed pillow close to her chest as she talked to the doctor. While Kae talked, Dr. Mitchell made notes on a pad she either held in her hands or had laying on the small table near the right side of her chair.

Kae's voice would change as she talked which caused Dr. Mitchell to ask to whom she was now speaking. The first change in Kae's voice was that of a personality called Connie. While the session

A Birthday to Die For

continued, Kae's voice changed two more times, revealing the additional personalities of Maxine and Cathleen.

"Well, Doc, that was sure confusing," Riggs said as the first tape rewound. "How do you know it's not just an act? The only thing I got out of this video is the possibility that Kae has multiple personalities. Until now, this is something I've only read about in paperback novels and seen in the movies. However, I'm not convinced that this isn't just an act. Maybe after I see the rest of the videos, I'll have a different opinion."

"Jerry, I can understand your skepticism, but please wait until you've seen all the videos before coming to any conclusion."

"Okay, bring on the second tape and another cup of coffee, please. You wouldn't have a stray donut lying around anywhere, would you?"

"Never touch the foul things," she replied with a smirk. "How about a granola bar?"

"I'll pass."

Riggs watched the second through the sixth videos seeing nothing new which sparked his interest or caused him to believe he was seeing anything but an act on the part of Kae. It wasn't until the seventh and final tape he started to feel there might be some validity to what Kae was claiming. The stiff body, rigid jaw line, angry eyes, and the hostility in her voice towards the foster mother was the type of body language he looked for in persons he interviewed. The body language oftentimes reveals more than the spoken word.

"Doc, this last video is convincing. I believe there's some merit to what Kae has told you. I'd like to interview Kae myself, if it's alright with you." The information revealed in the last session about the guy with the knit hat had piqued his curiosity. He wondered what else could be pulled from Kae's memory through that of her other personalities.

Paula sat silently for a few minutes while Riggs waited for a response. In her mind she was trying to identify the risks which may be involved with Riggs going face to face with Kae. She also considered what would happen if Kae didn't react well to Riggs and his skeptical attitude. It might do more damage than help; however, she also realized there was no other way to protect Kae's life.

"Okay, but only if I'm present and Kae agrees to it."

"I don't have a problem with that. In fact, you might have to give me some guidance during the interview. Remember, I've never interviewed anyone with multiple personalities before and I won't recognize which voice belongs to which personality."

Paula smiled at the false doubt. "When do you want to interview Kae?"

"Can you have her here tomorrow, let's say, thirteen hundred hours?"

It took her a minute to catch on. "If you mean one in the afternoon, yes I can. I'll give her a call and ask her to cut class tomorrow—that is,

A Birthday to Die For

if she's going to class. She's attending Seattle Community College on a grant that covers her living expenses as well."

"How can she go to college with multiple personalities?" Riggs asked.

"Well, that's part of the problem. She hasn't been going to classes on a regular basis and her grant is in jeopardy unless we get her emotional problems resolved—or at least under control."

"Good luck, Doc, you're going to need it. I'll see you at one tomorrow," he said, already looking forward to the challenge he'd face in the interview of Kae and her personalities.

"What are you going to do between now and one tomorrow?" she inquired.

"I'm going to do the research I told you about. I need to know a little more about cults, satanic rituals, and devil worshipping in general before I talk to Kae. Also, I'd like to know—have you ever done any profiling?"

"What do you mean?"

"Doc, it would be nice to have some understanding as to the type of people drawn into satanic worship. What's their background? What are they seeking? If we had this understanding, it just might be of help in this investigation."

"I understand your reasoning. I'll do some research and see if I can come up with a profile you can work with. See you tomorrow."

As Riggs headed for his car, he thought about where to start. Having Dr. Mitchell do some

31

profiling would make her feel like an active member of the investigation and encourage her participation as needed. He remembered reading something about a church in Los Angeles being broken into and a ritual involving a possible sacrifice. *What was the sacrifice?* He couldn't remember. It had been a long time since he'd read about it, but maybe it would be good place to start his research. LAPD saw every crazy in the book, so why not this? This would match anything LAPD had, with some left over.

Chapter 5

First stop was the library. Riggs knew he'd call the Los Angeles Police Department as soon as he reached his office, but he wondered if anyone there would remember the incident he had read about. It had been years since he'd read the article and with the turnover in officers, both on patrol and in the detectives, the odds were against him finding anyone with first–hand knowledge about the church incident.

The reference cards in the library showed a number of books and articles on satanic cults, rituals, and devil worship. One reference card in particular was important. It had the name of Detective Al Turner of the Los Angeles Police Department. It identified Turner as a recognized expert on cults and as a detective who had given expert testimony on the subject in court. Riggs jotted Turner's name down and headed for the office. Turner was the person he wanted to talk to. If Turner was still with LAPD, he was the one person who could give him a fast education on cults. He might also offer some ideas which could help expedite the investigation.

When Riggs telephoned LAPD, he quickly learned Turner was still with the Department and assigned to a Special Investigations Unit. At his request, he was transferred to Turner's extension.

"Special Investigations, Detective Turner."

"Detective Turner, this is Detective Riggs with the King County Sheriff's Department in Seattle, Washington."

"Hello Riggs, how can I help you?"

"Well, I'm handling an investigation where a woman claims she was impregnated by the High Priest of a devil–worshipping cult. Since she failed to deliver a baby to be sacrificed, she is to be killed or sacrificed on her twenty–sixth birthday. I've never been involved in an investigation of this nature, so I need a little help understanding if what I'm being told could be true and if so, what do I need to be on the lookout for."

"Let me guess, Riggs, she was impregnated on her thirteenth birthday."

Riggs' feet dropped to the floor at the confirmation of Kae's story. "That's what she claims."

"The information you're getting is consistent with what I know about cults and their rituals; however, I've found each cult I've investigated followed its own philosophy. Just because they're identified as satanic or devil worshippers doesn't

A Birthday to Die For

mean they practice their beliefs or perform their rituals the same way. I do believe from what you've been told, your victim is indeed in danger."

Surprised and a little excited, Riggs asked, "Since I know nothing about cults or what to expect, can you tell me a little more about them?"

"I can do that. First, let's start with the word "occult." The word came from the Latin word "occultist," which means "hidden." Satanism is represented by two separate groups, secular and traditional Satanists. They believe Satan is Lucifer, a high–ranking angel who wanted to be exalted to the same position as God. It was because of this sin that Lucifer fell and became Satan, the Devil, leading a large number of rebellious angels who became demons or fallen angels.

Satanism is practiced through two rituals. One is defined as psychological, sexual, or physical assault on an unwilling human victim. It is committed by one or more people whose primary motive is to fulfill a prescribed ritual in order to achieve a specific goal to satisfy the perceived needs of their deity.

The second ritual is a need to gratify the needs of the Christian Devil. It involves a highly organized, secret, often multi–generational group which engages in mutilation, ritual killing, cannibalism, drinking blood, and other disgusting things."

Riggs sat in stunned silence.

"Did you get all that, Riggs?"

"Yeah." He was overwhelmed with the information. He was impressed with Turner's knowledge, realizing he didn't learn all that overnight. The history on cults and Satanism was more than interesting—it gave him further reason to believe what Kae had told Dr. Mitchell was true.

"Yes, I got it. Thanks for all the information. I'm still wondering how the hell these people get away with it. Isn't there a record of the birth or death of the person being sacrificed? How do they discard the bodies of their victims? Where do they conduct their rituals? Why don't we hear more about these sick bastards?"

"Good questions. First, you must understand these cults are extremely secretive. Their membership is made up of people from every walk of life—doctors, lawyers, teachers, judges, military personnel, police officers, and just about anyone else who may come to mind. The secrecy is protected by the members. A doctor will deliver a baby for the purpose of sacrifice, after which a mortician will dispose of the body through cremation. There is no paper trail showing the baby ever existed, which more or less explains how they get away with it."

"How did you get involved in these types of investigations?" Riggs asked, amazed at the knowledge Turner had already shared with him.

"It started with a sacrifice in a church some years ago. I was a beat cop and responded to a

A Birthday to Die For

burglary at the church. When I got there, people dressed in red robes were running in every direction. I didn't have a back–up and I was unable to catch or arrest anyone. I secured the scene and detectives responded and processed the scene for evidence. In the end, the detectives found no fingerprints of any value and to this day the case is still unsolved. The one thing they did find that got our interest was the altar set up and the presence of blood, which tested to be human."

While Riggs digested the information, he asked, "I read an article a few years back regarding a church burglary and the evidence of an occult ritual. Is that the one you're talking about?"

"That's the one. The Department decided to create a special investigations unit to investigate cults because members in the top brass thought this was a bigger problem than first believed. Turns out they were right. I've been involved in hundreds of cult investigations with several successes, as well as some that weren't so successful. The one thing I've learned, Riggs, and something you need to be aware of, is these devil worshippers are very dangerous. They will kill you and anyone else they think has knowledge of them or if you're getting too close."

A chill of something unexpected raced down Riggs' spine as Turner described the risk associated with the unveiling of a cult and its members. "What can you tell me about their rituals, like when and where they hold them?"

37

"They will sometimes use a house or church, but most of the time they'll find an isolated place in the desert or in your case up north, the forest."

"How do you find these ritual sites?"

"Generally, you don't. Someone might stumble onto a site while hiking or hunting, but if that doesn't happen, you'll need someone who knows where it is and will guide you to it. Also, they often change the locations to avoid detection."

"Riggs, there's one more thing you need to know about ritual sites. When a ritual is being held, there will be an outer and an inner perimeter with armed guards at each. The guard on the outer perimeter will warn the inner perimeter guard if an intruder approaches. The inner guard alerts the worshippers who hide or flee. If the intruder gets too close, the inner guard will kill them."

"Damn! I sure wouldn't want to be some poor son–of–a–bitch who just happens to wander into the area where these assholes are doing their mumbo–jumbo routine."

"You got that right. You've got a tough investigation ahead of you. You'll need to pay attention to animal mutilations, church break–ins, and anything else suspicious in nature around a church. You should probably respond to the scene of any animal mutilation or church break–in because you just might discover a clue that will be of some help. I'd also recommend you give George Douglas a call. He's a psychologist who has counseled women associated with cults

A Birthday to Die For

in numerous jurisdictions. He's located in San Bernardino, California. You can get hold of him through the San Bernardino County Sheriff's Department. I can't think of anything else to tell you at the moment. If you have any more questions, give me a call. I'll be glad to help any way I can."

"I can understand the need to pay attention to what's happening at the churches, but why the animal mutilations?" Riggs asked, looking for some clarification.

"George Douglas will do a better job of explaining it than I can, but it has to do with whatever ritual they're conducting. Both satanic worshippers and believers in witchcraft use animal organs for their rituals."

"Turner, thanks for the information, but if you don't mind, I have one more question."

"What is it?"

"During the last session with the psychologist, my victim revealed that she believed she was being followed. What's the likelihood the cult would put a tail on her?"

"Based on what you've already told me, I believe the sacrificial date is getting close enough that there's a strong likelihood they'd put a tail on her. They'll probably abduct her at the appropriate time. I'd consider putting your victim into protective custody."

"Thanks for the information and advice. You've been a lot of help. I'll let you know how things go and I'll give you a call if I have any more questions," Riggs said, knowing it would be nearly impossible to convince the brass to spend department money on protective custody, but another thought popped into his mind that just might accomplish the same thing.

Riggs leaned back in his chair and propped his feet on the front edge of his desk, staring at the ceiling. The information he'd received from Turner was enlightening, giving him a better understanding as to how the devil worshippers operate, but would it help him protect Kae?

While still somewhat ambivalent regarding the existence of a satanic cult, what Turner had told him was undeniable. Satanic cults do exist and Kae's life was in jeopardy. Maybe it was time to put a tail on the tail. He needed to find out if there's really a man with a knit hat and if so, if he's a member of the cult.

Recognizing the probability that a satanic cult is the root of Kae's fears and accusations, Riggs pondered the investigative trails he'd need to follow, trails that would confirm Kae's story and identify the members of the satanic brotherhood responsible for the threats against her life. The way he saw it at this time, identification of the cult members would be the only way to save Kae's life. *If what she claims is true, the man in the knit hat may just have the answers. This is going to take time and help.* He opened a new file folder and started filling out the forms. It was time to let the sergeant in on what he was investigating.

First, he'd have to convince Sgt. Ashley of the

A Birthday to Die For

threat to Kae's life. He might have a hard time believing a satanic cult actually exists and why they hadn't been discovered before this.

On his way to Sgt. Ashley's office, Riggs spotted Sgt. Mary Francis coming out of her office. The sight of her immediately brought to mind his idea of putting a tail on Kae and maybe capturing the guy in the knit hat. She was in charge of the undercover narcotic detectives and who better to do the tailing than her detectives?

"Sgt. Francis, can I have a minute? I need to talk to you," Riggs called down the hallway.

"Riggs, what can I do for you?"

"It's like this, I need some surveillance help. I need someone who can blend into the college crowd. Can you help me?"

"Tell me what it's about and then I'll let you know."

"Well, it's like this. I have a young woman who is scheduled to die at the hands of a satanic cult. She has described a male individual wearing dark clothing and a knit type hat who she believes is following her when she leaves her home and goes to school. I believe if we put a tail on her, we just might catch the guy in the knit hat and identify the cult members. I'd like to use whoever you can give me to tail her and I'd like no one other than myself, you, and your detectives to know about this. What do you think?" Riggs asked.

Sgt. Francis looked at him with wide–open eyes that reflected disbelief at what she was hearing. "Are you kidding me?"

"No, Sarge, I'm deadly serious," answered Riggs.

"How long will you keep the tail on her?" she asked, rolling over in her mind which detectives she could spare for this assignment.

"The way I see it, I'll keep the tail on her until we either catch the guy in the knit hat or the scheduled time for her sacrifice has passed, which is only a couple of weeks from now."

"What if your guy in the knit hat turns out to be nothing more than a stalker with no connections to a satanic cult?" Francis asked.

"It may be a long shot, but right now I've nothing more to work with; but if I'm right, we'll save a young woman's life."

"Why not use someone in the homicide unit?"

"What I've learned so far about satanic cults leads me to consider the possibility that they already know I'm conducting this investigation. If so, they may also know who I am and the other members of the homicide unit, which would burn us before we even get started," Riggs explained, hoping Sgt. Francis was buying into his suggested need for help.

"You present a good argument. I'm willing to go along with it for a few days, but if I get backlogged on my unit's investigations, I'll pull my people back. Is that understood?"

"I understand. I appreciate any help you can give me. So which detectives are you going to assign so I can brief them?"

"Do you know Mike Hatch? Everyone calls

A Birthday to Die For

him 'Mad Dog.' Also, John Decker, who goes by the nickname, 'Squirrelly John.' " Francis had a broad smile on her face.

"I've seen them, but don't really know them."

"Believe me, you'll get to know them. I'll have them meet up with you for their briefing."

"Thanks, Sarge, I'll keep you briefed on what's going on," Riggs said, turning towards Sgt. Ashley's office.

Sergeant Dale Ashley was seated behind his desk when Riggs knocked on the door. Hearing the knock, Ashley glanced up and motioned Riggs towards the chair beside his desk.

"What's up, Riggs?" he asked.

"Sergeant, I need to let you know I've been working on a case I took over the telephone a few days ago. It involves a victim by the name of Kae Carlson."

Ashley quietly listened to Riggs describe the peculiar circumstances in his investigation, then asked, "Do you really believe this is true?"

"Yes, I do," Riggs replied, seeing the look on the Sergeant's face and feeling his request for future help might be in vain.

"Riggs, I've known about this case since the day you took the call. I've been waiting for you to own up to taking it in the first place and wondering if you'd closed it yet. This case sounds like so much bullshit that I'm surprised you even considered it," he admonished, obviously surprised that Riggs hadn't come to him sooner.

43

"Sarge, I apologize for not bringing it to your attention before now, but I needed some convincing one way or another before jumping into the investigation. I now believe there may be something to it. I've talked to the doctor, who has convinced me there's a strong possibility her patient is telling the truth and her patient's life is in jeopardy. I've talked to Detective Al Turner with LAPD, who is considered to be an expert in the investigation of Satanism and the weird bastards that partake in its practice. He confirms the existence of these cults and tells me the story relayed to me via the doctor is consistent with investigations he's handled. I believe we need to follow up on this and do everything we can to identify the cult members and save a life. This may all be bullshit, but then again, it may not."

"Okay, Riggs. I can't believe I'm doing this, but I'm going to keep you on this case. Keep me apprised and don't take forever closing this one."

"Thanks Sarge! One more thing…I may need some help. Time is running out. I've only got a few days before this gal's birthday when she's to be sacrificed. I also may need to put her into protective custody."

"Fat chance on the protective custody. No one but you believes this is for real and the brass isn't going to cough up any money to put her in a safe house."

"No harm in asking, just in case. Also, how did you find out I was already working this case?"

Ashley propped his feet on the desk. A smile

A Birthday to Die For

spread across his face. "I know everything and that's all you need to know."

"Okay, Sarge! How about some help, if I need it?"

"Who do you want?" Ashley asked, shaking his head back and forth, still amused with himself.

"La Moria. He and I work well together and he's got the kind of imagination needed for this investigation."

"If he can put his cases on hold for awhile, it's okay with me," said Ashley, wondering if this was all a waste of time.

"I'll ask him," said Riggs. He walked out the door feeling he'd just pulled off a major coup.

Chapter 6

The day was half gone by the time Riggs pulled into a parking spot in front of Dr. Mitchell's office. It had started out like most days in the Seattle area—wet and the forecast indicated that it wasn't going to change any time soon.

Riggs had a funny feeling in the pit of his stomach as he sat in his car going what approach to take when interviewing Kae Carlson. He'd interviewed hundreds of people during his career, but this was the first time he'd interviewed someone with multiple personalities. He knew he needed more information to help substantiate Kae's story and give him some leads to follow. He even thought maybe a medical examination would be in order to confirm whether or not she'd really been pregnant and miscarried; however, he was certain an examination at this juncture would not be approved by Dr. Mitchell. The risk of further psychological damage would be too high for her patient. Question after question popped into his mind, questions to which he needed answers. He still carried doubts. He needed to be completely convinced that Kae's story was true. He needed to believe there was a reasonable chance he'd be able to protect her.

The cell phone attached to his belt rang just as he was getting out of his car and heading to the front door of Dr. Mitchell's office. "This is Riggs. How can I help you?"

"Riggs, this is Hatch. I understand Decker and I will be doing some surveillance of a chick you think is going to get sacrificed to the devil, is that correct?"

"Yes, it is. Are you alone or is Decker with you?"

"He's here and we're alone."

"Put your phone on speaker and I'll talk to you both at the same time."

"Done, so what do you want us to do?"

"Sgt. Francis has told you why I need your help. I want you to tail a woman and try to capture a guy who's been following her. The only description I can give you is that the guy wears dark clothing, a knit–type hat that can be pulled down over his face, and he may have a beard and mustache. The woman is Kae Carlson. You can start your tail of her at Dr. Paula Mitchell's office up by Seattle University. I'm currently parked in front of the doctor's office where I'm about to go in and interview Kae. You can set up on her as soon as she leaves, in a couple of hours. Any questions?"

"Riggs, this is Decker. Do we know the race of

A Birthday to Die For

the guy in the knit hat?"

"No, we don't. Kae thinks he's white, but she isn't sure."

"What about a car? Does Kae have a car or has the guy with the knit hat been seen in or near a car?" Hatch asked.

"We have no information regarding a car associated with the guy with the knit hat. Kae did have a car, but got rid of it after someone left a message written in blood on the windshield. She now walks or takes a taxi wherever she's going," explained Riggs.

"Okay, Riggs. Decker and I will post ourselves somewhere outside the doctor's office and see where Kae leads us when she comes out. We'll let you know as soon as we learn anything or we put the arm on the suspect."

"Thanks, I'll have my cell phone with me all the time until I hear from you," said Riggs, hoping their assistance would pay off.

When Riggs walked into the doctor's office, he was met almost immediately by Paula. He could see the worry in her eyes as they greeted each other and shook hands. He knew she was torn between protecting the doctor–patient privilege and doing what she knew needed to be done to protect Kae's life. He tried to reassure her that everything would be okay, that he'd be cautious and gentle in his interview of Kae. He held her hand as he assured her, "I'll try not to frighten her during the interview, but I really need her to give me enough information to work with."

"I know you will. I know you need a lot more information than we have right now, but you know my concerns," she said, turning on the video recorder with the remote laying on the table beside her.

Riggs nodded his agreement. "I do and I'll keep them in mind."

The room was the same as in the videos he'd watched. Kae was seated on the couch only this time she was wearing a yellow pantsuit with a white belt and white shoes. She looked frightened, like she was ready to bolt at the least provocation. Her eyes seemed larger than shown in the videos as she followed his every move. She had the appearance of a scared or abused animal that had to be approached in a slow and non–threatening manner in order to get close. He decided to stay on the opposite side of the room when Dr. Mitchell introduced him. He began to talk in a low, unassuming voice, telling her that he was there to help Dr. Mitchell protect her. As he talked, she listened. Soon he could see the fear in her face start to ebb and the tension disappear.

While Riggs talked to Kae, he wondered if and when one of the other personalities would appear. The wait wasn't long. A scream shattered the calm. An eerie silence settled over the room as the hair on the back of his neck stood at attention. Since Kae hadn't spoken earlier and he'd never

A Birthday to Die For

heard her voice, he wasn't sure whether it was Kae or a different personality he was hearing. He looked over his shoulder at Paula. She whispered, "Maxine."

Riggs took his time settling in a chair in front of the couch. The added minutes gave him time to steady his voice. "Hello, Maxine. I'm Detective Riggs."

"I know who you are," Maxine answered, hostility oozing out with each word.

"Maxine, are you talking for Kae?" Riggs asked.

The girl shifted on the sofa. "Kae who? I don't know any Kae."

"Well, if you're not talking for Kae, who are you talking for...yourself?"

"I'm talking for myself. That damn Connie is always telling lies. Isn't that why you're here?"

"I don't know, is it?" Riggs asked, trying to reconcile the fact that Maxine was not Kae, but a figment of her imagination, someone she'd created to hide behind.

"Didn't Connie tell you she was going to be killed?" Maxine asked in an angry voice.

"Is she?" Riggs asked, trying to get direct answers to his questions.

"No."

"Maxine, how do you know Connie isn't going to be killed?"

"They told me," she said, avoiding Riggs' gaze.

He studied her face and body language. "Who

51

told you?"

"The people in the red robes."

"When did they tell you this, Maxine?"

Her eyes shifted back and forth. "Some time ago."

Paula remained silent as she watched Riggs pull information from Maxine. He spoke in a calm voice, asking direct questions that required direct answers. Each question seemed to set up the next, as if he knew what the answers were going to be before the question was even asked. She was amazed at his ability to keep Maxine talking. His method or technique for interviewing was far different than her own, but very effective. Where she tried to be calm and soothing with her technique, he was gentle, but aggressive. He had told her he needed information and he was clearly going after it.

"Maxine, did they tell you that more than once?"

She looked directly into Riggs' eyes, leaning towards him. "Yes." Her body language was somewhat of a surprise to Riggs. The movement displayed sincerity and truthfulness, which he found encouraging.

"How many times?"

Her fingers fluttered as she said, "I can't remember, but I know it was more than once."

"Well, was it more than twice?" he asked, trying to pin her down.

"Yes, at least five times, maybe more."

Riggs didn't know why the number of times

A Birthday to Die For

seemed so important, but he felt he needed to know, perhaps because the whole story was so far–fetched that he needed some specifics to make it feel real.

"Where were you when they told you?"

The answer was a little slower in coming this time. She was silent, looking away from him. "Different places."

Again, it was the specifics he was looking for and in this case, information that would lead him to a crime scene. "How many different places?"

"At least three," she answered without hesitation.

Riggs could feel his investigative juices flowing. "Do you remember what roads or highways you used to get to these places?"

"I remember we used Interstate 5 each time," she replied.

"Did you go the same direction each time?" Riggs asked, trying to fill in the blanks.

As she followed the progress of the interview, Paula started to feel the excitement building inside her as Maxine revealed more and more information that would help Riggs. The more she watched him, the more impressed she was with his skills. *He's already gotten more information out of Maxine than I did in seven previous sessions.*

"No, we went in both directions on Interstate 5," Maxine said, any hesitation now gone.

Riggs felt he was onto something with this line of questioning. *If only she could remember how to get to the ritual sites. Did she visit these*

53

sites enough times to remember? He thought back on what Detective Turner had told him about the difficulty of finding the ritual sites without a guide.

"Do you remember how many times you visited each ceremonial site?" he asked, Maxine's lack of hesitation and apparent sincerity encouraging him to press on.

"Maybe ten or twelve times over a year's time," she said.

Surprised at the answer and the frequency of the rituals, Riggs asked, "How many years are we talking about?"

"Maybe three or four," Maxine answered, glancing at Dr. Mitchell.

"Where would you start from?" Riggs asked.

"My home."

"Is this the same home where Connie, Cathleen, and Kae live?"

"Kae doesn't live there, but that lying bitch Connie lives there. So does little Miss Goody–Goody Cathleen," Maxine answered, resuming her hostile attitude.

"Maxine, do you remember how to get to the places they took you?" he asked, ignoring the hostility.

A frown appeared on her face. "I don't know, maybe."

Riggs picked up on the vagueness of her response. "Do you know the names of any of the people wearing the red robes?"

Almost sarcastically, Maxine said, "No, I

A Birthday to Die For

never got a good look at their faces."

"Maxine, is it okay if I talk to Connie?"

"I suppose so, but you know she's going to lie to you."

"Why would Connie lie to me?" Riggs asked.

"Because she's weak. She's afraid of everything."

"Is that why you don't like Connie?"

"Yes, she's such a baby."

"Okay, I understand. Maxine, can I talk to Connie now?"

She heaved a sigh. "Yeah, go ahead."

The information Maxine offered created excitement in Riggs. One of the things he liked most about being a detective was the pursuit and he was starting to feel he had the scent. Maxine had revealed the possibility that either she or one of Kae's other personalities might be able to lead him to one or more of the ritual sites. Whether or not she'd intended to, Maxine had given credibility to the story he'd been told. Now he faced the immediate challenge of getting Connie to come forward and talk to him.

"Connie, I'm Detective Riggs. I'd like to talk to you."

Riggs waited for a response from Connie, but received none. He looked at Paula, shrugging to signal that he didn't know what to do next.

"Connie, please talk to Detective Riggs. He wants to help and protect you. It will be okay to talk to him. I'll be right here the whole time."

"Connie, can you tell me why you're afraid?"

he asked.

Riggs nearly jumped out of his chair, surprised with the change in voice as Connie began to speak. It was almost like he was talking to a different person. Connie's manner of speech was much softer than Maxine's. It was like Kae's body was inhabited by strangers. The movie "The Exorcist" came to mind as he witnessed the change from Maxine to Connie. These personalities weren't evil spirits like those depicted in the movie, but they sure as hell inhabited and controlled her body. An eerie feeling settled over him.

"Because they're going to kill me on my birthday," she murmured with obvious fear in her voice, the same fear Riggs had seen in the videos.

"Why your birthday?"

"When I was thirteen, I didn't deliver a baby for them to sacrifice. They told me I'd be sacrificed in place of my baby when I turned twenty–six."

"Why didn't you deliver a baby?"

Her head dropped forward and her voice quivered. "I had a miscarriage."

Her voice and body language told him she was about to bolt, a complication he couldn't afford. As much as he felt the need to console her, the risk that she might flee forced him to restrain himself. *What's my approach now? I must calm her and give her a reason to keep talking. Back off, give her a little time to relax.*

Minutes passed. No one spoke as he watched the rigidity in Kae's body disappear and her gaze

A Birthday to Die For

return to him. He gave her small smile. "Connie, do you really believe you're going to be killed on your birthday?"

"Yes, I do. They told me it was a calling—my divine obligation...and it had happened to others in the past."

"Who told you this?"

"The men and women wearing the red robes."

Trying to identify a specific place or locale, he asked, "Connie, where were you when they told you this?"

She seemed to mull this over in her mind for a few seconds. "It was at my home, in their car, and the places they took me." She glanced around, as if looking for an escape route.

He was convinced his line of questioning was starting to bear fruit and he need to push for specifics, but her body language told him she was ready to flee, so again he paused to allow her to regain her composure. He touched the back of her hand before asking the next question. "When you say your home, what do you mean?"

She seemed surprised at the question. She'd assumed Riggs already knew the answer, so why was he asking? Still confused, she replied, "My foster homes, of course."

Paula was intrigued with what she was witnessing. She saw how Riggs dealt with Kae's fear. *Why is he pushing and pulling every bit of information out of the personalities of Maxine and Connie when he already knows the answers?*

Every once in awhile, Riggs would glance in

57

Paula's direction to see if there were questions in her eyes, but the absence of a signal from her to the contrary or any indications of fear from Kae told him to continue with his interrogation.

"Connie, did your foster parents or other foster children know anything about this?"

"No, they'd come after everyone was asleep and take me to their car and drive to where everyone was meeting."

"Did you know they were coming for you before they came into your bedroom?" he asked, mystified as to why the cult members would risk being caught abducting her. Did they actually believe she was that vital to their ritual?

"Never. I would have hidden somewhere if I'd known beforehand."

"Didn't you refuse to go?" Riggs inquired, wondering if maybe the foster parents were involved.

"Oh no! They would have killed me," she said, fear evident in her voice again.

"Why do you believe they would have killed you?"

"Because they told me they would. They held a knife to my throat or against my chest."

"How many foster homes have you been in?" Riggs asked, puzzled about how someone could enter and remove a child from the premises without the foster parents' knowledge.

"Four," Connie replied without hesitation.

"Couldn't you have run away and gotten some help?"

"Where would I have run to? Who would have believed me? They told me they'd kill everyone in the house if I did anything to wake them. I was afraid."

"Connie, why did you wait so long to see Dr. Mitchell?"

"I thought enough time had passed that they weren't after me anymore. My last foster parents helped me get a job and a place to live when I turned eighteen. They told me as long as I kept my job, paid my bills, went to school, and stayed out of trouble, I'd be safe."

"What happened to change all that?" Riggs saw Paula's look of amazement.

"I don't know, unless it was the phone calls I started receiving at odd hours of the night. The phone would ring and I'd answer it, but no one said anything. All I heard was heavy breathing."

"Could the calls have been sexual in nature? You know that strange people make calls and get off on just listening to a female voice, don't you?"

"I thought about that, but I didn't believe it. Then I spotted the guy with the knit hat following me to and from school. Each time I tried to approach him, he ducked into a building real fast or would cross the street."

"How long ago was it since the last time you saw the guy in the knit hat?" Riggs asked, starting to understand why so much time had passed between the rape and now.

"A few days ago. The phone calls continued after the last time I saw the man following me. I know they're after me."

"At any time did you get a good look at the guy wearing the knit hat?" Riggs asked, knowing he'd be surprised if she had.

"No! I couldn't get that close to him."

"Were you able to check your telephone bills to determine if any of the calls were from someone or place you don't know?"

"No, I didn't even think about doing that," Connie answered, looking somewhat embarrassed at the oversight.

Riggs also noticed that Connie's breathing had changed to short gasps and he could see a trace of perspiration on her upper lip. It was obvious to him that his questions were forcing her to perceive these events as threats. He knew he needed to get her into a state of mind so she'd feel anger and want payback from the people who'd done this to her.

"Connie, what do you do for fun?"

The question caught both Connie and Paula by surprise. Connie stared at Riggs, while Paula analyzed the reason behind it.

"Come on, Connie, there's got to be something you do just for fun. What is it?"

"I like to ski or play in the snow."

"Why do you like that so much?"

"The air is clean and the snow is bright...it makes me feel good inside."

"How would you like to be able to play in the snow or do anything you want without worrying about the people in the red robes?" Riggs asked.

A Birthday to Die For

"I'd do anything if that could happen, Detective Riggs."

"Well, Connie, the way I see it, there's something you can do. You can stop them from ever bothering you again. You can make them pay for what they did to you. Together, we can stop them if you'll tell me everything you remember. What do you say about that?"

In that moment, the fear left her. Connie held her head high, looked directly into Riggs eyes and said, "Let's do it."

"Okay, let's start where we left off earlier."

"Connie, did they ever cut you with a knife?"

"Not counting the carving on my back, only once. They nicked my neck under my chin. I bled for a little while, but it wasn't a serious cut."

"Can you describe the knife?"

"It was scary–looking. It had a crooked blade with a shiny silver handle that had the face of Satan engraved in it."

"Did you ever see any guns?"

She paused, then said, "Only at the meeting places."

Riggs' doubts quickly disappeared as he listened to the answers given to his questions. The information Maxine and Connie had given was consistent with one another and with what Detective Turner had told him. He was starting to understand and appreciate the fear Kae was experiencing.

"Where were these meeting places?" Riggs asked, knowing if she gave the right answers, he

61

might have a starting point in this investigation.

"Most of the time, they took me to a building, but sometimes they'd take me to the mountains and into the forest."

"Do you think you could find the building they took you to?"

"I don't think so. It was always dark outside and they turned on so many streets that I just can't remember."

"Okay, I understand. You're doing great, Connie. Keep it up and we'll get to the bottom of this."

"Okay, I'm trying to remember things."

"Tell me about the meeting places in the forest. What did they look like?"

"Well, I remember two different places they took me to in the forest. They looked almost the same. It was a clearing below the trees where a circle had been formed. Logs had been moved around the circle where I would sit with the people dressed in the red robes. In the center was a table made out of logs tied together and placed on huge wooden blocks."

A picture was starting to form in his mind as he listened to Connie's description of the ceremonial sites. He could envision the satanic world created during the ceremonies, with a ritual sacrifice of an animal and probably a human every once in awhile. The thought of Kae as a thirteen year–old girl witnessing a ritual sacrifice, surrounded by people in red robes representing evil, would be beyond the wildest imagination of the average

A Birthday to Die For

citizen. The forest vaguely lit up from the glow of makeshift torches and filtered moonlight through the trees casting threatening shadows everywhere would be enough to scare most adults and certainly a young girl.

"Do you know what the table was used for?" Riggs asked in a calm, reassuring voice. He was having difficulty trying to conceal the anger he felt for the sick bastards who put a young girl through such an evil, frightening ordeal.

"They told me it was the sacrificial table."

"Did you ever see them sacrifice an animal or a person?"

"No, but I did see something red that looked like blood coming off the table and soaking the ground beneath it."

"Connie, I want you to think about the next question before you answer. It's very important and I want you to be sure of your answer. Can you take me to the ceremonial sites you were taken to in the forest?"

Paula was on pins and needles as she watched Connie lean forward and rest her chin on the palms of hands. Several seconds went by as they both looked at Connie, sitting there with her eyes closed, waiting for her answer. While Paula felt the tension building in her own body, she wondered about Riggs. *How can he be so calm? Does he already know what Connie's answer will be?*

"I think so," Connie said at last. "I remember we turned off Interstate 5 onto Highway 2. We

63

took Highway 9 and I saw a sign to Granite Falls. When we went the other way, we turned off Interstate 5 onto Highway 12 where I remember seeing a sign for Mayfield. I think I might be able to find them if we drove around those areas, but I'm not absolutely sure."

"That's great news, Connie. You've got a good memory. Would you be willing to take a ride with me tomorrow or the next day and see if we can find those places?"

"Only if Dr. Mitchell goes with me."

"I think that can be arranged. How about it, Doc?"

Paula couldn't believe what she had just witnessed—the interview of her patient with multiple personalities, two of them being in conflict with one another most of the time, and a detective who in one interview had developed a rapport with them. *Absolutely unbelievable!*

"Yes, I'll come along, but it will have to be day after tomorrow. I need to change some appointments around before I can take off for a day."

"Good, but maybe you should clear your schedule for a couple of days. The places we're trying to find are on opposite ends of the county."

"Okay. When do you want to meet?"

"Eight o'clock in the morning, here, day after tomorrow."

"Okay, we'll be here."

Riggs took Kae's hand. "You've done very well.

A Birthday to Die For

I'm looking forward to seeing you again, day after tomorrow." He motioned for Paula to follow him into the adjoining room.

"When and if we catch these guys and we go to trial, their defense attorney is going to ask about proof of a miscarriage. Can you arrange with a medical doctor to examine Kae for the proof we will need?"

She was surprised at the request, but impressed with how thorough Riggs was in the investigation. She hadn't realized Kae's claim of being impregnated and having a miscarriage would be challenged in court. "Yes, I'll make sure it's done, but can we wait until we know we're going to court? I think an examination at this time would be counter–productive. It could further traumatize Kae, make her feel we don't believe her and we won't get any further information."

"We can wait until we know we're going to court," Riggs responded, not surprised at the request.

"Good, I'll make sure it gets done when it's time."

"Oh…one more thing, Doc. Did you get a chance to do anything on the profiling?"

"I'm working on it. I've made contact with some of my colleagues for their input. They'll get back to me as soon as they can."

"That's good! I'll also make an inquiry to the Behavioral Science Unit of the FBI. Between them and your colleagues, we'll have something to work with."

Paula watched Riggs as he left the office. She went over the events of the day in her mind. *I can't remember ever having a day like this one with the same degree of tension and excitement. Being asked to put a profile together on cult members and feeling like an essential member of an investigative team, I think I'm having an adrenaline rush.*

Chapter 7

A quick breakfast with Toby and the boys was a good way to start the day. Listening to his sons banter back and forth across the breakfast table about who was better at basketball and their challenge that they could beat him if he'd just come to the basketball court brought a smile to his face as he drove to work, but soon faded as he refocused on the investigation at hand.

As he drove, he went over in his mind the things he had learned so far. The review of the videos identified Rebecca Shelby, the foster mother, as being the first person who introduced Kae to the cult. This was a promising lead, but in order for it to be of any value, she had to be located. The ceremonial sites were other possible leads, as well as the guy in the knit hat. If they could be located, one could only wonder what they would reveal.

The realization that leads were starting to build and time was running out, he knew he was going to need some help. Asking for help was one thing Riggs wasn't good at. He knew the other detectives had their own caseloads and to ask them to help him would cause them to fall behind in their own investigations, possibly risking their solvability. He didn't take his responsibilities lightly and he knew the other detectives were of the same mind, although he also knew that when asked, he'd do anything within his power to help another detective who needed it. This was one of those times and he was the detective in need.

In most cases, the victim was already dead and it was just a matter of identifying the suspect and filing charges with the prosecutor. In this case, he had a live victim and the challenge was to keep her that way.

The office was coming to life as he walked in—detectives were joking with one another, discussing their individual cases over coffee. This was a ritual that took place every morning and allowed an exchange of investigative ideas. To ask for assistance on a particular problem or arrest wasn't unusual, just out of character for him.

Riggs found Bob La Moria at his desk reading through some files. Bob was a close personal friend and the one person Riggs knew he could rely on for help. They'd worked numerous homicides together and found their individual talents complemented one another, making them a very effective team. La Moria always presented a low–key, laid–back demeanor, a personality more representative of a minister or a priest than a cop. He spoke in a soft

A Birthday to Die For

voice when he interviewed or interrogated, a tone which almost seemed lackadaisical, drawing the suspects into the web that Bob created to catch them in a lie. Once he discovered the lie, his disposition changed dramatically, making the suspect realize they'd been had.

"Hey Bob! I talked to the Sarge about you helping out on my investigation. He agreed, as long as it doesn't screw up any of yours. Is there a chance you can put your cases on hold for awhile and give me a hand in this cult investigation?" Riggs asked, seating himself on the corner of La Moria's desk.

La Moria glanced up, his over–the–counter glasses slipping down his nose. "I think I can manage that," he smiled. "Besides, I've kinda wanted to get involved since I've never had an investigation involving Satanism." Bob arched his eyebrows and with the expression of a child about to get a treat, he asked, "Do they wear weird clothing, drink blood, howl at the moon, or do any of those things described in novels?"

"Hell, they just might. You know as much about them as I do. This investigation is so weird nothing would surprise me, but one thing I know for sure—I need your help. I'm running out of time and I could use a hand with following up some of the leads. If I don't get to the bottom of this in time, there's a good chance my victim is going to die."

Riggs handed La Moria his file. "Read through this. It'll bring you up–to–date on what I've done so far and what I've learned. When you finish, we'll get together and discuss strategy."

Bob sobered immediately. "Sounds like a plan. Give me a few minutes and I'll get back to you."

While La Moria was bringing himself up–to–speed on the investigation, Riggs sent out an All Points Bulletin to all police agencies up and down the Interstate 5 corridor from Portland, Oregon to the Canadian border. The bulletin requested any and all information regarding alleged cult activity within their jurisdictions.

The memory of what he'd been told about the ritual sites and their proximity to Interstate 5, the City of Granite Falls, and Lake Mayfield caused Riggs to wonder if maybe he could get some help from the Department's Air Support Unit. The helicopter would have the capability of flying over both areas during the hours of darkness without raising suspicions. The flight crew could look for any lighting from torches or any other source. They could also use the infra–red imaging device to detect heat cast off by the bodies of humans or animals. The trick was going to be persuading the Commander, Captain Osborn to allow use of the helicopter for fly–overs of the areas that were in other jurisdictions.

Riggs was leaning back in his chair with his legs propped across one corner of the desk, gazing up at the ceiling and deep in thought when La Moria walked up. "I see you're in your thinking position," he quipped.

"You're right! I'm trying to come up with some

A Birthday to Die For

innovative ideas that will help create some leads for us to follow up."

Bob planted himself in the suspects' chair beside Riggs' desk. "What ideas have you come up with so far?"

"A couple, like a bulletin to other agencies up and down Interstate 5 for one and asking Captain Osborn for assistance with helicopter fly–overs of the possible ceremonial sites. I've also got another thing I need to let you know about, but in private," Riggs advised, not wanting the tail on Kae to become public information.

La Moria wasn't surprised at Riggs' ideas, but was a little surprised at his wanting to tell him something in private. It was their individual imaginations that had brought them so much success in solving homicides. "Sounds good to me. When are you going to talk to Captain Osborn? Are you going tell me about the other thing before or after you talk to him?"

Riggs winced. He hated talking to brass. "I'll tell you about the other thing when we're alone. In the meantime, I'll go talk to Osborn while you contact the Department of Health and Social Services to get an address for Rebecca Shelby."

"I'll do that and while I'm at it, I'll try to get the names and addresses of any references she listed in order to get the job as a foster mother."

As he watched La Moria gather up his raincoat and notebook, Riggs hoped the information gained from the Department of Health and Social Services would identify the references as well as friends and relatives. The more names they got, the more leads they'd have, which would increase the possibility of gaining reliable information that would eventually lead to the cult.

Riggs left the office shortly after La Moria and headed towards Captain Osborn's office, located at the southeast corner of the King County Airport, away from the Courthouse. Osborn had seen him through the window when he arrived and met him at the front door. Osborn ran a tight ship when it came to productivity and discipline. His subordinates respected him as shown through their loyalty. He carried with him a high degree of integrity and work ethic which he acquired growing up on his parents' farm in Kansas and while serving in Vietnam assigned to the Army's Criminal Investigation Division. He'd been around and by no means was he a pushover in any sense of the word.

Captain Osborn crossed his arms. "What can I do for you, Riggs?"

Riggs tried a smile, but it didn't work. "What makes you think I want something, Captain?"

"Don't play games with me, Riggs. I know you homicide guys don't come slumming unless you need something. So, what is it?"

Riggs remembered that Osborn was known for his eagerness to get to the point on any subject brought before him. He was also well known for his ability to make the Department brass and local politicians squirm with his directness. "I need the help of your helicopter crew," Riggs said,

A Birthday to Die For

looking directly into Osborn's eyes.

Osborn was aware of Riggs' intensity as he made his intentions known. The request was without hesitation and to the point. He was aware of Riggs' reputation as a 'no holds barred' investigator with a case solvability record that was the envy of some detectives who felt they had to compete with him. "Okay, Riggs, come into my office and tell me your reason before I agree."

They had no sooner gotten seated when a large fly started dive–bombing Captain Osborn's head. The Captain kept swatting at it while trying to maintain some semblance of rank and authority. Riggs watched in amazement.

"Damn it, Riggs, wipe that grin off your face. It's hard to carry on a conversation when you have a damn fly the size of a B–52 trying to land on your head."

Riggs knew his request for assistance would go nowhere as long as the Captain's attention was diverted to the fly. Knowing this, he leaned over and removed a rubber band from top of the Captain's desk. In one fluid motion, Riggs wrapped the rubber band around the tip of his right index finger, stretched it back to his thumb, took aim, and fired. The rubber band struck the fly in mid–air, killing it instantly. Unfortunately, as the fly exploded, its innards landed on the Captain's tie.

"Damn, Riggs! That was one hell of a shot, but you better hope I can get this bug juice off my tie. If I ever need a fly killer in SWAT, you're my man. Now let's get back to business. What do you have?"

Riggs leaned forward, resting his right elbow on the Captain's desk and proceeded to tell him the story of Kae Carlson. As he spoke, Osborn shook his head in disbelief. He sat back in his chair listening to Riggs describe the possible ritual sites and his need to utilize the helicopter and flight crew. He stressed the fact that time was running out and the girl could very likely die if he didn't get the help he needed.

"You make a strong argument," Osborn acknowledged as Riggs finished his summation.

"It sounds like an old Hitchcock movie. I think you have your work cut out for you. I'll alert the flight crew to assist you any way they can. I'll take care of getting permission from the Sheriff to fly over those areas in Snohomish and Lewis Counties."

Riggs could feel a sigh of relief building in his chest. "Thanks, Captain, I owe you."

Osborn waved him away. "It's my job. You don't owe me anything."

"I know, Captain, but I still want you to know how much I appreciate the help," Riggs said sincerely, feeling the tension leave his body.

On his way back to the office, Riggs stopped in the Office of Natural Resources where he picked up copies of maps for the areas in both state and federal forests where he believed the rituals were being held.

A Birthday to Die For

Back at the office, Riggs was barely inside the door when La Moria motioned for him to hurry over to his desk, anxious to share what he'd learned. "The records at Health and Social Services show a Rebecca Shelby was appointed as a foster mother fifteen years ago. They also show that she left their employment about two years later, a time consistent with the time period when Kae was introduced to the devil worshippers."

"That's interesting. How about the references—family or friends?" Riggs asked.

"I don't have their names and addresses yet, but I do know the references consist of a school teacher, a social worker, a neighbor, and believe or not, a police officer," La Moria explained.

"When will we have their names and addresses?" Riggs asked, knowing the names were vital to the investigation.

"I'm working on that. They're going through their records now and they'll call me as soon as they locate it."

"Good. I'll be out tomorrow with Kae and Dr. Mitchell trying to find the ritual sites. I'll be on my cell phone if you need anything. I think it'll help us in any interviews if the sites are located first. Let's wait until after I check out these locations before we contact any of the references."

"Sounds good. In the meantime, I'll get caught up on some of my own investigations," La Moria commented, picking up a file.

"If I find anything, I'll pass it onto Captain Osborn so the flight crew can narrow their search of the areas," Riggs said, watching La Moria tuck a file under his arm and head for the door.

On the drive home, Riggs could feel the adrenaline build inside him, a feeling he'd experienced many times in the past whenever he was involved in a life–threatening situation or about to discover a lead that could possibly break a case wide open. *What will tomorrow bring?*

That thought was suddenly interrupted by an emergency broadcast on the police radio. "Radio traffic closed to emergency transmissions only. Units in the area of Northeast 124th and 116th Northeast, there's been an armed robbery of the 'Mom and Pop' grocery at that location. Suspect is described as a black male wearing a dark–colored trench coat and a black knit ski hat. Suspect is carrying a sawed–off shotgun and is considered armed and dangerous. Boy–Two will be primary."

"10–4. Do we have a direction of travel or information on the suspect's vehicle?" asked Boy–Two as others listening in heard the whine of the engine in his police car as he put his foot to the metal and activated his emergency equipment, lights, and siren.

"No vehicle or other suspects seen or heard. Direction of travel unknown."

Riggs caught the excitement in the voice of the dispatcher as information was relayed to Boy–Two and other responding units. He too felt the adrenalin rush as he instinctively turned his car

A Birthday to Die For

in the direction of the robbery location, a habit all officers within hearing range and distance had, especially because the description of the knit hat piqued his interest. He was acutely aware of the risk involved in this diversion. It could result in him being tied up for an extended period of time and complicate the cult investigation. His gut was telling him it was unlikely the suspect wearing the knit hat was the same sick bastard who'd been following Kae, but on the other hand, he couldn't be absolutely sure. He felt the need to check it out, but he also didn't want to risk the possibility of driving right by the suspects while he was in the area. Besides, it would be dereliction of duty and unprofessional to do otherwise.

He kept his eyes open to anyone or anything out of the ordinary as he drove through the area. He knew he had a slight advantage over other responding police units because his car was unmarked with an undercover license plate. Except for the spotlight on the driver's side of the car, it looked nothing like a police car. It was unlikely that the suspect would identify his car as a police car in time to avoid detection. He also knew the suspect would be in a hurry to put as much distance as possible between himself and the Mom and Pop grocery store.

Visibility was impeded by the darkness and the glow from the streetlights as Riggs scoured the alleys, businesses, and side streets for anything suspicious. While he was still two blocks from the grocery store, he noticed an older vehicle stopped at the stop sign on the intersecting street. He watched the car as he approached, wondering, *Why don't they pull into the intersection to cross the street or turn one way or the other? I'm the only other car on the street and there's more than enough time for the driver to continue on safely.*

When Riggs passed in front of the older vehicle he could see it was a green 1973 Chevrolet two–door sedan with two occupants in the front seat. He was unable to clearly see anything other than their silhouettes. *Why in hell are they staying at the stop sign so long?* Riggs mulled over the information given by the dispatcher. No other vehicle or suspects had been seen or heard, yet this car was within two blocks of the robbery scene, sitting at a stop sign for an unusually long time. If they were involved in the robbery, wouldn't they be speeding from the location or were they trying not to attract attention to themselves? If that's it, they're wrong.

Riggs turned right at the next intersection and onto the street where the Mom and Pop grocery store was located. Just after he made the turn, he immediately turned off his headlights, made a U–turn, and pulled to the curb. His gut was telling him there was something out of the ordinary with the car he'd just passed. He waited for only a moment before the green Chevrolet crossed in front of him. Not a person to argue with his gut feelings or to rationalize away suspicious circumstances, he turned on his headlights and pulled in behind the Chevrolet. *Should I call in*

A Birthday to Die For

*the stop or not? If it isn't the suspects, the real
suspect will get away when the other units on scene
respond to my location. Then again, maybe there's
a legitimate reason for the driver's conduct.*

While Riggs ran these questions through his
mind, he hit his bright lights hoping to at least
get a look into the interior of the Chevrolet and
maybe see whether one of them was wearing a
trench coat or a knit hat...or better yet, a red–
hooded robe saying 'I'm a member of a devil-
worshipping cult and you've got me!' Conscious
of the cult investigation, he knew that was just
wishful thinking; however, if he discovered the
knit hat and trench coat, his gut feeling would be
confirmed and justify a call for assistance.

The bright lights did nothing to allow him a
glance into the vehicle, instead serving only to
have the driver slow to a near crawl. He'd certainly
gotten the attention of the driver who appeared
to be waiting for Riggs' next move. Next was a
quick flash of his spotlight across the rear window
which resulted in the driver suddenly slamming
on his brakes as if he was trying to cause a rear–
end accident or evade detection. For what reason,
Riggs wasn't really sure, but every fiber in his
body was telling him he was in danger. While he
applied his brakes and skillfully avoided rear–
ending the car in front of him, he got a glimpse of
the occupants. In the right front passenger seat
sat the suspect wearing the trench coat and knit
hat.

Struck by the realization that he had the

suspects, he pulled his gun as he rolled out of his vehicle. He had no time to call in his location or call for a back–up. He knew the odds were in favor of the suspects. His mind went into warp speed as he analyzed his predicament. *The driver will come out with a handgun because the steering wheel will keep him from handling the shotgun. Kill the driver as soon as he gets out of the car and shows his intentions. This will leave me with some cover between me and the passenger. It may give me enough time to retrieve my own shotgun and even the odds.*

Riggs watched as the suspects looked over their shoulders trying to see exactly where he was standing in order to decide what they'd do. "Stay in the car," Riggs shouted. "If either of you gets out of the car, I'll kill you."

He'd never been in a situation exactly like this one, but on other occasions where his life was suddenly in jeopardy, he'd convinced the suspects he was going to kill them and enjoy it if they gave him the opportunity. This was one of those situations where he felt his life was being held in the balance between the suspects' desire to escape and their belief that he'd actually kill them if they tried.

The tone of his voice was almost like that of a drill instructor in the Marines—no–nonsense, which screamed out the desire to do serious harm to anyone not willing to follow orders. "I know you can't see me, but I can see you. I guarantee you'll die if you don't do exactly what I tell you."

A Birthday to Die For

He barked orders. "Put your hands against the windshield so I can see them. Do it now. Passenger, keep your hands against the windshield. Driver, with your left hand, reach through the steering wheel and remove the keys from the ignition. Throw them out the window onto the pavement. Do it now." When the driver complied, Riggs said, "Now put your hands back against the windshield so I can see them."

The suspects kept looking over their shoulders and into the side mirrors trying desperately to locate Riggs and weigh their odds of escape. Riggs was surprised they hadn't tried to get out of their car, wondering whether or not his tone of voice and orders had convinced them he was looking for any provocation to kill them. The reasons escaped him, but he didn't really care as long as they stayed in the car. He knew the slightest mistake on his part could change the scenario and he'd be in whole lot of shit.

He kept a steady watch on the back of the suspects' heads looking for any indication they were going to make a hostile move—one that would cost them their lives. While he maintained a constant vigilance, he reached for his radio transmitter. His call for help was immediately answered with the wail of sirens in the distance, heading his way.

The suspects also heard the sirens and knew their opportunity to escape was evaporating. Riggs could see them twisting around and talking to each other. He couldn't hear what they were saying, but he figured they were telling each other that if they didn't do something right then, they'd never have another chance. Believing the suspects were about to make a desperate attempt to escape, Riggs picked up a large rock from the roadway and lobbed it into the air so it would come down on the top of their car. The impact of the rock on the roof had miraculous results. The suspects started screaming, "Don't shoot! Don't shoot! We're not gonna do anything!"

Riggs felt great pleasure with the results and the fact he'd even come up with the idea. He knew they'd never teach that as a restraining method in the academy, but then again, he'd done a lot of things that didn't exactly fall within the framework of proper police training procedures.

Within moments, police cars and uniformed officers surrounded the suspects' vehicle. It sounded almost like an explosion when the officers crawled from their vehicles bringing shotguns with them and jacking a round into the chamber at the same time.

As if the rock on the roof wasn't enough, the sound of shotguns coming to the ready scared the hell out of the suspects. Riggs could almost imagine the sweat pouring from their bodies as they wondered if they were going to die. They both had that deer–in–the–headlights look as they were pulled from the car one by one and placed face down on the road. As they were being handcuffed by Officer Dave Bennett, Riggs leaned over and advised them that they were under

A Birthday to Die For

arrest and that they had the right to an attorney before saying or signing anything.

After going through the Miranda warning and asking them if they understood their rights, Riggs asked them why they didn't try to jump out of their car and run. "Because you would've killed us, man."

"How long have you had that hat?" Riggs asked the passenger suspect.

"Couple of days."

"Where'd you get it?"

"Pike Place Market on the waterfront."

"Why'd you buy it?" Riggs asked, trying to determine if there was a connection with his cult investigation.

"I want a lawyer. I'm not saying anything else."

"Okay, you have a right to an attorney, but your hat is going into evidence showing the eye holes you've cut into it so you could use it as a mask. Tell your attorney that."

Riggs knew he was pressured for time in his investigation, so he handed the arrest off to Officer Dave Bennett, who confirmed he'd be booking the hat into evidence. He was a good officer. He'd supervised the removal of the suspects from their vehicle and the recovery of the stolen money, but no red–hooded robes.

After writing out a quick officer's witness statement and handing it to Bennett, Riggs got into his car and headed for home. *Damn, it sure would've been nice if there'd been a connection to my cult investigation, but deep down I'd already come to the conclusion there was none.* The thought was a stretch of anyone's imagination, which showed just how desperate he was for a lead. The thought stayed with him until he fell into bed, hoping to get a little sleep before his meeting with Dr. Mitchell and Kae Carlson.

Chapter 8

A block from Doctor Mitchell's office, Riggs used his cell phone to call the number for Detective Hatch.

"This is Hatch, what can I do for you?"

"Mike, this is Riggs. I'm calling you to let you know Kae Carlson will be with me today. We're going to try to locate the ritual sites where she'd been taken. I'll be returning her to the doctor's office sometime around sixteen hundred hours. You can set up on her again at that time. How's that sound to you?"

"Sounds good. Decker and I'll have her in our sights as soon as you drop her off at the Doc's office."

When Riggs pulled to the curb, Kae and the doctor hurried out of the warmth of Paula's office and ran to his car. Kae climbed into the front passenger seat while Paula seated herself in the right rear directly behind Kae, an arrangement that he and Paula had previously agreed upon. The idea was that Kae might see signs or landmarks which would spark a memory of roads, turns made, and so forth in order to reach the locations where the rituals had been held.

"Good morning, ladies! Are you ready to have a fun day of exploring?" Riggs asked with a sarcastic smile, trying to lighten the dread that showed on Kae's face.

Kae nodded, while Paula responded, "We're looking forward to it."

"Good, but first we're going to make a stop and get something that'll help us get through the day," Riggs explained as he maneuvered the car into the westbound lane. Riggs glanced back and forth between the two women, believing he could detect a certain amount of excitement in their body language, which came as a pleasant surprise.

The first stop was a coffee shop a short distance away, one to which Riggs had been many times before. He purchased tea for Kae, coffee for himself and Paula, a dozen bagels, cream cheese, and bottles of water for all of them.

"What do you think?" he asked. "Will this get us through the day?"

"I'm certain it will, as long as you remember that we're women and we'll need potty breaks," said Paula.

Riggs grinned. "I'll do my best to remember that."

It was nine–thirty by the time they reached the southbound lanes of Interstate 5. The morning commute traffic was starting to thin,

A Birthday to Die For

allowing them to pick up speed. Things were looking pretty good for the day trip. The weather was cooperating. It wasn't raining and the sun broke through the clouds as they pulled onto the freeway.

This could be a good day. The weather's good, the ladies seem to be excited about this adventure. Maybe it's an omen that we'll be successful in finding the ritual site and bring me a step closer to identifying the cult members. It was something he wanted very much. He was looking forward to learning the identity of the High Priest, a mortal who had raped a thirteen year–old girl and plunged a knife deep into the chest of sacrificial victims. He wanted nothing more than to bring him to justice.

Riggs chuckled when he caught himself using the word, "omen." The investigation of occults, devil worshippers, rituals, and what have you must be rubbing off on him. Sometimes he felt like he'd walked into an old D–rated horror flick.

They were approaching a sign that read "Downtown Tacoma" when Riggs glanced at Kae. "This would be about where you'd get onto the freeway after they picked you up at your foster home, so be on the lookout for signs or anything else that might help you remember where they took you." Kae acknowledged his comment with a slight affirmative nod of her head. Riggs wondered which of her personalities was going to accompany them on this trip.

They'd been traveling a little over an hour

southbound on Interstate 5 when he heard the voice of Connie say, "Turn here."

The road was a little south of the city of Chehalis heading due east towards Lake Mayfield. He'd traveled here before, but had never explored the back roads and wooded areas. He couldn't help but wonder what secrets would be revealed as they continued into the isolated forest area. *Will it reveal the secrets of the cult...secrets that might identify who the crazy bastards are and bring an end to their miserable existence?*

As they traveled through the forest they could see the snow–covered mountains through breaks in the trees. They could see where loggers had left only stumps and broken branches where clear–cutting left behind blemishes on the beautiful, lush hillsides.

At the intersection of a paved highway and a dirt road, Connie gasped. "Turn right here."

"How did you know to turn here?" Riggs asked.

Connie pointed to a half–burned stump on the northeast corner. After a quick glance in his direction, she said, "I've been to this place before. I remember that stump."

Riggs turned onto the dirt road and drove northbound on a road covered with large potholes filled with water. He drove in a zigzag fashion, trying to miss the majority of them as they climbed higher in elevation. He began to wonder where the cult members attending the rituals parked their cars. *How would they escape if someone just happened upon them?*

At the crest of a hill, in the distance they could see a wide spot in the roadway where oncoming cars could pass one another, park, or turn around. This spot was in a hollow obstructed from view until you crested the hill on either side. Riggs felt his investigative juices start to race as he surveyed the terrain, letting his imagination run free. In his mind he could see the possibilities, how easy it would be to hide or camouflage a clandestine operation such as a sacrificial ritual. The deeper they traveled into the forested area along the pock–marked logging road, the more he was convinced that Kae, through the personality of Connie, was taking them to the ritual site she'd been to before. How many times was still a question. His mind was reeling with all the things, the evidence that might be concealed and exposed with the discovery of the ritual site. He literally jumped when Connie shouted, "Stop here! This is the place!"

"How do you know?" Riggs asked, pulling the car to the side of the road.

"See how the road drops down? I remember getting out of their cars right here," she said, pointing to the turn out on the downhill side of the road.

"Okay! Where did you go after you got out of their cars?" Riggs asked, cutting the engine. Taking out his pad, he scribbled some notes and made a quick diagram of the road.

"We walked down the hill from here. I think

the trail we took is over there somewhere," Connie explained, her voice trembling. Her body was shaking as she pointed her finger in the direction slightly to the south of where they'd parked.

Riggs stood at the west edge of the dirt road looking down the hill in the direction Connie had indicated. He could see no obvious path to follow, but the small opening between the bushes seemed to be the best route to take. He asked Connie and Paula to remain in the car while he did some exploring down the hill and under the trees. The last thing he needed right now was a surprise, especially with two civilians in tow.

Riggs had walked about two hundred yards into the forest and under some tree branches when his attention was drawn towards a small clearing off to the left. It was in the form of a circle, with what looked like a bench or table situated on the high side. The top was made out of pieces of log about six inches in diameter and six feet long, tied together with rope. The top was resting on blocks of wood, which brought the top of the table about four feet above the ground. Around the circle there were round logs which appeared to be arranged for seating.

Riggs looked around the circle. *Damn! This matches the description previously given by Connie and Turner from LAPD. Her description is exactly what I'm looking at. The details she recalled when describing the site are astoundingly accurate. There's no doubt she's telling the truth about what she saw.*

A Birthday to Die For

Out of habit, Riggs stood still at the edge of the circle, which he now looked upon as a crime scene and stored in his memory all that he could see, hear, and smell, as well as his gut–wrenching feelings. The survey of the scene and the memory of what the personalities of Maxine and Connie had told him allowed him to visualize the ritual as it was performed. He could see the actual sacrifice of a baby. The blood from the stab wounds seeping into the wood table top, ropes, and the dirt below...blood that would become evidence.

When Riggs returned to the car, the two women were seated in the front holding hands, anxiously awaiting his return. As he approached, they got out of the car and looked at him, their eyes filled with questions. He noticed the shaking in Kae's body had disappeared.

Paula broke the silence. "Did you find anything?"

He nodded, though a worried frown marked his brow as he waited for Kae's reaction. "Yes, it's exactly the way Connie described it."

Riggs opened the trunk of his car and gathered up his camera along with other evidence collection paraphernalia. "I'd like the two of you to come with me to the site. I want to see if Connie can remember anything else. While I'm collecting some evidence, if the two of you will please remain on the perimeter of the circle you're about to see, it would be helpful. I don't know what the evidence will eventually reveal, but I can't take any chances of having to argue that it wasn't contaminated by either of you before I collected it."

Dr. Mitchell turned to Connie. "Is it alright with you? Do you think you might be able to remember anything else?"

Riggs watched Connie as Doctor Mitchell asked the question. He could see her back stiffen and her body began to shake. A stern look came over her face. "If I must, I will." The answer was almost as if another personality had come into play, but he wasn't sure.

Paula moved closer to Connie, placing her hand under Kae's chin and lifting it to look into her eyes. "Thank you, Kae, for being so strong."

Riggs picked up on Paula telling Kae she was strong, knowing it was the personality of Connie who'd given the information. Obviously Paula was taking every opportunity to encourage Kae to stop hiding behind the personalities she had created.

The apprehension was clearly visible on Paula's face as they walked to the site. Riggs knew she was concerned about Kae's reaction when she saw the site which was the cause of so many of her fears. He knew she was asking herself if this would cause Kae to slip further into her fantasy world or if it would be a step towards recovery.

A glance at Riggs told Paula he was wondering about her thoughts, almost as if he was trying to read her mind. She had never experienced the return to a location, what Riggs referred

A Birthday to Die For

to as a crime scene, especially with a patient or as Riggs would say, 'a victim.' She knew the return was necessary to reconstruct the events leading to Kae's bizarre behavior and help in the identification of those responsible. While she recognized the upside of the return, she also knew there could be a downside. Would Kae be able to handle it or would it push her deeper into the psychological nightmare she'd been living? The shaking of Kae's body and the tremble in her voice had not gone unnoticed.

As soon as they entered the circle, Kae began to cry, her body wracked with sobs. Paula immediately moved towards Kae, wrapping her arms around her, telling her softly, "Don't be afraid. Detective Riggs will protect us."

While Paula tried to comfort Kae, Riggs asked, "Does this help your memory any?" Kae's only response was a shake of her head in the negative. Riggs examined the table and with a knife cut several small pieces of wood from different locations on the table's top, sides, and bottom. Each sample was placed into small individual envelopes. He also cut from the rope binding the logs on the table top together. Again, each sample was placed into a small paper envelope and labeled. He bent down and gathered dirt samples from different locations on the ground beneath the table, placing each of these samples into glass containers. Each envelope and glass container was sealed with a sticker bearing Riggs' name, the date, time, and place from which the sample was taken.

Paula watched Riggs as he gathered his samples for evidence and understood his reasons for doing so; however, she became confused when she saw him lean over and pick up a handful of dirt to rub on those areas he'd cut samples from.

While they were walking back to the car, Paula could no longer contain herself. She had to know why Riggs had rubbed the dirt on those areas from which he'd taken the samples.

"Can you tell me why you rubbed the dirt on those places you took samples from?"

Riggs was somewhat surprised at Paula's observations—and also quite impressed.

"Doc, it's called 'planning ahead.' You never know what might happen during an investigation. It may turn out that another ritual is in the works and the cult members will return here to hold it. If they do, I don't want to frighten them away or cause them to find another location for their rituals. I want it to be here. With the help of the Department's helicopter, I hope to have the chance to catch them in the act. This just might be the place."

"What do you think the chances are of that happening?" asked Paula.

"I don't really know, but anything can happen in any criminal investigation. You just need to plan ahead whenever possible."

On the ride back to Dr. Mitchell's office, Riggs could see Kae starting to relax as she laid her head back against the headrest and closed her eyes. He wondered what was going through her mind. *Is she starting to feel some hope of escaping the death threat which has hung over her head for so many years? Maybe she's trying to escape the fantasy world she's created and is attempting to regain her own identity. So many questions, yet I might never have any answers.*

The two women looked exhausted from the trip and hastily got out of the car when Riggs pulled to a stop in front of the doctor's office. He was almost afraid to remind them of their trip scheduled for the next day to locate the other ritual site. If Connie was telling the truth, it was near the City of Granite Falls in Snohomish County.

"Please remember, ladies, we have a date for tomorrow morning," Riggs told them, all the while trying to sound upbeat and encouraging.

"We'll be here at eight o'clock, but Riggs, you need to do a better job at remembering the potty breaks," Paula chided him with a wave of her hand in his direction.

"I'll try to do better tomorrow," he said through the car's open window. The dark look on the Paula's face did not go unnoticed.

As Riggs pulled away from the curb, he looked around trying to see if Hatch and Decker were in position to resume their surveillance of Kae. Even with his experienced eyes, he was unable to see them, but knew they were there somewhere as he drove in the direction of his office.

He'd planned to meet La Moria for an update and strategy session in the office, but then decided, *Why not meet at the coffee shop near the office?* This would give them the privacy and opportunity to let La Moria in on the information regarding Hatch and Decker. A quick phone call to La Moria diverted him to the coffee shop.

La Moria was already seated at a table tucked around a corner, the most private one in the shop. It was the same one they'd used on numerous occasions to discuss their investigations over a cup of coffee.

"Hi Bob! I thought this would be better than meeting in the office. I want to share some information with you without the risk of it getting in the hands of the wrong people."

"Sounds intriguing. What is it?"

"Well, it's like this. The interview with Kae revealed that there might be a tail on her—a guy in a knit hat. I thought I had the guy in the knit hat when the arrest was made in that robbery of the Mom and Pop grocery store, but I was wrong. I contacted Sgt. Francis and asked her for some help, which she agreed to do. As we speak, Detectives Hatch and Decker are tailing Kae in hopes of putting the arm on the guy wearing the knit hat."

"What a great idea, but why are you keeping this information so close to your chest?"

"I believe the cult may already know we're conducting this investigation. If so, they may try to gather as much information as they can

A Birthday to Die For

regarding what we're doing through whatever sources they have available to them, including someone within our department; so besides the two of us, Sgt. Francis, Hatch, and Decker, no one else knows about the tail."

"You're not going paranoid on me, are you?" La Maria asked, unable to conceal a smile.

"Hope not, but you've got to admit, this case is different than any we've handled before. We don't know a lot about cults, but what little we do know tells us there are a lot of possible surprises ahead of us."

"I don't disagree with what you're saying, so I'll head back to the office while you drop your evidence off at the lab," La Moria said, getting up from the table feeling a little paranoid himself.

Just as the two of them were heading for the coffee shop's exit, Riggs' cell phone rang. "This is Riggs."

"Jerry, this is Paula. I think you should come by my office right away. I think someone broke into my files while we were out with you today."

"I'll be right there. Lock your doors until I get there."

"What's going on?" La Moria asked upon hearing one side of the conversation Riggs had just concluded.

"That was Dr. Mitchell. She thinks someone has broken into her files while she and Kae were with me today. I need to go by her office and see if her assumption is correct."

"Want me to go with you?"

97

"No, if I need any help or backup, I'll call SPD. It's their jurisdiction anyway."

"Okay! I'll see you in the office when you get there."

In less than ten minutes Riggs was knocking on the front door to Dr. Mitchell's office.

"Hi Jerry. You made good time," Paula said as she grasped his arm and pulled him inside.

"Is Kae here?" Riggs asked, glancing around office for any evidence of a forced entry.

"No, she left for home as soon as we got out of your car and you drove off."

"Okay, now tell me what's caused you to believe your files have been compromised."

"When I approached the entry to my office, there was a note taped to the door which had been left by the building's security officer. He informed me that he'd found my front door unlocked while I was away. He also informed me that he checked the interior of my office, but found nothing disturbed or evidence of a break–in."

"Okay Doc, go on. Tell me why you feel someone broke into your office and files."

"Jerry, I always lock my doors when I leave. I also make sure my filing cabinet is locked since I have patient files in there. When I found the note from building security, the door was still unlocked, as well as my filing cabinet. I never forget to lock either."

"Okay, I believe you. I want you to call SPD and have them come out at once. I want an official

A Birthday to Die For

police report made. I also want them to process the front door and filing cabinet for possible fingerprints. I'll stick around until the officer arrives."

It seemed like it had only been two or three minutes since Paula made the phone call to SPD when the officer walked through the door. Riggs immediately identified himself and clued the officer into why he was there. The officer agreed to process the front door and filing cabinet for fingerprints. He also agreed to put in his report that should a match come back on the latent prints, the SPD investigating detective would notify Riggs.

"Doc, I'm going to leave you with this officer. Are you going to be okay?"

"I'll be fine, Jerry. Thanks for coming back."

"I've got some things I need to do back in my own office, so I'll see you in the morning."

When he got back to his office, Riggs immediately went to the Evidence Lab where he turned all the samples over to Lab Technician Joyce Reese. He explained the need to examine the samples as soon as possible. He had to know if they contained any human blood.

Joyce shook her head with a smile. "Riggs, you never cease to amaze me. Now you tell me about a cult, devil worshippers, and human sacrifices. If this is for real, it presents some interesting possibilities, something different for a change. I'll get right on it."

"Thanks! I owe you one," Riggs smiled wearily, agreeing with her that this case was different than other investigations he had worked on and for which she'd done the lab analysis.

"I've heard that from you before," she retorted. "When am I going to collect on the hundred and fifty other times you said that you owe me?" she said, turning away, ambling into her lab and shutting the door.

Riggs yelled after her, "Whenever you need something from me."

La Moria was seated at his desk reading through some files when Riggs walked up and looked over his shoulder at the paperwork on the desk.

"I forgot to ask you while we were at the coffee shop if you have any information for me?" he said, hoping La Moria had something to offer, maybe a positive lead or idea that would advance the investigation.

Bob let his feet drop to the floor. "Aren't you forgetting something?"

"Like what?" Riggs asked, knowing full well that La Moria wanted to know about what happened at the Dr. Mitchell's office.

After quickly bringing La Moria up–to–date on what had occurred at the Paula's office, La Moria advised, "I have the names of the references for Rebecca Shelby and their addresses."

"Good. Let's hang onto them until I get back from my trip with the Doc and Kae tomorrow. Maybe we'll find the other ritual site up around

A Birthday to Die For

Granite Falls and I'll find something which might be of help when we interview the references."

"Sounds okay to me, but if I were you, I'd keep an eye peeled on my rearview mirror tomorrow."

"Why's that?"

"The way I see it, the Doc's office has been broken into and the only conclusion I come up with is the cult is trying to find out just how much the doctor knows. They may also be trying to determine the best time to abduct Kae. I think that if they discover we know the locations of the ritual sites, they'll move to another unknown location and prevent us from keeping a knife out of Kae's chest."

"I see your point and it's a good one. I'll pay special attention to the vehicles behind and around me."

"Good! While I'm waiting for you to get back, it'll give me a chance to do a little more work on my own cases."

"Sounds good, but I got the name of a George Douglas from Detective Turner with LAPD. Douglas may have information that could be of some help to us. Would you mind giving him a call through the San Bernardino Sheriff's Department and see what he can tell us about satanic cults? Turner says this guy has interviewed and counseled several women who have escaped from cults."

"I'll do that and let you know what he has to say when you get back."

Riggs and his partner were thinking the same

101

thing—the more information they had before an interview, the better the chance of discovering a lie or other discrepancy which would give them a lead to follow up.

As Riggs drove home remembering La Moria's warning for tomorrow, he noticed a store with "Supernatural Beliefs" painted on the front window. He didn't really give it serious thought, but made a U–turn in mid–block and pulled into the small parking lot at the side of the store. What had popped into his mind was the possibility that the store dealt in material used by people who practiced devil worship, Satanism, and other evil things. Why else would the store be called "Supernatural Beliefs?"

The store was dimly lit and had a strange odor, probably from burning incense, which seemed to hit you in the face as you walked inside. The interior was painted black with the only other colors being those reflected off the papers lying on the counter and garments hanging on the wall. The garments were made mostly of black cloth with some in glossy red satin. Each garment resembled a long robe with a hood attached, matching the description given to him by Kae's personalities, Connie and Maxine.

The clerk behind the counter fit right in with the décor and garments hanging from the wall. He was a thin man with eyes that looked sunken in his head and dark, almost black rings around them. He was a person who looked like he'd just risen from the dead—a scary sight for sure ... a

A Birthday to Die For

great–type cast for another movie.

The clerk's gaze had been on Riggs the moment he walked through the door. "How can I help you?"

Riggs walked over to the counter, displayed his badge, and identified himself to the clerk. "If possible, I'd like some information regarding some of your customers."

"I'm not sure I should give you any, it might piss off the owner."

"Does the owner have something to hide?" Riggs inquired.

The guy turned a shade paler. "I don't think so."

"Then what's the problem?" Riggs asked, his voice changing to a deeper, almost sinister tone. "Do you or do you not know the names of specific people who practice devil worship or anyone who may have purchased a knife with the head of Satan carved in the handle?"

The clerk was quick to recognize that he was heading for disaster as he backed away from the counter putting as much space between him and Riggs as possible. He had a distinct feeling Riggs was about to pull him across the countertop and maybe put some hurt on him.

"There are really strange people who come in here for supplies they use in séances or other really weird crap, maybe sacrificial rituals, I don't know. I'm not into that shit. I think most of the people who come in here are involved in witchcraft."

103

"What's the difference between satanic worship and witchcraft?" Riggs asked.

"I don't fully understand the difference," the clerk confessed. "They both believe in demons. In witchcraft they believe in and use curses, hexes, what have you. It doesn't make any difference which group it is, they're both scary."

"It sounds like you don't really believe in your work," Riggs commented.

"I think you're right. It's just a job. The weird bastards who come in here freak me out."

"In what way do they freak you out?"

"Sometimes it's the way they look and other times it's the stuff they ask for," he said.

"Give me an example," said Riggs.

"Well, sometimes they come in with a glassy stare, like maybe they're high on something or they'll ask for ashes of bat wings or other crazy ingredients for whatever they're cooking up."

"Do you practice any of this stuff yourself?"

"You've got to be kidding. I work here because I need a job."

"Well, I'd appreciate it if you'd call me if you come up with anything that might be of help, such as the names of people who purchased red robes from your store," Riggs said in a much friendlier tone of voice, handing the clerk a business card.

"Be glad to…if I come up with anything."

"Thanks! By the way, what's your name?"

"Bud Jackson."

"Thanks Bud!" Riggs called out as he left the store.

A Birthday to Die For

* * *

The rest of the drive home went smoothly. Riggs wondered if this last contact would produce any helpful information. He knew it was a long shot, but you never know what's going to pay off. This thought was still going through his mind when he arrived home. Toby and the boys met him at the front door.

Riggs tried to play a few games with the boys before their bedtime, but his mind kept straying back to the investigation and the little time remaining to solve it. The boys knew his mind wasn't on the games since he offered no challenge to them and they won easily. They eventually got bored and decided to watch one of their favorite TV shows instead, leaving their dad deep in thought.

The night was like so many others when Riggs was involved in a complicated investigation. It seemed like he couldn't turn off his mind. He kept having flashbacks to the one ceremonial site already found, wondering if the second site would be similar. He also wondered what the test of the wood, rope, and dirt samples from the first site would reveal.

Chapter 9

When Riggs awoke, he quickly dressed and grabbed a cup of coffee and a donut as he headed out the front door. He was excited at what the day might bring and didn't feel like wasting any time.

Just a few block away from Dr. Mitchell's office, he made a quick call to Detective Hatch, again arranging for Hatch and Decker to resume their surveillance of Kae around sixteen hundred hours in front of the doctor's office. They agreed and informed him they had not been set up on the doctor's office at the time of the break–in the day before.

As Riggs pulled to the curb, he observed Paula and Kae as they walked towards him. They were dressed in clothes more appropriate for the outdoors—Levis, long–sleeved shirts, boots, and heavier jackets. Paula carried a large picnic basket which she placed on the rear seat of the car before getting in.

"What's in the basket, Doc?" Riggs asked.

"Food, good food, no bagels," she said, directing a laugh in his direction when he grimaced.

"You mean you didn't like my bagels yesterday?" Riggs asked, pretending to be offended.

"Bagels are fine, Riggs, as long as there's something else to eat with them. Eight hours of bagels was a little too much. It felt like we were back in the old days when travelers ate hard tack and jerky to survive."

"You've got to be kidding. I thought the bagels with the cream cheese were good," he shot back.

"It wasn't that they weren't good, but it would have been nice to have some fruit or a salad, something that would keep all of our bodily functions working," she said, glancing at Kae for support.

As they pulled away from the curb, Riggs couldn't help but notice Paula looking towards her office. He guessed that she was worried her office might be broken into a second time while she was away. "Doc, did you ask Building Security to keep a closer watch on your office?"

"I sure did. I also asked the SPD officer if he could stop by now and then."

"Sounds like you've covered your bases."

It was about eight–thirty when they turned northbound onto the freeway. The roads were dry and you could already feel the sun as it glared through the front windshield. Traffic was flowing smoothly as they pulled into the northbound express lane of Interstate 5 and settled back for

A Birthday to Die For

the long ride.

Riggs didn't know which personality he should start with today—Connie, Maxine, Cathleen...or Kae herself. Whoever he chose, it was a crap shoot. There was no way to tell which one it would be. If he picked wrong, he ran the risk of increasing Kae's paranoia and jeopardizing the trust between them. The whole thing was intimidating. He remembered Connie being the most talkative and knowledgeable personality regarding the ceremonial site they'd found yesterday, so he decided to start with her.

"Connie, what do you remember when they drove you to the site near Granite Falls?"

Kae's eyes blinked, then a visible change settled over her. "I remember driving through Seattle on Interstate 5 to Everett," Connie replied without hesitation.

He'd guessed right and mentally patted himself on the back. *One down and only a thousand to go.* He looked for a response in Paula's eyes as he glanced in the rearview mirror. He didn't see a reaction, so he was convinced she was comfortable with him talking to Kae and her personalities.

"I'll stay on Interstate 5 until you tell me to turn. Keep an eye out for the road or highway that looks familiar," he said, increasing their speed.

They had been on the road for about forty minutes, just passing the exits to the city of Everett when Connie reacted. "Turn here." They exited onto a highway leading toward the mountain range in the southeast portion of Snohomish County. It wasn't long before he heard Connie tell him to turn again. He followed the directions she gave him, all the while thinking, *This trip is going more smoothly than our trip yesterday. I wonder why this route seems easier for Connie to find.*

"Why is it you remember this route better than the one we took yesterday?" Riggs asked.

"So far it's been easy because I remember the signs. We also went this way more than the other way, but I may have trouble farther ahead," she said, falling back into a more submissive mode.

As soon as Connie saw a sign that read, "Granite Falls eastbound," she said, "Turn here."

They made the eastbound turn and drove for another twenty minutes before hearing anything more out of Connie. Once again she was sitting forward in the seat, resting her elbows on the dash as she peered through the window. "Stop here," she said, motioning for Riggs to pull off the road.

He pulled onto the dirt shoulder, directly under power lines stretching across the road and up the hillside. He glanced over at Connie, whose head was now against the headrest and her eyes were closed. She remained in that position for several minutes. When he glanced over his shoulder at Paula, she held her finger to her lips signaling for him to stay quiet.

Connie finally spoke. "I can remember power

A Birthday to Die For

lines like these and a dirt road under them. They drove me up the dirt road over the top of the mountain to where they held the ceremony."

"Are you sure these are the same power lines?" Riggs asked.

Connie frowned, a look of determined concentration on her face. "I think so, but I can't be absolutely sure."

Riggs noticed the tremble had returned to Connie's voice and a slight shaking of her body. He asked them to remain in the car while he checked for a road under the power lines. The area under the power lines had been cleared of trees and underbrush, but there was no road. Disappointed, he returned to the car and reported that he didn't find a road.

"Connie, could the power lines you remember be somewhere farther up the road?" Riggs asked, looking into her eyes and mentally crossing his fingers.

"They could be, but they'd have to look exactly like these," she said, the frown becoming more apparent.

"I understand," said Riggs, hoping there'd be another set of power lines up the road.

They decided to continue in the same direction since Connie seemed positive that they were on was the right road. They'd traveled about ten miles farther before they saw the next set of power lines. Riggs pulled to a stop. They could clearly see a road winding up the hillside beneath the power lines.

The road was constructed of dirt and whatever natural rocks had been exposed during grading, which made for a rough ride. The ruts left by previous vehicles and frequent rains made the trip even more perilous as Riggs navigated around the hazards. As they climbed the hill, the narrowness of the road and the abrupt drop–off on the right side sent chills down his spine. He'd never liked heights and this was no exception.

When they reached what they believed to be the top, the road suddenly dropped into a valley covered with a blanket of trees and surrounded by snow–covered mountain peaks. If it hadn't been for the power lines stretching across the valley floor, one could easily imagine being the first person to discover this place. The forest was so vast that a person could become lost without the power lines and road to follow.

As they drove down the hillside onto the valley floor, awed by the beauty around them, the silence was suddenly broken by Connie. "This is the place. I've been here before." She pointed towards a cluster of trees off to the right about a hundred yards from the dirt road. "There. That's it."

Looking in the direction she pointed, Riggs could see what looked like an animal trail leading into the circle of trees—at least it looked like it was made by animals, not humans, but it was hard to tell.

"Doc, I'm asking you and Kae to stay here by the car until I get closer and check out the

A Birthday to Die For

site," Riggs said, looking at Kae to ascertain her emotional condition.

"We'll do that. Be careful." Paula responded.

He followed the trail, walking into the cluster of trees and under branches that were so heavy with foliage that it was like having a roof overhead. He'd only walked a short distance into the stand when he came upon a clearing very similar to the one found yesterday. *There's no way this site could belong to anyone other than the cult who built the site we discovered yesterday.* The log table at the top of the circle and the round logs situated for seating were almost exact duplicates.

In anticipation of the find, Riggs had brought the evidence collection paraphernalia with him. He collected wood, rope, and dirt samples, just as he'd done at the other site, then returned to the car for his camera.

Paula watched Riggs approach carrying paper envelopes and glass containers similar to what he'd used to store evidence from the previous site. She knew without asking that he'd found the ceremonial site Connie had described. She also knew he'd want Connie to return to the site to check her memory. That frightened her because there was no way for her to predict how Kae would react.

It took Paula several minutes to persuade Kae to follow them into the trees. She theorized that showing Kae the location where she'd been brought more often than the other site would be more traumatic for her. They had just walked

113

into the clearing and were standing at the edge of the circle when Kae burst into tears and started to babble incoherently. Her body tremors increased. But for Paula's firm grip on her arm, Kae would have bolted. Paula drew her close, wrapping her arms around her. She spoke softly, trying to console and reassure Kae that she was safe. When Kae appeared calmer, Paula asked, "Can you tell Detective Riggs anything more about what happened to you or anyone else at this location?"

Riggs watched in silence as Paula questioned Kae. He recognized the emotional state Kae was in and felt it was necessary to allow Paula to do the questioning. To do otherwise, could cause further psychological damage to Kae and he certainly didn't want to be responsible for doing her more harm than she'd already suffered. Paula pressed Kae to draw more information from her memory, but without success. Kae continued to weep and shake her head back and forth, denying that she remembered anything more than what she'd already described. Paula consistently used Kae's real name while soliciting information, but Kae didn't respond verbally, nor did any of the other personalities.

They walked back to the car in silence. Riggs was convinced the DNA test of the evidence samples would show the presence of human blood. Paula feared for Kae's life. After seeing what Riggs had collected at the site, she was convinced a human life had been sacrificed there. She only

A Birthday to Die For

hoped she could conceal her growing fear from Kae.

"Are you okay, Doc?" Riggs asked, seeing the worry in her eyes.

"Riggs, I've never been more convinced than I am right now that Kae will die unless you find these bad men and women before her birthday. Can you do it?"

"It's going to be close, but with a little luck and hard work, I think I can," Riggs told her, mentally crossing his fingers—something he'd been doing a lot lately.

The ride back to Paula's office was quiet, each of them caught up in their own thoughts. The hour was late and the sun was starting to disappear beyond the horizon as they got back on I–5 southbound. Riggs pulled out his cell phone to call Joyce Reese in the Crime Lab, while Paula and Kae napped—or at least had their eyes closed.

"Lab Tech Reese, how can I help you?"

"Joyce, this is Riggs. Have you gotten any results on the DNA request I made?"

"Yes! Your samples all show traces of both human and animal blood. I think the victim in your case is telling the truth about human sacrifices," she said without a hint of doubt in her voice. "In fact, I've been able to distinguish at least three different DNA specimens."

"Thanks for the information, Joyce. I'll be bringing similar samples into you sometime tomorrow for the same tests."

115

"I'll be here."

Even though he'd expected it, it was still a surprise when Joyce confirmed that the evidence samples contained human blood. There was no doubt in his mind that humans were being sacrificed during the ceremonies described to him. *The evidence is indisputable—the Satanic cult is planning to sacrifice Kae on her birthday. Now, if it will only point to at least one of the worshippers, I can save her.*

Riggs decided to keep the information regarding the DNA results to himself. He was convinced their knowledge of the results at this time would only enhance their fears and possibly do more harm than good. He knew that Paula should know, but not right now. She had enough to worry about. The break–in at her office made her feel like a victim as well.

Today's trip ended where it started, in front of Dr. Mitchell's office. They wiped the sleep from their eyes, gathered up their belongings, and got out of the car. Before leaving, Riggs checked the doors to Paula's office. "I'll stay in touch and let you know when I have anything positive to tell you."

Riggs looked at Kae and took hold of her hand. He held her stare. "I won't let anything happen to you. I promise."

As he drove away, he thought about the promise he'd just made to Kae, one he hoped he could keep.

Chapter 10

La Moria knew this call could provide some information that would give them a better understanding about how satanic cults work, perhaps give them an avenue they hadn't seen before. The motivation behind satanic worshippers or why they felt the need to inflict harm on others, to sacrifice a baby or any other human being, was something he and Riggs couldn't fully comprehend.

The phone rang twice before a male voice answered. "This is George Douglas, can I help you?"

"Yes! I'm Detective Bob La Moria with the King County Sheriff's Department in Seattle, Washington. I've been referred to you by Detective Turner with the LAPD. He says you've counseled women who have escaped the clutches of satanic cults and you might be able to help us out a little as it relates to our case here in the Seattle area."

"I know Turner. He's a good detective. If he referred you to me, he must think I can help you in some way. What kind of help you looking for?"

"Well, it's like this. My partner and I are trying to save the life of a young woman who claims she's to be sacrificed to Satan on her twenty–sixth birthday. We believe her story, even though she tells it through different multiple personalities. We're looking for ways to save her life. Since we don't know anything about satanic cults, any information you can give us would be of help."

The story had a familiar ring to it. Douglas knew the best way to get to the cult and save the victim's life would be to identify the members, a task that had proven to be impossible in the past. In all the meetings and counseling sessions, either groups or individually, the identity of the cult members had never been revealed.

"Without giving any names, I'll share with you the information I've received during my sessions with women who have escaped their capture, involvement, imprisonment, and anything else I can remember that might be of help. If nothing else, it should help you realize the difficulty of your investigation and give you a better understanding of the satanic culture."

"Any information or education you give us is something we need and should help our investigation," La Moria advised, readying his pen to take notes.

"I've had the privilege of meeting with at least thirty or more women over the last ten or twelve years who have claimed to be fleeing from different cults. They've come primarily from

A Birthday to Die For

Southern California, but some from Nevada and Arizona, too. They've informed me they were introduced to their cult through family members, friends, fellow employees, and some even joined the cult after attending a party."

"You're kidding?" gasped La Moria.

"No, I'm not. These women all had something in common...the fear they developed after attending rituals and realizing the mistake they'd made by getting involved. Each and every one of them still feared being caught and forced to return to the cult for whatever reason. They felt that if they returned they'd be sacrificed or forced to attend rituals or have a baby they'd never see again."

"Have they ever gone to the police or tried to file charges against the cult members?" La Moria asked, still confounded by what he was hearing.

"The closest most of these women ever got to making a report to the police is me. They either can't or won't identify the cult members. I know that on two or three occasions the police have conducted investigations, but came to dead–ends and closed their investigations due to lack of supporting evidence or cooperation on the part of the victim. In those cases, the police were taken to sites believed to be where the rituals were held. The police did find what they believed to be altars which were made either from rocks being piled up or a rock formation. They did find evidence of human blood at one site, but no other evidence to help them in the investigation. So as you can see, the police didn't have a lot to work with and out of frustration deactivated their investigations. I've certainly tried to get the women to file official complaints when they hadn't done so and to cooperate fully when they had. The primary reason they give for not filing a report or cooperating is they're afraid that in doing so their whereabouts would become public record and they'd easily be found by the cult. These women are truly in fear of their lives."

"Have any of these women actually witnessed the sacrifice of a human being?" La Moria asked.

"Yes, they have. Some have described the ritual, the altar with a human stretched across it, and the plunging of the knife into the victim's heart as the cult members chanted their praise to Satan. The descriptions they've given me are so vivid I have no doubt that what they're saying is true. They've even told me about having babies while active in the cult and never seeing their baby again after it was delivered by a cult member. They've told me about being forced to witness the gutting of an animal or the severing of the animal's testicles. Apparently the way the organs fall from the stomach carries a message known only to them."

"Mr. Douglas, why do the cult members do what they do?"

"There are lots of reasons. In their eyes they view Satan as a real god. They are rebellious against Judeo–Christian worship of God. They try to infiltrate churches to undo its work and decrease the power of Jesus. They want to destroy

A Birthday to Die For

free will and to control minds without conscious knowledge. They want to create cult–loyal followers with mind control systems to serve the cult and to protect its secrets. They want to share the power of Satan and demons. Their rituals are very complex, but practiced to ensure obedience. They terrorize their weak members to reinforce mind control."

"Do you believe the red liquid on our victim's windshield, the phone calls at all hours, and the person she believes to be following her are terror tactics conducted by the cult she's trying to escape?"

"Yes, I do. I also believe she'll be killed unless you and your partner can pull off a miracle."

"I was afraid you were going to say something like that." La Moria was feeling the weight of the world on his shoulders.

"Sorry about that, but that's the way I see it. I wish I could help you more, but I don't see how. I'll be available anytime you feel I might be of help. Good luck!"

"Thanks for the information. I'm sure we'll put it to good use."

La Moria leaned back in his chair, exhausted from the information he'd received. There was no longer any doubt in his mind that he and Riggs were working a very dangerous and impossible case. He couldn't wait to share the information with Riggs and wondered how they could use it to save Kae's life, much less identify the cult members and arrest the sick bastards.

Chapter 11

With the interviews of Kae, her alternate personalities, and Dr. Mitchell completed, it was time to put a full court press to the investigation. Riggs had always looked on his investigations as a game of wits between himself and the bad guys. In most cases involving petty crimes, the actions of the bad guys lacked the sophistication it took to make it a real game, but in premeditated crimes such as murder, fraud, and others, the intellectual challenge is always present. Nonetheless, the game of wits starts like any other game—you play the cards you're dealt.

Riggs' first stop was the Crime Lab where he handed the evidence collected at the ritual site near Granite Falls to Joyce Reese. "I'd appreciate it if you'd do the same DNA test on these samples as you did on the samples from the Lake Mayfield area. I suspect your findings will be the same."

"You're probably right, but let's make sure. I'll get right on it and let you know as soon as I have an answer."

123

Riggs turned to leave, then paused and looked at Reese. "Joyce, did your test of the items at the first ritual site reveal enough DNA to make a match should I find the donor?"

"More than enough. Just bring me who you think is the donor or something of theirs that I can draw a sample from and if it's the right person, I can make a positive match."

His eyes gave off a mischievous sparkle. "Glad to hear that. I'll see if I can find the donor."

Riggs left the office knowing he could rely on Joyce to do her job. He'd always been impressed with her and her willingness to get involved. She got excited about cases, especially when she knew her lab work was critical to the investigation. The more complicated the case, the more interest she had in getting the lab work done as fast and as carefully as possible. She often voiced her objection about not being included in the arrest of suspects. She truly believed herself to be a partner to each and every detective she'd done lab work for and would never let them forget it.

Back in his office, Riggs phoned Captain Osborn as La Moria walked in. He listened as Riggs explained to the Captain exactly where the ritual sites were located. On the desk in front of him, Riggs referred to the latitude and longitude shown on a map, which specifically identified the locations for the flyover by the helicopter crew. He also recommended that the flyovers be conducted between twenty–three hundred and zero two

A Birthday to Die For

hundred hours, a time during which he believed the rituals were being held. La Moria could tell from Riggs' reaction that the Captain had agreed to pass the information on to the flight crew.

"Sounds like we have one of the bases covered," La Moria said.

"I believe so. Now if these assholes will only cooperate by performing a ritual right away, we'll have a chance at nailing some of them and maybe close them down."

La Moria knew where Riggs was coming from. They'd worked so many cases together that they actually knew what the other was thinking most of the time as it related to an investigation.

"Bob, I think Rebecca Shelby is the key to this whole thing. If we can find her and persuade her to talk, we'll know who we're looking for."

"You might be right, unless we catch the guy in the knit hat first. In any case, finding this Shelby woman is going to be a challenge. She disappeared about the same time Kae was introduced to the cult. We haven't been able to locate any friends or relatives, no proof of her ever being married, and no activity on her credit cards or Social Security number. If I didn't know better, I'd think she never existed," La Moria said, leaning forward in his chair.

Riggs frowned. "I don't believe it's just a coincidence that she disappeared after introducing Kae to the cult. What was her connection to the cult? Did she become a foster mother so she could funnel young girls...virgins...to the cult for sacrificial purposes? Is that why she introduced Kae to them? If we can find her, we can get some answers."

"I've asked myself those same questions and I agree—I don't believe her disappearance was just a coincidence either," said La Moria.

"I'm going to see Barbara Pope from the Missing Persons Unit. If Shelby can be found, Barbara will find her," said Riggs.

"Good thinking. While you're talking to Pope, I'll contact the teacher, Patricia Mohon. She's listed as a reference on Shelby's foster parent application. She currently teaches Biology at South Seattle Community College. I'll meet you back here after I talk to her."

"Maybe I should go with you on that interview?" Riggs suggested.

"It's just one woman and unless she's seven feet tall and weighs three hundred pounds, I think I can handle her. I'll be talking to her at the school, so I don't really see her as a threat at this stage of the game."

After La Moria left the office, Riggs made his way to the office for the Missing Persons Unit located one floor above the Homicide Unit. Barbara Pope was a go–getter, a compassionate person who paid attention to details. She didn't fit the cop stereotype, which explained her tremendous success as a Missing Persons Detective. She approached each investigation as if the missing person she was trying to find was her own

A Birthday to Die For

mother.

Raising a skeptical brow, Pope asked, "To what do I owe the pleasure of this visit?"

"I've got a weird one and I need your help," Riggs said, trying to peer around an oversized rose blossom in a vase parked in the center of Pope's desk.

"Come on, Riggs. Everything you're involved in is weird, so why should it be any different this time?"

"Well, maybe it's because I have a twenty–five year–old woman who suffers from multiple personalities and believes she's going to be sacrificed in a satanic ritual on her birthday, which is less than ten days from now." Riggs paused for effect.

Surprise bloomed across Pope's face as large as the flower in front of her. "You're kidding me?"

"I need your help to find the foster mother, Rebecca Shelby, who introduced the victim to the satanic cult."

"This is a joke, right? I'm one stupid cop, right?" she laughed, her eyes sweeping around her office for cameras or others who would burst in to witness the joke being played on her.

Riggs shook his head. "Sorry Charlie, but this one's for real and here's a copy of my file."

Pope gingerly took the file. "That's hard to believe Riggs, but I'll play along. I'll contact Health and Social Services for any information they may have on the Shelby woman and your victim...uh...Kae Carlson," she read. "They

127

should be able to provide me with the last known address, phone number, Social Security number, date of birth, as well as names of friends or relatives and anything else they may have that will help in finding Shelby. Who knows, maybe I'll find some of Carlson's kin."

"I'd appreciate anything you can do. We've already gotten Shelby's credit card information and Social Security number, but our preliminary check has revealed no activity on either. La Moria has also gotten the names of the references she used on her application for the job. He's out interviewing one of them right now."

"I'll have all the information they have on Shelby and Carlson within the hour."

Riggs stood up to leave. "Thanks, Barb. We can use anything that will expedite this investigation. Oh, before I forget, I need to know...do you still have your contacts with the telephone company?"

"Yeah, why?"

"Well, I need another favor," Riggs said, shooting a sideward glance in her direction.

"Okay, spill it. What do you want me to do?"

"I'd like you to pull the telephone records for Kae Carlson for the last three or four months and check her incoming calls. If possible, I want to identify the callers. She tells me she's been getting calls at all hours of the day and night, but no one speaks when she answers."

"I'll do it, but if you keep asking me to do all these things, I may as well take over your

A Birthday to Die For

investigation."

"I'd gladly give it to you, but you've no idea what's really involved or you wouldn't even entertain the thought."

"I suppose you're right. You do have a habit of getting involved in some difficult cases."

"Well, I can remember some of your missing persons being a little weird as well and sometimes showing up dead."

"I know what you mean. By the way, if you ever get the chance, I could use a little help finding four missing prostitutes. Who knows, they might be related to this case? Prostitutes are thought to be the carriers for the devil, so I'm told."

"You're kidding, aren't you?"

"I don't know, Riggs. I've hunted down a lot of missing prostitutes over the years and heard every explanation in the world about why they do the things they do, so your guess is as good as mine. Maybe they did meet their fate at the hands of the Grim Reaper."

"Thanks Barb, I'll keep that in mind." *Why not have prostitutes involved, too? It's not like I have a whole lot of other leads.* The phone rang just as he turned to leave.

"Missing Persons, Pope. Riggs wait." She handed him the phone. "It's La Moria."

"I made contact with Patricia Mohon in the teachers' lounge at the school. She denies having any knowledge regarding cults, devil worshippers, or anything of the sort. She also denies knowing Kae Carlson or why Shelby disappeared. She

129

does recall being Shelby's reference, but says she didn't know Shelby. She claims a detective with the Pierce County Sheriff's Department asked her to do it. Get this, it's Paul Trickey."

"Trickey? Do you think she's telling the truth?" Riggs asked.

"After what you told me about who can be cult member and how secretive they are, I'm not willing to stake my reputation on it," La Moria replied.

"Did you ask her to take a polygraph examination?"

"Sure did, but she refused."

"Press harder. Tell her if she still refuses, we'll be forced to contact her fellow teachers, administrators, friends, relatives, and neighbors in an attempt to verify her story."

Barbara watched his eyes narrow to a squint as she listened to Riggs' side of the conversation. She knew she was witnessing some hardball being played by Riggs.

Riggs paused before exiting her office. "Do you by chance have a DNA sample from any of your missing prostitutes?"

"Yeah, one…Hazel Cunningham. Why do you ask?"

"I've recovered blood from two ceremonial sites. It might be a long shot, but why don't you have Joyce down in the lab run Cunningham's DNA against the samples I collected?"

"Like you say, it's a long shot, but why not?"

"Good! Let me know the results."

A Birthday to Die For

On his way back to his office, Riggs stuck his head around door of the Crime Lab looking for Joyce Reese, but saw no one. Just as he turned away, he heard Joyce yell at him to come back.

"I was just checking to see if you've had a chance to complete the test on those samples I brought you from the Granite Falls site?"

"Perfect timing, I just finished," she replied.

"What did you find?" he asked, feeling he already knew what her answer would be.

"The test screams you're looking for some real bad dudes. I found traces of human and animal blood in each of the samples you submitted, same as in the Lake Mayfield samples. I think you'd better find these sick perverts before they kill anyone else."

"I know, Joyce. I'd like nothing better than to do just that. If you could tell me who was killed and by whom, the case would be solved and we'd all be happy," he said, only half kidding.

"If I could do that, we wouldn't need you," Joyce said, smiling back at him.

"By the way, Barbara up in Missing Persons will be asking you to compare the DNA of one of her missing prostitutes against what I've submitted to you. Let me know what you find."

"Will do."

Riggs made his way back to his office, thinking about the ritual sites and the presence of blood. While the evidence of human blood helped verify Kae's story, whether or not it was murder remained a mystery. The phone on his desk was ringing.

"She's complaining that it's unfair to force her to take a polygraph, but she finally agreed," La Moria said. "We're enroute to the office, so alert the Polygraph Examiner we'll be in his office in a few minutes."

"I'll make all of the arrangements," Riggs advised. "See you when you get here."

For La Moria it seemed as if the drive to the office was a hundred miles. Mohon talked nonstop. "I don't understand why my honesty is in question. I'm going to file a complaint against you and sue you for defamation of character." *Blah, blah, blah.*

The polygraph office was located a short distance down the hall from the Detectives' office. The door was open when Riggs walked in. Karl Hutchinson, a man with vast experience in the law enforcement field, grunted at him. Hutch had given several hundred polygraph examinations over the years and had even obtained several confessions without ever hooking the suspect up to the polygraph machine.

Riggs handed his case file to Hutchinson, pointing out the need for the polygraph. As Hutchinson browsed through the file, he jotted down notes in order to formulate the questions he would ask Patricia Mohon which would either

A Birthday to Die For

confirm her involvement or her lack of knowledge of the cult.

After reading the file and asking a few question of Riggs, Hutchinson decided the relevant questions should be: "Are you a member of any group that worships Satan?" and "Have you ever been present during the ritual sacrifice of any animal or human being?" The final relevant question would be "Is the statement you gave to Detective La Moria the complete truth?"

"Hutch, I think these questions pretty much cover my concerns. Depending on her answers, I'll know which way to go with regard to her."

"Remember what I've always told you, they have to lie to pass the polygraph," he said with the hint of a smile on his face.

"Yeah, I remember. If they lie to the relevant questions, they're guilty of the crime, but if they lie to the control questions, they're innocent."

Their attention was drawn to the door as La Moria walked in with Patricia Mohon. She was a thin woman, nearly blonde hair, and very well dressed. Had he not known, Riggs would have guessed her to be an executive of some kind. The outfit she wore screamed expensive.

La Moria quickly introduced Mohon to Riggs and Hutchinson. As Hutchinson started to talk to Mohon, Riggs and La Moria left the office, closing the door behind them. They moved to the small room located next to the polygraph room which had a one–way mirror in the wall between the two rooms. Hutchinson advised Mohon of her rights and how the polygraph worked as Riggs and La Moria settled back to watch the proceedings.

Mohon acknowledged her understanding of her rights to an attorney, but waived them and agreed to take the examination. Hutchinson went on to explain about relevant and control questions to her. When she nodded indicating she understood, Hutchinson advised her that she needed to answer each question with a yes or no, that a shake of the head or any other body movement could create a false response and negate the test. "If that were to happen, Ms. Mohon, the investigators will assume you did it on purpose and that you're hiding something."

They watched the needles moving up and down on the chart as each question was asked and answered. Both thought they detected an indication that she was being deceptive in her answers to the relevant questions, but they were proven wrong when they heard Hutchinson tell Mohon she had passed.

"I told that detective I didn't have anything to hide," she said indignantly.

"I'm sure Detective La Moria believed you, but because of the serious nature of his investigation, he had to be absolutely sure," explained Hutchinson.

Realizing they were at a dead end as far as Mohon was concerned, they apologized for the inconvenience caused her and La Moria drove her back to the school.

A Birthday to Die For

* * *

Slightly disappointed that the Mohon lead had evaporated, Riggs decided to contact Detective Pope to see if she had come up with anything on Shelby. Pope was on the telephone when he walked into her office. He took a seat in the chair beside her desk and waited for her to finish her call.

"I've been expecting you," she said as she hung up the phone.

"I thought I'd stop by for an update on Shelby. I brought coffee for you," he said, handing her the cup of coffee.

"Oh please, Riggs, you can't call that coffee, not with the mocha and whip cream in it."

"I thought it might sweeten your disposition a little."

"Ha, there you go again, Riggs...thinking."

"See Barb, that's what happens when I try to be a nice guy."

She shrugged. "Well at least you try. Here's the information I have so far. Internal Revenue has informed me there has been no activity on her Social Security number for at least ten years, which would be consistent with the time your victim, Kae Carlson, was transferred to another foster home. I didn't find any additional information through the credit check, which is highly unusual unless the person is incarcerated or dead. I don't have an answer for you, but I'll keep working on it. If I come up with anything,

135

I'll let you know right away."

"One more thing, Riggs. Shelby's application indicates she was an orphan and raised in a foster home herself. There was no record of a spouse, children, parents, or siblings. The records on Carlson indicate she was abandoned by her parents whose whereabouts are unknown. She has a younger brother and sister who were placed in different foster homes and later adopted. The adoption papers are sealed, so we're at a dead end as far as finding them without a court order to unseal the files."

"Thanks for what you've done. If you come up with any more ideas, let me know. I doubt the unsealing of the adoption records will be of any help due to the young age of the brother and sister when this all happened," Riggs said.

"Wait, there's one more thing I can do for you."

"What's that?"

"I can send an alert nationwide to the Medical Examiners and Coroners asking for any information they might have on a Jane Doe corpse they may be holding in their morgue. It could be they have an open case pending the identification of a female victim. If so, it would explain why it appears Shelby fell off the face of the earth."

"Good idea. Let's do it! Anything on the telephone records yet?" Riggs asked.

"No, not yet. I should have the records either later today or sometime tomorrow."

"Good. Let me know if you learn anything

A Birthday to Die For

from the telephone records or you get a response from any of the morgues."

"Count on it. By the way, I did submit my request to the lab to check Cunningham's DNA against what you found at the ceremonial sites."

The facts so far caused Riggs to consider the possibility that Shelby was also a victim of the cult. *Why would they sacrifice her too? Had she done something to fall out of favor so they killed her?* Riggs was still pondering the question regarding the whereabouts of Shelby when he received a call from La Moria.

"Riggs, I tried to contact Beth Williams, the social worker who's also listed as a reference for Shelby. She no longer works for the Department of Health and Social Services. Their records show she's retired and currently resides in Monroe, up in Snohomish County."

"Okay, let's meet at the Pierce County Sheriff's Office in the morning. We'll interview Paul Trickey, who is now the Chief of Detectives, before we contact Beth Williams.

"Sounds good. I'll pick up the coffee and meet you in their parking garage at zero eight hundred hours."

Chapter 12

A light rain was coming down as Riggs drove to Tacoma. The clouds hung a little lower than usual, turning everything a dismal gray. The streets were wet with the oil coming to the surface, mixing with the rain water and trash flowing into the gutters. Riggs pulled into the parking garage at the Pierce County Sheriff's Department. He could hear the sound of thunder in the distance, familiar because Riggs had lived in this area most of his life. He was used to the rain and thunder, but lately he found himself looking forward to the approach of summer with days of sunshine and the opportunity to go somewhere without a raincoat. However, today was just another normal day in the Northwest where people considered three days without rain a signal that summer had arrived. Four days without rain and they began to worry about the possibility of drought conditions and the threat to the forest around them.

As Riggs stepped from his car, La Moria

approached, handing him a cup of coffee. Both of them enjoyed their coffee as well as the occasions they spent together, whether at work or on their own personal time. This gave them an opportunity to discuss cases or just shoot the bull. They always had something they could talk about.

"How do you want to approach this interview?" La Moria asked.

"I'll take the lead with you jumping in any time, especially when further clarification is needed."

"You mean just like you do on my interviews?" La Moria teased.

"Something like that, but remember, Paul Trickey is the Chief of Detectives and will be well–tuned to our approach. He's pretty young to hold that position, so he must be pretty sharp. Either that or he's well connected. On top of everything else, he's a fellow officer and our superior. He'll expect a certain degree of respect as well as candor," Riggs mused aloud.

La Moria slapped him on the back. "I hear you loud and clear. Glad you have the lead on this."

The main lobby had several entrances leading off of it to the Detective Offices. A receptionist was seated at her desk behind the counter, which was separated from the lobby by a bullet–proof window, which extended from the countertop to the ceiling. The window had a small hole with a screen over it to protect her, while still allowing her to communicate with anyone on the other side. She controlled entry to all the offices by way

A Birthday to Die For

of a button on her desk which sent an electrical signal to the door to be opened and deactivating the lock for a brief moment. She didn't even glance up when they approached.

Riggs spoke through the small opening while at the same time he and La Moria held their badges and identification against the window for her inspection.

"We'd like to speak with Paul Trickey, Chief of Detectives," Riggs said.

As they waited for her response, he couldn't help but wonder why an attractive young woman who looked to be in her early twenties would pierce her nose and bottom lip, which detracted from her appearance and looked unsanitary. He could only imagine what other parts of her body had been pierced. *Ouch!*

While punching some numbers on a keypad, she asked, "Is he expecting you?"

"We didn't call ahead if that's what you mean, but I'm sure he will talk to us. Just let him know we're here," Riggs said. They watched as she picked up the telephone and dialed the Chief's Office.

"He said to send you in. He'll meet you just inside that door and escort you to his office," she said, pointing to a door on the left side of the lobby.

"Thanks," Riggs replied, surprised at her professionalism, despite the pin in her lip.

Just inside the door, they were met by two men, both about six feet tall with slim, muscular

141

builds and well–trimmed hair. It was almost like they'd come from the same mold. They both wore short–sleeved white shirts which were tight around their biceps in an obvious attempt to draw attention to their physiques, something commonly seen with bodybuilders.

The first one to approach held out his hand to shake theirs and identified himself as Paul Trickey, Chief of Detectives. He then introduced his sidekick, Detective Sergeant Dennis Ryker.

"Denny and I go back a long ways. We worked patrol and narcotics together for a few years. He's such a great backup, so I brought him into the Criminal Investigations Section to serve as my assistant. You know how it is, you always need someone you trust behind you," said Trickey as they exchanged handshakes.

"Nice to meet both of you, Chief. I'm Jerry Riggs and this is my partner, Bob La Moria."

"What can we do for you boys?" Chief Trickey asked, looking first at Riggs, then at La Moria.

"We'd like to talk to you about satanic cults and a woman by the name of Rebecca Shelby," Riggs advised, paying close attention to their body language or some sign of surprise. He'd hoped to see their reactions, but both had turned away as they escorted them to the Chief's office.

Chief Trickey moved to his chair behind the desk, motioning for them to sit in the two chairs facing him. Ryker seated himself in a chair slightly behind them, next to the door—a power move often used during interrogations to intimidate

A Birthday to Die For

and control, as well as allowing signals to be passed from the person seated behind the person being interviewed. Riggs and La Moria picked up on it immediately, which brought a slight smile to their faces because the Chief and Ryker had things turned around. It was they who were going to be interviewed or interrogated, depending on how the exchange of information flowed.

The Chief sat for a moment, studying the faces of Riggs and La Moria. "Can I get you some coffee?"

Riggs shook his head. "We just had some, but thanks anyway."

"Sounds like you want to get right down to business, so obviously this isn't a social call."

"Chief, we're up against a short timeline and we need as much information as possible to prevent the murder of a young woman. We think you might have some information which will help us do just that," Riggs advised, settling back in his chair, appearing relaxed in order to send a signal to the Chief and Ryker that he was not intimidated.

Trickey planted his elbows on his desk and interlaced his fingers, touching the tips of his index fingers. "Okay, I don't know what information you're looking for, but let's hear your questions."

"What do you know about cults, satanic rituals, or devil worshippers?" Riggs inquired.

"Nothing! I've heard and read a little about these alleged activities over the years, but have never witnessed or been involved in any

143

investigation regarding anything of that nature. Frankly, I don't believe they really exist to the extent some claim," Chief Trickey responded, glancing past Riggs' shoulder in Ryker's direction, a gesture not unnoticed by Riggs.

Riggs and La Moria turned their attention to Ryker when he interrupted their questioning of Trickey. "This young woman who is to die, do you have her in protective custody?"

"Let's just say, we know where she is at this time," answered La Moria, surprised at the question. Riggs turned back to Trickey, feeling annoyed and surprised at Ryker's question.

La Moria listened and watched as Riggs resumed his interrogation of the Chief. He wasn't impressed with Trickey or his answers. He wondered why Ryker remained in the room and why he was concerned about the Kae's whereabouts. *Is there more to their involvement than meets the eye?* He'd also noticed the exchange of glances between the Chief and Ryker. In his opinion, the Chief's answers came too fast. He didn't pause to think about the question or his answer. He sensed that Riggs had already come to the same conclusion that the Chief is a showboat kind of guy. Bob knew if the right people were asked, they'd say that the Chief is a person who believes he's God's gift to women...or maybe not. *Maybe Trickey's more interested in guys with big biceps.* He watched Riggs' body language and listened to his tone of voice, which clearly indicated that he'd had enough of the Chief's

A Birthday to Die For

arrogance and wasn't buying any of his answers.

There was a pause as Riggs leaned forward and looked directly into the Chief's eyes. "Would you agree there's a possibility that satanic cults and rituals do actually exist?" Riggs asked, his eyes narrowing and his demeanor becoming more intense.

"Anything's *possible*, it's just that I've never seen any concrete evidence which proves that they do."

Riggs suddenly swiveled his chair around and looked at Ryker. "How about you? Do you believe in the possibility of devil worshippers, satanic cults, and human sacrifices?"

Riggs' sudden move caught Ryker off guard. He reacted by pushing his chair against the wall and sitting up straight. "Maybe!" he sputtered.

"What makes you think there may be satanic cults?" Riggs asked, seemingly ignoring the Chief and focusing on Ryker, a move which La Moria believed caught the Chief off guard.

"I've heard rumors, but only rumors, nothing solid," Ryker replied, now looking somewhat uneasy as they focused on him.

"I thought you were here to talk to me," said Trickey, trying to regain control of the situation. "Like I said, I've seen no real evidence to support any theory that satanic cults or devil worshippers really exist," he repeated.

La Moria couldn't believe what he was hearing. A Chief of Detectives has access to all the bulletins and other sources reporting mutilation

145

of animals believed to be related to some type of satanic ritual or activity, yet he still refuses to accept their existence. *This is unbelievable! How the hell did he ever make Detective, much less Chief of Detectives with such a closed mind? And Ryker, he's nothing but a kiss ass.*

"Chief, do you know a teacher by the name of Pat Mohon?" Riggs asked, pushing on, knowing he now had both Trickey and Ryker off balance.

Trickey looked perplexed. "No, should I?"

Riggs chose to ignore the Chief's comeback question, which he recognized as an attempt to gain information before being asked the next question. "Do you know a Social Worker by the name of Beth Williams?"

Again the Chief answered in an officious tone of voice, "No. Now boys, if you've come here to ask me about people I don't know, then you're wasting your time and mine. I don't appreciate your attitude or tone of voice and I'll make sure your Chief hears about this."

La Moria couldn't believe what he'd just heard. Neither he nor Riggs were known for wasting anybody's time. Trickey's comment was like waving a red flag in front of a bull—it pissed him off. He saw a cold steely stare in Riggs' eyes before all pretense at diplomacy went out the window.

Riggs stood up and leaned over the desk towards the Chief, then asked the next question slowly, emphasizing every word. "Do you know Rebecca Shelby?"

A Birthday to Die For

Clearly agitated, Trickey replied, "No."

Out of the corner of his eye, Riggs noticed that Ryker was now standing, as if he was going to come to the Chief's defense. Ignoring Ryker's obvious attempt to show support to the Chief and regain some degree of intimidation, Riggs again leaned towards the Chief. Placing his hands palms down on the desk, he spoke quietly. "That's strange since you were one of her references for her foster mother application and you also encouraged others to recommend her."

Riggs knew the Chief had stepped in it and miscalculated the two of them. They'd done their homework and were paying very close attention to his answers and body language. Neither he nor La Moria were impressed or intimidated by his rank or Detective Sergeant Ryker's presence. If he wanted to complain to their Chief, they could care less and Trickey knew it.

Riggs watched as the Chief squirmed in his chair, then finally picked up his coffee cup and turned away. Ryker had returned to his chair and was attempting to look officious and threatening, not realizing how ludicrous his actions appeared to Riggs and La Moria. In their opinion, there was nothing he could do now to help the Chief save face. Riggs knew he had the Chief by the balls. He'd caught him in a lie and he'd done it in front of one of his own. He knew Trickey would attempt to save face, as ridiculous as it was, in order to minimize the impact of his last answer.

Trickey turned and set his cup down on the

desk, obviously trying to come up with a plausible excuse for his answers and actions. "My memory isn't what it used to be. While I was looking out the window, I was trying to recollect where I might have known this Rebecca Shelby. I don't recall the name, but I do remember several years ago when I was a beat cop, I handled a domestic violence detail where both the husband and wife were beat up pretty bad. I arrested both of them and sent the wife to the hospital in an ambulance. I can't remember their names, but they had three children in need of foster care. A neighbor, who may have been this Rebecca Shelby, came forward and agreed to take charge of the children until either parent returned home. This was before it became mandatory to release children only to Children's Protective Services, so I placed the children into her custody. This is the only thing I remember that would explain my being a reference for her."

The Chief was now matching stare for stare with Riggs as he waited for Riggs' reaction to what he had just been told when Ryker cut in. "Chief, I think I remember backing you up on that call, but it's been a long time and I'm not really sure," Ryker volunteered in another lame attempt to show support for the Chief.

La Moria knew Riggs wasn't buying it and waited for Riggs' reaction. The Chief's explanation was viable and he didn't see any reason for further questioning at this time. Apparently, Riggs felt the same way. He stood up and extended his hand

A Birthday to Die For

to Trickey. "Thanks, for your time, Chief. Do what you think you have to regarding my Chief."

They stood to leave and just outside the door to the Chief's office, Riggs stopped and turned to the Chief. "One more question, if you don't mind."

"What is it?"

"How about Kae Carlson? Do you remember that name?"

There was slight pause before Trickey answered. "Not that I can recall."

"How about you, Sgt. Ryker? Do you remember the name Kae Carlson?" Riggs asked, not wanting to let Ryker off the hook.

"No, it isn't familiar to me either," Ryker said.

"Well, thanks again to both of you. Maybe we'll talk another time," Riggs said as he and La Moria walked towards the lobby.

Once out of their earshot, Riggs said, "What do you think, Bob? Can you believe those dimwits?"

"No, I can't. If the Chief thinks he can trust Ryker, he'd better think again. That guy's a real snake in the grass. He'll do anything to climb the ladder."

Back in the lobby, La Moria motioned to Riggs to follow him as he walked over to the receptionist. "Hi, I'm Detective Bob La Moria. What's your name?"

"Jan, why do you ask?"

"Well, Jan, we just met your boss for the first

time. I was wondering if he's a pretty good boss," La Moria asked casually.

"You mean 'muffin buns'?" she replied.

"Is that what you call the Chief of Detectives?" La Moria asked with a sly smile.

"We sure do. Didn't you notice his tight ass? He struts around here like a rooster in heat, flexing his muscles, combing his hair, and flirting with every girl in sight. Some of the guys said they've seen him and Sgt. Ryker standing in front of the locker room mirror flexing their muscles and admiring each other. Neither one is easy to ignore...they won't let you."

"Just as I thought," La Moria said, laughing, as he and Riggs exited the building.

The glass door hadn't fully closed when they heard someone call out their names. They turned around and saw Jan Ice approaching.

"Oh no, not her," Riggs groaned.

"Yeah, our favorite TV news personality. What a pain in the ass she is," La Moria commented, watching Riggs simmer at the thought of having to talk to her.

"Riggs, what are you doing here in Pierce County? You're working on something big, aren't you?" Ice asked, once again trying to worm inside information out of them to share with her TV audience during the evening broadcast. She didn't care what the "big news" was, all she cared about was impressing her boss in an attempt to justify the big bucks she was being paid.

A Birthday to Die For

"Jan, I'm going to tell you and Bob is going to tell you, we're just visiting," said Riggs as he moved away.

"Come on, Riggs, I know you and La Moria better than that. You two are working on something and I'd like to be on top of it if it's breaking news."

"Jan, *if* we have a story for you, you'll be the first to know," La Moria advised, trying to get Riggs off the hook. He was aware of the hard feeling Riggs had towards her. If she'd done the same thing to him, he'd be pissed too.

"I've heard that from you two before and every time I get the story after it breaks with another reporter. How long are you going to hold that one little thing against me, Riggs?"

"Little thing? Jan you almost got a person killed! You promised me you'd keep the information I gave you off the record, but you didn't because you were showing off for your boss. Until I believe I can trust you, I'm not going to give you the scoop on anything."

"That's not fair! I've learned my lesson. I won't burn you again, I promise!"

"Okay, then this is the closest I'm going to come to giving you anything on our investigation at this time," said Riggs, glancing at La Moria for some kind of response.

"Okay, okay, I promise I won't release it until you tell me it's safe," said Jan, pulling out her note pad.

"Jan, we're working on something we feel

could be very dangerous, not only for us, but anyone closely associated with us. Your life could be in danger if it's suspected you've got any inside knowledge about what we're doing. That's all I'm going to tell you."

"Come on, Riggs, you've got to tell me more than that. I can handle myself. I'm not worried. I need a story," she implored with unconcealed excitement in her voice.

"That's it. I'm not telling you anything more. Come on, Bob, let's get out of here."

Ice watched them walk away, peeved over the fact that Riggs had gotten her investigative juices flowing, then left her hanging. She knew them well enough to know they were working on something which would turn into a good story. *If those bozos think they're going to keep me from the story, they're dead wrong.*

On their walk back to the garage, they agreed to leave La Moria's car there while they contacted Dan Fowler, another person listed as a reference for Rebecca Shelby. They'd contact this individual together since his address indicated that he lived in the seedier part of town, an area heavily populated by juvenile gangs always looking for a fight with anyone encroaching on their territory. These gang–bangers hated cops, considered them challengers to their self– perceived authority.

The home of Dan Fowler was a small, single–story house painted white and in serious need of another paint job. The once white latex on the

A Birthday to Die For

side of the house was curled in spots with the paint chipping and falling off. The lawn hadn't been mowed for some time and a garbage can was laying on its side with garbage spilled around it. A chain–link fence surrounded the property and parallel with both sides of the driveway. An old, grey–colored Toyota pickup was parked in the driveway with the hood up and tools laying on top of the engine. A Harley Davidson motorcycle that had been converted into a chopper was parked in front of the pickup truck.

"Well, this picture says it all," La Moria muttered with a scowl.

"It sure does. What do you want to bet this guy is big, ugly, and dirty?" Riggs asked.

"No thanks. I also believe these guys who ride choppers work at looking as dirty as they can, which also relates to being ugly."

"That sounds about right," Riggs replied, exiting the car.

They approached the front porch through the swinging gate on the chain link fence. A white male about five feet eleven inches tall, with a full beard and mustache walked out and stood in front of them. Their attention was immediately drawn to the tattoos on both arms. On his left bicep was a tattoo in the design of a banner with the words "Go Navy" while the one on his right bicep was the image of the Devil mounted on a horse, carrying a banner that read, "Welcome to Hell." Riggs and La Moria looked at each other

153

and smiled. They couldn't have been more right. This guy was indeed big, ugly, and dirty.

"What do you want?" he asked, doing a good "bad guy" impression in a tone of voice that was quite unnecessary as his looks alone would scare most people.

They held up their badges. "I'm Detective Riggs and this is my partner, Detective La Moria. We'd like to have a few words with you about Rebecca Shelby…that is, if you're Dan Fowler."

"I'm Fowler, but I don't talk to cops, so get your sorry asses off my property."

"Can't do that," Riggs replied, continuing towards the porch.

La Moria moved slightly to the right and a step behind Riggs as they approached, knowing anything could happen when confronted with a person like this. Fowler knew Riggs wasn't intimidated by him and would be ready for anything he might decide to do.

"When did you last see Rebecca Shelby?" Riggs asked.

"I don't know a Rebecca Shelby and even if I did, I wouldn't tell you a damn thing."

Riggs was now standing in front of Fowler, almost nose to nose, as La Moria watched for any threatening moves by Fowler. He knew what Riggs was doing—trying to get Fowler to do something that would put him in a compromising position, like maybe face down on the porch. Time was running out for Kae Carlson and Riggs wasn't about to walk away from someone who

A Birthday to Die For

might have some valuable information.

It happened so fast that La Moria almost missed what Fowler had done to deserve being laid out on the porch with his right arm extended behind and above him in a reverse wrist lock, a controlling move practiced over and over again in the police academy and during refresher training. Fowler had placed his right hand on Riggs' chest to push him away. Riggs reached across and over Fowler's hand, peeling it off his chest, twisting it away from Fowler's body and bending it back at the wrist. The movement caused considerable pain and brought Fowler's knees to the porch as he tried to prevent his arm from being broken.

"See what you've done, you ugly bastard? You've given me enough to throw your sorry ass in jail. So let me ask you again, do you know Rebecca Shelby?" Riggs said, keeping the pressure on Fowler's arm and wrist as he waited for an answer.

"Yeah, yeah, I know Becca. She was a neighbor a few years back."

"Now that was easy, wasn't it?" Riggs said, applying a little more pressure to emphasize what would happen if he continued to be an asshole.

"Do you know where she is right now?"

"No, I don't," Fowler shouted, trying to move back and forth to alleviate the pain Riggs was applying to keep him under control.

The information was forthcoming, but slowly. La Moria wondered how long he was going to keep the pressure on Fowler's arm. He knew from his

155

own experience how severe the pain from that hold can be. He wished he could be as proficient with it as Riggs.

"Do you remember being a reference for Shelby to become a foster mother?" Riggs asked.

"I might have, but I don't remember," Fowler answered, trying to push away from the hold and relieve some of the pain.

"How can you live right next door to her, but you don't remember her or being a reference for her on a job application? Seems like you have a selective memory."

"I'm telling you, I don't know anything and even if I did, I wouldn't tell you."

"What about devil worshipping? Do you know anything about that?" Riggs asked, applying a little more pressure.

"I told you, I don't know anything. I don't know anything more about Becca and I don't know anything about devil worshippers."

"Okay, I guess I have to accept what you're saying for now, but if I find out you're lying, I'll be back. In the meantime, if you agree not to be an asshole and you promise to call me if you remember anything, I'll let you up."

"Okay, okay!"

Riggs stepped back while Fowler clambered to his feet. "Here's my business card. If you remember or find out any information on the whereabouts of Rebecca Shelby, I expect you to give me a call. Understood?" Riggs advised, knowing it would be a cold day in hell before this guy ever called the

A Birthday to Die For

police for anything.

"Yeah, I understand." Fowler said, rubbing his arm.

"Just two more questions before we leave. Do you know Kae Carlson?" Riggs asked.

"No, but if I hear anything, I'll let you know," Fowler replied with a smirk.

"Second question…and you'd better give me a straight answer. Which neighbor was here when Shelby lived here?"

"The people living in the yellow house, second from the corner."

"Thanks. I appreciate you cooperation," said Riggs, sarcasm reflecting the obvious disgust he felt.

Riggs walked along the sidewalk to the yellow house while La Moria pulled the car up. Their knock on the door was answered by Susan Dixson, a woman in her late sixties. She was still wearing her bathrobe even though it was well past noon.

"Hello, I'm Detective Riggs and this is my partner Detective La Moria. We're trying to locate the whereabouts of Rebecca Shelby. Do you know her?"

"She used to be my neighbor and she took in foster children."

"When was the last time you saw her Ms. Dixson?"

"Just call me Susan. I've been a widow for the last six years. I lost my husband, John, to cancer."

"I'm sorry for your loss. When was the last time you saw Rebecca?"

"It's been a long time… nine or ten years ago. I woke up one morning and she was gone. She'd stopped taking in foster children before that. Some man stopped by every once in awhile. I thought it was strange that she left without saying a word."

"Do you know who the man was?"

"No! He looked like a professional man. He was tall and looked like he was in very good physical shape. He drove a dark–colored car that looked official. He might be an inspector with Health and Social Services because of the foster children. I thought I got a glimpse of a badge attached to his belt one time, but I'm not really sure."

"Would you recognize him if you saw him again?"

"I don't think so. There's been so much time that's passed and my eyes aren't what they used to be. The man would be much older now."

"Thanks for your help, Susan. Here's my business card. If you think of anything else that may help us find Rebecca, please give me a call."

"I will, officer. You have a nice day."

Back in the car and enroute to where La Moria's car was parked, they agreed there wasn't much more they could have done to get Fowler to cooperate or get further information from Susan Dixson.

"I enjoyed your demonstration of the reverse

A Birthday to Die For

wrist lock. Maybe one of these days you'll teach me how to remember which direction to peel the hand off my chest," La Moria said, grinning.

"Any time!" Riggs answered, knowing La Moria always had trouble with the hold, but was quite effective with the hair hold.

"What's next?" La Moria inquired.

"Next is the retired Social Worker, Beth Williams."

Chapter 13

Riggs' mind was going in every direction as he reviewed the facts of his investigation, a thought pattern that was suddenly interrupted by a routine radio transmission to a beat officer. The dispatcher had just dispatched the Boy–Three car to an animal mutilation scene. Recalling that Detective Turner had recommended he respond to a report of this nature, he detoured to the scene since it could produce some physical evidence related to the cult investigation. He was looking forward to the interview with retired Social Worker Beth Williams, but this call had potential that he just couldn't afford to pass up.

The farm was located on the north side of the city of Duvall near the Snohomish County line. As he drove through the city, he saw a few pickup trucks parked along the street and in front of the feed store, leaving one with the impression this was definitely a farmers' town. It had a peaceful look about it and lacked any evidence or indications that its residents would be involved in satanic cults or the mutilation of their animals.

As Riggs rolled up to the scene, he saw a police officer standing over the carcass of a black and brown spotted horse. Officer Bartell was talking to a man wearing a dirty, tan–colored cowboy hat, bib overalls, and high–top rubber boots.

As Riggs approached, Bartell turned to face him. "Riggs, I'm surprised to see you out here in farm country. I've got a dead horse, but no dead humans, so why are you here?"

"I've got an investigation going that may be parallel with this one, so I thought I'd stop by and see what type of evidence you have," Riggs advised, glancing at the farmer.

"Riggs, this is Winfred Matson, the owner of this property and the dead horse. He discovered the dead animal early this morning as he was driving by the field enroute to town. At first he thought the animal had been struck by lightning or from natural causes, but when he saw the mutilation, he knew better and called the police."

"Nice to meet you, Mr. Matson. I'm Detective Riggs with the Homicide Unit. I've been doing some reading regarding animal mutilations, trying to understand the motive behind them, so I decided to drop by and see what kind of evidence there might be. Hope you don't mind."

"Not at all, Detective. If you can help, more power to you. I'd like to see you catch whoever's responsible for this and send them to prison."

"I understand your feelings. I'll help Officer

A Birthday to Die For

Bartell anyway I can."

"What have you got so far?" Riggs asked, returning his gaze to Bartell.

"Well, Mr. Matson didn't hear anything last night or early this morning that would have attracted his attention to this location. He doesn't remember seeing anyone recently who made him suspicious, so we don't have a lot to go on. I don't see any real evidence such as tire tracks or footprints. I don't see any tools or weapons that may have been used. All I see is the mutilation and I don't really know its significance."

"Have you called anyone from Animal Control to come out? They'd be in a better position to examine the carcass and explain to us the missing parts and what significance that may have," Riggs asked, noticing Matson looking back and forth as they talked.

"Dispatch notified them. Animal Control Officer Tailor Masterjohn is responding. She should be here any minute."

A moment later their attention was drawn to the roadway as they watched the Animal Control truck turn onto the property and pull in behind Bartell's patrol car. Tailor Masterjohn was obvious an animal lover as the expression on her face changed from disgust to anger as she surveyed the mutilation of the dead horse.

"Hi guys. I'm Tailor Masterjohn. What can I do for you, other than make a report and file it with the other mutilation reports which never seem to get solved?"

163

"We'd like you to tell us what happened to this animal. Is it something you've seen before?" Bartell asked as Riggs looked on.

"Yeah, I've seen this before, not often, but enough times to make you sick. This animal was mutilated by human beings."

"Besides the obvious, how do you come to that conclusion?" Riggs asked, looking for clarification and information which would lead to a satanic cult.

"Well, it's like this. You can exclude natural predators such as dogs, coyotes, and cougars. If a predator had attacked this animal, you'd see teeth marks around the hocks and the nose because those areas are usually attacked first. There would be tearing of the flesh and blood everywhere. In this case, I see the edges where the skin was peeled from the horse's neck are straight and regularly serrated, which suggests they used an instrument such as a surgical tool to make the cut. They used other instruments of this nature to remove the horse's tongue, ears, and testicles. Since I don't see a lot of blood, the only thing I can think of that would explain the absence of blood to the degree I think there should be is they put the animal down somehow before performing the mutilation, so the animal was dead at the time. If the animal was already dead, the heart would not have been pumping and therefore, very little blood."

"Can you explain why the animal was mutilated this way? Why they took the tongue,

A Birthday to Die For

ears, and testicles?" Riggs asked, still looking for satanic cult involvement.

"No, I really can't. There are shared theories among many that either UFOs are involved or satanic cults are taking the animal parts for rituals. Take your pick since neither has been proven beyond a shadow of a doubt, but if I had to go with one, I'd go with the satanic cult version."

"Thanks for the information and your opinion," said Riggs. Bartell shook his head in agreement.

Riggs headed back to his car satisfied that there was no collectible physical evidence at this scene. Animal Control Officer Masterjohn and Officer Bartell were still talking to Mr. Matson and coordinating the disposal of the dead horse.

On his drive back to the office, Riggs recalled what Detective Turner had told him about the use of animal parts in rituals and wondered what was next. A quick call to Turner gave him the answer.

"This is Detective Turner. From my caller ID, I'm guessing it's you Riggs."

"Yeah, it's me. Sounds like you were expecting a call from me."

"I've been wondering how your investigation is going and whether or not I'd hear from you again. What can I do for you this time?"

"I remember you telling me to pay attention to animal mutilations and to respond to the scene, if at all possible. Well, I just now responded to one. I remember you saying the animal parts were used in rituals. I'd like to know what kind of rituals and if you think this animal mutilation will lead me to something else?"

"The only thing I'm reasonably sure of is there's a better than even chance that there will be a burglary of a church somewhere in the area of the mutilation. There may be an actual break–in, but it'll be unlikely you'll find any evidence of the animal organs at the scene unless you actually catch the suspects in the act. In the numerous investigations I've conducted regarding animal mutilations, I've found that a day or two later, a church burglary showed up on the crime bulletin circulated among the detectives. I also discovered the burglaries were within close proximity to the site of the animal mutilation and that the churches were more or less isolated from business or residential areas, they had large parking lots, very few lights, no obvious alarm systems, and no caretakers on premises. So, I guess what I'm trying to tell you is that you should do whatever you can to get the jump on any church burglaries within the area of the animal mutilation you just responded to," Turner advised.

"Thanks for the information, Turner. I hope someday I might be able to return the favor."

"If I have anything up your way, you'll be the first person I'll call," Turner said.

"Hey, before you hang up, I've one more question. Have you ever found any connection between the cults you investigated and prostitutes?" Riggs asked, trying to find a reason

A Birthday to Die For

to believe Pope's missing prostitutes might be connected to his investigation of the cult.

"Yes and no. I've had leads pointing to prostitutes being involved, but I've never been able to find them to interview."

"Did you find that kind of strange?"

"As a matter of fact, I did. However, knowing the prostitutes use aliases and work the circuit up and down the west coast, I didn't want to use up the resources I had available to me at the time to really go after them."

"Been there, done that on the resources, so I understand. Well, thanks again for your assistance. Talk to you later."

Riggs had just ended his call to the communications supervisor when he pulled into the county parking garage. He asked the supervisor to post a note at each of the call receiver stations advising them to call him on any church burglaries that occurred in the area of the mutilation.

As he was placing his cell phone into his jacket pocket, it rang. "Riggs here!"

"Jerry, this is Paula. I don't know if it's going to be of much help, but I just got off the phone with my colleagues and this is what we've come up with a profile for you to work with. The participants in the cult or devil worshipping can be of any race and involve both sexes. Some may have gotten involved because they're angry at God for their own personal reasons, such as feeling they were abandoned by God during a

167

period of need. Some just like the power it gives them over others. They're the ones who probably get off on the sacrifice of another human being or animal. Some do it to justify their sexual or violent behavior.

"Is that it, Doc? That's pretty broad and general. It doesn't give me anything specific to work with."

"I know, Jerry, but this is the best we could come up with. Our research of the subject, even looking at the criteria used by the FBI, gave us only these general unspecific details. Sorry, but I hope it helps a little."

"Thanks, Doc, and tell your colleagues I really appreciate what they've done."

"I'll do that, Jerry."

Chapter 14

The office was vacant when Riggs walked in. He was surprised to find La Moria missing as he was almost always the first one there, ready to hit the field. Last night they'd agreed to meet in the office early to prepare for their meeting with Beth Williams. He knew La Moria would be there any minute. He pulled out his map for Snohomish County and located the address for Williams. Her residence was located just outside the city limits of Monroe, in unincorporated Snohomish County, clearly in the jurisdiction of the Snohomish County Sheriff's Department.

While he was weighing the procedure to follow, La Moria walked in with two cups of coffee. "I think it's going to be a long day, so I brought you a super–sized coffee mocha to sustain you on our drive to Williams' house," La Moria said, revealing how well he knew Riggs.

"Thanks, I'll get lunch today and tell you about the mutilated animal call I rolled on while enroute to the office this morning," Riggs said, gratefully accepting the coffee.

"You did say 'mutilated animal' didn't you?" La Moria asked, not wanting to wait until later to hear about it.

"Sure did. I remembered what Turner told me, so I rolled on it when I heard the call. I thought it might be related to our case, but if it is, there sure as hell wasn't any evidence to confirm it."

"Why doesn't that surprise me?" La Moria said, wondering if they were ever going to come up with a solid lead in this investigation.

"Here's the address for Williams. Before we make contact with her, I'll give Detective Sergeant John Goldsmith of Snohomish a call and see if he'll meet us there since it's in his jurisdiction," said Riggs, handing the piece of paper with Williams' address on it to La Moria.

"Good. While you're calling Goldsmith, I'll contact Pope and see if she's found anything more on Rebecca Shelby."

As he held the receiver to his ear, Riggs motioned for La Moria to wait a moment. He picked up a note from his desk and handed it to him. The note was from Pope advising Riggs to come to her office for an update on her search for Shelby. Before Riggs' call to Goldsmith went through, he hung up the phone. "Let's go see what Barb has before we coordinate things with Goldsmith."

When they walked into Barbara Pope's office, she was seated at her desk going through some papers. She looked up as they approached and

A Birthday to Die For

pulled her notebook from her top drawer.

"We're ready for the update, Barb," said Riggs, pulling a chair in front of her desk while La Moria took a seat at the desk next to hers.

"It's like this, guys. I found an old copy of Shelby's driver's license photo. I also found a set of her fingerprints taken at the time she applied for foster–parent status and a criminal background check was made. A copy of the driver's license photo has been given to the Crime Lab with a request to do a computerized age enhancement to her face, adding thirteen years. This should be of help if you decide to put out a flyer anywhere."

"Were you able to come up with anything on the telephone records?" La Moria asked as Riggs studied Shelby's old photo.

"Yes I did, but it's not going to be of any help," Barb advised, referring to her notes.

"Why's that? Riggs asked.

"The records show that she received eight telephone calls lasting less than a minute during the late evening hours. The incoming phone numbers are assigned to disposable cellular phones with no record of the owner. These are throw–away telephones. A person buys them for a designated amount of minutes and when those minutes expire, they just throw it away," she explained.

"What you're saying then is we've reached another dead end?" Riggs said, a frown returning to his face.

"Yes, that's what I'm saying as it relates to

the telephone calls."

"What about the requests you sent out to other agencies regarding any Jane Does they may have stored in their coolers?" La Moria asked.

"Sorry to say, but I've got nothing on that either."

As Riggs and La Moria stood to leave, the phone on Barb's desk rang and she motioned for them to stay.

"You guys aren't going to believe this, but that was Joyce down in the Evidence Lab. She said she's been trying to track you two down. She says her test of the DNA sample you recovered from one of your sites comes back a positive match for my missing prostitute, Hazel Cunningham. It looks like my missing person was sacrificed during one of your cult ceremonies." Barb recognized this was the first lead regarding what happened to Cunningham.

"It sure appears that way, Barb, but absent her body, it's only an educated guess. Before the prosecutor will let us call her a murder victim, they'll want corroborating evidence such as a confession, an eyewitness, photographs, or body parts," Riggs explained, weighing the information and its value as a lead.

"Riggs, I now have a vested interest in your cult investigation. I want to be included any way you see fit."

"Count on it, Barb. There's one more thing you can do for me. Call your contacts at Children's Protective Services and see if anybody from

A Birthday to Die For

their office did follow up inspections of the foster home controlled by Rebecca Shelby. If they report that they did not send a guy out to do the inspections, then run down photographs of the Pierce County Chief of Detectives Paul Trickey and his assistant, Sergeant Detective Dennis Ryker. If I think of anything more that requires your expertise, I'll get back to you."

"Thanks, I'll get right on this. It'll probably take them a little time to hunt down their old records and get back to me."

"I understand," said Riggs as he turned away.

Back in their office, Riggs placed a call to Goldsmith. He knew he was calling a friend who was also in a position to help. They'd met a few years back while attending classes at the Police Academy and remained close friends ever since. In fact, Goldsmith had married his old partner, Lorie Torgerson, who now ruled the Goldsmith clan. The friendship included La Moria and his family. He'd also worked with Lorie on a few cases before she decided to retire and raise her son. She loved her new job as "Supreme Domestic Commander."

"Riggs, how you doing?" Goldsmith asked.

"Doing great, but we need some help," Riggs said, awaiting an inquiry about Toby.

"Before we go there, I want to know what Toby's been up to. What's that five–foot bundle of energy pulled on you lately?" Goldsmith asked,

173

unable to conceal the chuckle in his voice.

"Come on, John, I really do need your help," Riggs pleaded.

"Not until you tell me about Toby. Remember, we know she can't go very long without pulling something on you."

"Okay, okay, she sewed up the fly of my shorts," Riggs confessed, knowing full well that John wouldn't give up until he'd heard all the sordid details.

"She did what?"

"Yep! The last trip I made out of town to follow up a lead in California, I discovered she'd sewn up the fly on my shorts. I was at the airport trying to take a leak and I couldn't get the damn thing out. I had to take my pants down just to take a piss."

"Now that's funny! When did you discover your other shorts were sewn up?" John asked, not even trying to conceal his laughter at this time.

"In my hotel room after I'd taken a shower."

"And?" John was relentless.

"I called Toby at home. She was laughing so hard, she couldn't even talk. I told her it wasn't funny. I damn near peed my pants and the guy standing at the urinal next to me thought I was playing with myself, like I was some kind of pervert. She said she was sorry, but her laughter told me otherwise. Now if you'll please stop laughing, I'll tell you why I called."

"I can't wait to tell Lorie about this, but go ahead, tell me how I can help."

La Moria sat silently watching Riggs describe

A Birthday to Die For

the last trick Toby had pulled on him. He could hear Goldsmith's laughter. He knew John and Lorie were good friends of Riggs or he wouldn't be admitting to the joke Toby had pulled on him. He knew Toby too and had witnessed other tricks she'd pulled on Riggs in the past. *I wonder what it'd be like to be married to a woman like Toby, a person with a never-ending imagination and willing to play a trick on anyone.*

A few minutes passed before Goldsmith calmed down enough to write down the address for Beth Williams. "Okay, I'll see you there."

Goldsmith was waiting for them when they arrived at William' home. The house was older, probably built in the late sixties, painted white with blue trim. The front door was covered with a screen door controlled by a spring attached to the side of the house...crude, but effective. It had a small window in front at the north end covered with some type of cloth material. At the south end of the house there was a single car detached garage with a gravel driveway and grass growing between the tire tracks leading from the street. The gravel and grass in the driveway showed no signs of recent use.

There was a wooden fence around the back yard with a gate between the house and the fence, which ran parallel with the south end of the garage. Wind chimes were hanging from the roof overhang, just to the north side of the front door, close enough that it would be nearly impossible

175

to miss as you entered the house. From the street there were no visible signs to indicate that anyone was home—no light showing through the windows, no smoke coming from the chimney.

They approached the house from the front with Goldsmith moving to the front door while Riggs and La Moria stood at opposite ends of the house to back up Goldsmith at the front door and to make sure no one went out the back door unseen. Goldsmith knocked on the front door, announcing himself as a police officer. Getting no answer, he repeated the knock and announcement several more times, with no results.

Goldsmith remained at the front door while Riggs and La Moria met in the backyard at the rear of the house. The lawn was overgrown with knee–high, wet grass. A picnic table with two chairs situated just off the patio had been turned on their sides, probably to allow rain to run off. As they continued toward the rear sliding door, Riggs whistled softly to get La Moria's attention. He pointed to tracks left in the unkempt lawn showing that someone had walked around the house earlier. How early was impossible to determine, but certainly this morning. The grass was pressed to the ground in several places showing the path taken by an individual. Closer examination failed to reveal a shoe print, so there was no way to determine the size of the shoe or the possible gender.

Riggs and La Moria moved close to the backside of the house and peered through the

A Birthday to Die For

windows into the interior. La Moria motioned Riggs to join him at the sliding glass door. Inside, light–colored curtain panels hung from the wall on either side of the door. It was difficult to see inside because of the gray dirty film, but Riggs noticed what appeared to be the shadow of a person hanging from the ceiling. He could also see a lone shoe on the floor by a chair that was laying on its side just inside the doorway leading from the kitchen into the adjoining room.

"Damn, this doesn't look good," Riggs declared.

"It sure as hell doesn't. If it's Williams, we'll be at another dead end...no pun intended," La Moria muttered.

"Let's get John around here and see how he wants to handle it," said Riggs.

While La Moria walked to the front of the house to give Goldsmith the bad news, Riggs inserted the blade of his pocketknife between the door and the doorframe to see if the door was locked. As he pushed, the door opened, which led him to surmise that this may have been the escape route if there was foul play involved. Using the knife blade helped avoid any contamination of possible fingerprints if it turned out there was a need to lift them, providing the suspect left any to be lifted.

"Let me take a look," Goldsmith requested as he peered through the sliding glass door.

"Riggs, you and La Moria check the rooms for possible suspects while I check out the victim. I

177

hope it's not the witness you're looking for, but who else could it be?"

Riggs used his knife again and pushed the door open. With guns drawn, Riggs and La Moria quickly moved past Goldsmith and checked each room and closet in the house, looking for someone who might be hiding to avoid detection. When they found no one present, they returned to the dining room area where Goldsmith was noting the condition of the female body hanging from the chandelier.

"We can come back and finish our examination of the scene after we get a search warrant," Goldsmith said, as they moved back through the open sliding door to the rear porch.

The warrant was something they all knew would be mandatory after the preliminary search for suspects had been concluded and whether or not there was need for life support measures to be taken. Whether or not the victim was the sole owner of the house and in no way able to give permission for a search to help determine her killer apparently did not concern the United States Supreme Court when they ruled a search warrant would be required should the suspect have a residential claim to the property being searched and a constitutional right against unreasonable search and seizure, a decision most police officers did not agree with. It wasn't the search warrant in and of itself that pissed off the officers, it was the time it took away from the processing of a fresh crime scene and the possible

A Birthday to Die For

contamination of evidence it created that always concerned Riggs. Fortunately, the local judges and prosecutors created a means to obtain a search warrant by means of a phone call made from the crime scene.

While Riggs and La Moria remained on the rear porch, Goldsmith completed the affidavit for the search warrant, describing what he'd seen inside the house and his probable cause to search the house for evidence which would help determine whether or not the hanging was the result of foul play and, if so, who the suspect might be. It also included any evidence connecting the victim with devil worship or membership in a satanic cult. He used his cell phone hooked up to a portable recorder and called the Presiding Judge of the Snohomish County Superior Court. After reading the affidavit to the judge and getting the warrant approved, he placed the tape from his recorder into an evidence envelope, which he would log into evidence when he got back to his office.

"The telephonic search warrant has been granted, so let's take a closer look at the body," Goldsmith said as he again entered the house through the back door.

The deceased female was Caucasian, slight of build, with dirty blonde hair that had obviously been colored since gray roots could be seen next to the scalp. Her eyes were open displaying brown eyes which were somewhat glazed over. The whites of her eyes were extremely blood shot, typical for victims of strangulation. No necklace or earrings were visible, but she did have a gold–plated wristwatch on her right wrist, indicating she was probably left–handed.

She was wearing a light brown, short–sleeved, pull–over sweater, dark brown pants, and a brown shoe on her right foot which matched the shoe on the floor beneath her. She was also wearing knee–high nylon stockings. There were no visible signs of bleeding, but she had soiled her pants, which was quite common upon all deaths. In this case it was unknown whether the release of her bodily fluids was the result of a struggle or had occurred after death.

She was hanging from the chandelier by a small nylon rope, commonly used as a clothes–line, attached to the chandelier chain next to the ceiling. The rope had been tied in a double knot configuration right up against the ceiling, then allowed to hang down between the decorative arms of the chandelier to her neck. The end of the rope around her neck had been tied in a slip–knot fashion, which caused the rope to tighten as her weight pulled down on it. The slip–knot had been positioned to the left side of her neck, possibly, to increase the chance her neck would be broken when she stepped off the chair, which now lay on its side beneath her. The dining room table had been moved to the side to allow room for the hanging to occur.

"It just doesn't feel right," Riggs said.

Goldsmith frowned, "What do you mean?"

A Birthday to Die For

"If this woman is Beth Williams and she owns this house, it's unlikely she would do anything to destroy the inside, especially a decorative chandelier. Another thing, I don't see a suicide note anywhere in sight. It does happen every now and then, but it's generally the exception when you don't find a note. It just doesn't smell right," Riggs explained.

"I agree. At first glance it certainly looks like a suicide, but I see a few things that bother me," La Moria said, glancing around the room and at the victim.

"Such as?" Goldsmith queried.

"I know we have to wait until the Medical Examiner arrives, but I don't believe her feet would reach the chair. I think she was lifted to her hanging position, but I could be wrong," La Moria explained.

Riggs nodded in agreement. "Now that you mention it, I think you might be right."

"Let's get this show on the road. Riggs, if you and La Moria will do the diagram of the house, I'll take the photos. Let me put in a call to the M.E. before we get started because it'll take them a while to get here."

After the call was made to the Medical Examiner, Goldsmith proceeded to take photographs of the exterior sides of the house, including the street in front, as well as the garage, backyard, and the footpath through the grass. He also photographed the neighbors' homes to show their location and distance from Williams' home.

181

He then moved to the rear sliding glass door where he started photographing each room as he walked through, stopping at the entrance to each and describing everything he could see into his recorder. The position of every light switch, electrical outlet, color of the paint or wallpaper on the walls, color and type of material of the curtains and drapes on each window and the size of the windows and distance from the floor, whether locked or not, and any sign or absence of any sign of forced entry. He described each piece of furniture in detail and its location in the room. The floor covering was described in detail, including any damage to linoleum or tile, and spots on the carpet. Special attention was given to the temperature in each room, the thermostat settings, and location of the fireplace before he moved towards the victim and described what she looked like.

Riggs and La Moria followed Goldsmith and as he completed the photographs of each room, they took measurements while preparing a scaled diagram of the room. The diagram showed the exact position of each piece of furniture and the relative relationship to the hanging victim. They described and photographed the victim herself, paying special attention to the rope and the knot at both ends.

"Riggs, hold this tape measure up so I can get a photograph of the distance from her toes to the floor," Goldsmith said.

"Sure thing. I'll also hold the tape over here so

A Birthday to Die For

we can see the distance from the seat to the floor on this chair, which matches the one laying on its side beneath her."

"I'll be damned. You two were right when you told me things didn't seem right. The distance from her toes to the floor is twenty–one inches. The distance from the seat of the matching chair to the floor is nineteen inches. She couldn't have hung herself unless she shrunk two inches after she died," Goldsmith exclaimed.

"It sure looks like we have a murder here and you know what, I'm not really surprised," Riggs said, as a new frown appeared on his face.

Goldsmith gave him a quizzical look. "Why's that?"

"This case has been full of surprises when you consider the multiple personalities of Kae Carlson, the ritual sites having evidence of human blood, and the disappearance of the foster mother, Rebecca Shelby. What the hell, why not a dead body? I wonder what other surprises are in store for us?" Riggs said, moving to take a closer look at the victim.

Riggs had learned early on that when conducting a homicide investigation he needed to make notes about the condition of the victim's body as it pertains to injuries and rigor mortis. He touched the victim's face and detected a stiffness in the facial muscles not present in other parts of the body other than the fingers. Rigor mortis usually starts in the facial muscles and fingertips. Since it didn't appear the rigor mortis was fully set, he guessed the victim, who he now believed to be Beth Williams, had been dead for just a few hours. Whether he was right or not would be confirmed by the Medical Examiner.

"What do you think, Bob? Is this murder related to Kae Carlson?" Riggs asked.

"I don't know for sure, but it's certainly beginning to look that way."

"If that's a possibility, then we have to wonder what she would have told us, who got to her first, and why they didn't want us to hear her story? It seems a little strange that her murder occurred right after we talked to the others who served as references for Shelby," Riggs mumbled, obviously in deep thought.

"I agree. I'm starting to think Chief Trickey may be more involved than he let on. It would have been nice if we'd had the information on the positive DNA hit on the prostitute before we talked to him. It could have been valuable information knowing how many hookers he and his spineless assistant have arrested over the years. What a good way to come up with a sacrificial victim."

Trying to put two and two together in his mind, La Moria suggested, "What about the teacher? She might have passed the polygraph, but there's still something not quite right there either."

The sun was going down when the Medical Examiner showed up with her assistant, Tom Caldwell, who was a tall, bald individual, who

A Birthday to Die For

resembled the "Mr. Clean" commercial right down to the earring in one ear.

The M.E., Dr. Robin Spears, was well known throughout the state for her ability to determine the cause of death in a victim early on. She'd been a recognized medical expert in the area of forensic pathology for many years and her testimony in court was beyond reproach. Criminal defense attorneys hated to see her on the witness stand testifying against their clients. They knew her reputation and had been unable to challenge the results of her examination of the victim and her autopsy results. Riggs was one of her admirers. He had worked with her on other homicide investigations and sat in on some of her autopsies. He was glad she was the M.E. on this case because they needed all the help they could get.

"Hi guys!" Spears said, turning to each of them and shaking their hands.

"Hi Doc, glad you could make it. We have a female victim hanging from the ceiling, who we think is a murder victim. We're looking forward to what you have to tell us after your examination," Goldsmith said.

"Whose investigation is it?" Spears asked, knowing Riggs and La Moria were out of their jurisdiction.

"The death of this woman is mine, but we believe it's connected to an investigation Riggs and La Moria are conducting in their jurisdiction," Goldsmith explained.

185

Spears pulled on gloves. "Sounds interesting, so let's get on with it and see what we can find out."

Dr. Spears took her own photographs of the victim and the contents of the room, and the position of the shoe, the chair on the floor, as well as the table. She paid special attention to the rope and how the knots had been tied.

"How about you two holding the victim in place as I cut the rope? After I cut the rope, place her on the white sheet I've spread out on the floor. Lay her on her back when you do," she advised, motioning to Riggs and Goldsmith to help her.

While Riggs and Goldsmith held the victim, Spears cut the rope from around the victim's neck with the cut being about three inches from the knot. Based on her experience, she knew the knot and the style used in tying it could be a possible lead.

"We need to take the whole light assembly into evidence. I want you to leave the rope attached to the chandelier chain because I'd like to examine the rope and knot in my office."

Spears then moved to the victim who had been laid face up on the white sheet. She pulled the victim's sweater up to just below her breasts and pushed a temperature gauge through the skin and into the victim's liver.

"It will be just a minute or so before I know the victim's inner body temperature, which might give us a clue as to how long she's been dead," Spears told them, looking at her watch

A Birthday to Die For

and waiting for the seconds to pass.

Riggs cringed as he watched the tip of the thermometer pierce the victim's skin enroute to her liver, remembering what he'd learned in his homicide investigation course. The liver is an organ which is believed to hold the body temperature longer than most body parts, so it's considered a reliable aid in determining the time of death. *That damn thermometer looks like the one I've seen Toby use on our Thanksgiving turkey. How pathetic I am, looking at a dead body like it's turkey. The fact that I'm hungry is no excuse.*

"Well guys, the temperature within the liver is eighty–nine point four degrees," Spears announced. She checked the temperature of the room and recorded her findings in her notes.

"Okay, Doc, tell me how long she's been dead?" Riggs asked, remembering his earlier estimation.

"Well, based on the body's temperature of 89.4 degrees, the progression of rigor mortis in the muscles of the eyelids and lower jaw, I'd estimate death occurred within the last six hours. My estimation is also based on the assumption that the body had a normal temperature of 98.6 at the time of her death. The progression of rigor mortis is between two and nine hours. Together, the temperature and the evidence of rigor mortis, leads me to believe the victim has been dead about six hours."

Spears examined the victim's throat for discoloration and bruises. She checked the victim's rib cage and back pointing to what appeared to be abrasions with some bruising just under the arm pits, then went back to her examination of the bruising around the neck.

"The damage to the skin around the neck is wider than the diameter of the rope, which leads me to believe this victim was strangled before she was hung. You would expect the abrasions to move upward as the victim's body pulled down on the rope, causing the rope to damage the skin as it was pulled up in the area of the knot. While I see that type of skin damage, it still doesn't explain why the bruising around the entire neck is consistently larger than the diameter of the rope unless she was strangled before she was hanged. I believe this was staged to look like a suicide."

Riggs paid close attention to every word Spears uttered. He'd often found the information useful in his investigations and interrogation of suspects. He couldn't help but think, *John has the primary responsibility for this investigation, but I know this death is related to Kae Carlson.*

"Let's bag her hands before we haul her out of here. I wouldn't want to lose any trace evidence hidden under her fingernails," Spears instructed her assistant.

"I'll be doing the autopsy at seven in the morning if any of you would like to attend. I may have some more answers for you then."

"Thanks Doc, I'll be there," Riggs told her. Goldsmith nodded too.

A Birthday to Die For

"Before we leave, let's check with people living on this block to see if they saw anything out of the ordinary during the approximate time of our victim's death," Goldsmith suggested as they watched the Medical Examiner drive away with the corpse.

"Sounds like a plan. We'll take the east side of the street if you'll take the west, John," La Moria offered. They separated and headed to the houses on opposite sides of the street.

It took a little over an hour to cover the houses on the block and return to their starting location.

"What did we find out?" Goldsmith asked, exchanging glances with Riggs and La Moria.

"We didn't find out anything from the residents we contacted," Riggs explained.

"I didn't do much better, but there was an elderly lady two houses down on the west side who claimed to have seen a dark, official–looking car parked on the street just about where my car is parked right now. She can't identify the make of car, nor did she see the driver, but it was during the time frame we're interested in. She was unable to offer any further information," Goldsmith advised.

"Well, it's better than nothing at all," Riggs said, wishing the woman had at least gotten a glimpse of the driver.

On his drive home, Riggs was thinking about his tussle with Dan Fowler. *I wonder why   he has*

189

such a strong hatred for the police. Does he have something to hide or is he just an asshole? Could he be a member of a cult? The tattoo of the devil on his left bicep indicates he might be or could it be that he just likes to look bad and thinks the tattoo intimidates people? Anyway you look at it, he doesn't match Detective Turner's description of a cult member, but then again, who does?

As the thoughts churned inside his head, he took his cell phone out of his breast pocket and dialed the number shown on the business card tucked above his sun visor.

"Supernatural Beliefs, may I help you?"

Riggs immediately recognized the voice of Bud Jackson, the clerk he'd talked to while visiting the store a few days before.

"Hi Bud, this is Detective Riggs. I'm hoping you can remember some names if I say them to you."

"I don't know, but I'll try," Bud answered, recalling his first encounter with Riggs.

"Thanks Bud. Do the names Patricia Mohon, Beth Williams, Dan Fowler, Paul Trickey, or Rebecca Shelby sound familiar to you?"

"Dan Fowler rings a bell."

"Why's that?" Riggs asked.

"A few years ago, a guy by the name of Fowler worked here for awhile. I think his first name was Danny, but I'm not really sure," Bud said.

"Did you work with him?"

"Briefly, during my training, but he quit shortly after I started. I think I was hired to take

A Birthday to Die For

his place."

"While you worked with Fowler, did you notice anything strange about him?"

"Not really. He did take a lot of telephone calls in private."

"What do you mean 'in private'?"

"He'd always step outside or go into the restroom."

"Did you ever overhear any of the conversations he was having?"

"No! He always made sure he was alone when he talked on the phone."

"Bud, could you check the store's records and confirm the dates Fowler was employed there?"

"I don't have those records."

"Why not?" Riggs asked.

"The owner disposes of any records that are more than five years old. It's been longer than five years since Fowler worked here."

"I understand. Thanks for your help. You may have given me some valuable information anyway. Thanks again."

Riggs pressed harder on the accelerator. The hour was late and he needed to get some sleep before leaving for the Snohomish County Medical Examiner's Office in the morning. He knew it was just wishful thinking because he wouldn't get any sleep, even if he went to bed. Although not confirmed, the information he had just received from Bud about Fowler held some investigative possibilities. He was certain there would be another visit with Fowler.

Chapter 15

It seemed like he'd just gotten into bed when the alarm went off. He remembered thinking about the possible connection between Fowler and the cult before he dropped off to sleep, but this was ridiculous—only three hours of sleep and less than an hour to get to the autopsy. Toby was still snoring softly as he crawled out of bed, kissed her lightly on the cheek, and pulled on his pants. Sitting on the edge of the bed, he put on his socks and shoes. He finished dressing in the bathroom after shaving with an electric razor and splashing an extra dab of aftershave on his face. *Maybe it'll offset the odor which is always present during an autopsy.*

Before dashing out to his car, he stopped by the kitchen and took a cookie from the cookie jar, knowing he didn't have time for a good breakfast.

During the drive to the Medical Examiner's Office, Riggs thought about how fast the time had passed since starting this investigation. As he mulled things over, he realized that unless something was revealed in this autopsy that he wasn't already aware of or that he was wrong about Fowler, he'd be no closer to identifying the cult members than he was at the beginning of this investigation. With only four days left before Kae's birthday, it was looking pretty bleak that he'd be able to keep his promise.

When he pulled into the parking space in front of the Medical Examiner's Office, he saw La Moria's and Goldsmith's cars. He wasn't surprised that they'd gotten there before him. *Maybe they got a better night's sleep than I did.* A quick glance at his watch showed he still had five minutes before the doctor started the autopsy. He pulled his cell phone from his pocket and quickly dialed Dr. Mitchell's number.

"Dr. Mitchell, may I help you?"

"Hi Doc, this is Riggs."

"How are things going, Jerry?"

"Yesterday we found one of the references for Rebecca Shelby dead in her home. It looks like she was murdered. I still haven't got anything solid that will lead me to the cult and I'm concerned about Kae's safety. I was hoping you could move her into your home or another safe place until I come up with something? I don't have enough time to place her into protective custody with the department."

The call from Riggs wasn't really unexpected, but the request was. She'd never allowed one of

A Birthday to Die For

her patients to stay with her, feeling it would compromise her doctor–patient relationship. She also felt it was outside proper doctor–patient protocol, but she realized she'd already violated the established protocol in an attempt to save her patient's life. The way she saw it, this was no different.

"Okay, I know where she is and I'll pick her up. She's been staying at her apartment, but she's in fear they'll come for her there. I'll make sure she's safe, but you have to give me a call as soon as you have something solid."

"I'll do it, Doc...and thanks," Riggs agreed, while at the same time thinking he should have told her about Hatch and Decker. He wasn't worried so much about Kae's safety while she was being tailed by Hatch and Decker, but shit does happen and they could be pulled away for an emergency elsewhere. He knew it would be safer if she was hidden away in a safe house.

As soon as Riggs walked into the reception area, he was motioned to continue on up the stairs leading to the autopsy room where he found Dr. Spears standing over the body of Beth Williams with a scalpel in her right hand, ready to make the first cut. La Moria and Goldsmith were standing across the steel table from the doctor. Riggs moved to the immediate left of Spears so he could see close up the examination of each organ as it was severed and removed from the body, then examined for any flaw or injury which would explain the cause of death. Spears gave him a smile as he moved closer. "It's about time Riggs. I thought you were going to miss my show."

"Not a chance, Doc," he said, glancing at La Moria and Goldsmith.

Williams' body was positioned on a steel table which slanted downward from the head to the feet. This was to allow the water used to wash the body to flow into a drain on the floor beneath the table, along with body fluids. Williams was on her back, nude, ready for Spears to open her up and confirm how she died...and maybe, reveal some evidence that would help identify her killer.

Spears spoke into a recorder attached to a bar hanging from a tripod on wheels, the type normally seen in hospitals with intravenous medication bags hanging from them. She described Williams as being a white female, sixty–five years of age, five feet tall, and weighing one hundred and thirty–five pounds. She emphasized the bruising and abrasions around the neck and the inconsistency between the width of the abrasions and the diameter of the rope. She also included the fact that she had combed both the head hair and pubic hair for trace evidence, taken a blood sample for drug screening, as well as fingernail scrapings prior to proceeding with the autopsy. She then turned off her recorder and directed her assistant to ready the video camera for the taping of the autopsy. She looked at Riggs, La Moria, and Goldsmith and asked, "Are you ready to begin?"

A Birthday to Die For

"Yes, we're ready," Riggs answered for everyone.

"Showtime, let's get this thing over with," said Spears, donning her clear lens goggles for eye protection.

Riggs prepared himself for the first cut, which always seemed to bother him more than anything else he observed during an autopsy. The first cut was through flesh just above one of the breasts proceeding downward at an angle and stopping just above the belly button. The second cut started just above the other breast proceeding downward at an angle intersecting with the first cut above the belly button forming a "V" pattern. These cuts exposed a yellowish fatty tissue between the skin and the red flesh, which he found repulsive. Knowing this yellowish tissue was fat, he wondered why he had so much trouble staying on a diet.

Having made the "V" cut, Spears proceeded to peel back the layer of skin and fatty tissue exposing the rib cage. She examined each rib, describing what she saw into her recorder. "There are two broken ribs to the right side." She then cut through the ribs on both sides an inch or so from the sternum, then pulled the sternum up and over William's face, exposing the heart, lungs, and internal organs. Each organ was checked for any signs of trauma, such as bruises, lacerations, puncture wounds, and anything else not consistent with a healthy body. She described the lungs as being collapsed, indicating that

Williams had been deprived of air and absent any other indicators had died from suffocation.

Spears completed her examination of the internal organs located in the chest cavity, then moved on to Williams' head. Using the scalpel, she made a cut through the scalp and across the center of the head, starting the cut near the hairline above one ear, over the top, and stopping at the hairline above the other ear. She pulled the scalp towards the front and back of the head, exposing the top of the skull.

Her assistant moved in with a small electric surgical saw, cutting through and around the skull. He left a notch on each side to allow easy replacement after the brain and spinal cord were examined. Spears removed the skull cap, revealing the brain. She described the discoloration to the brain which she found to be consistent with the loss of oxygen and suffocation. Her final entry into the recorder was, "Based on the unusual width of the abrasion on the neck of one Beth Williams, the condition of her lungs, and the discoloration to the brain, it was my determination that the cause of death was the result of homicidal means, suffocation via strangulation."

As her assistant proceeded to replace the skull cap and sew up the cuts to the scalp and torso, Doctor Spears escorted the others to an adjoining room to discuss her findings.

"Could any of you use a cup of coffee to go with the sweet rolls over there?" Spears asked, knowing food and drink was the last thing on the

A Birthday to Die For

officers' minds after witnessing an autopsy.

"I could use a cup of coffee. I know Bob could too," Riggs said, looking into the pale face of Goldsmith, sweat beaded across his forehead.

As she handed Riggs and La Moria each a cup of coffee, she asked, "La Moria, what nationality is your name?"

"It's French," La Moria he replied.

"Come on, Bob, tell her what it means," Riggs urged with a grin on his face.

"Yeah, tell me what it means," Spears begged, knowing it had to be something good or Riggs wouldn't be enjoying the moment so much.

"Okay, I'll tell you. It means 'the lover,' " Bob explained, now feeling somewhat embarrassed and annoyed with Riggs for pressuring him into giving the answer.

"Well, are you?" Spears asked.

"I don't know, you'll have to ask Robin...my wife."

"Your wife's name is Robin, same as mine? La Moria, there's hope for you after all! She turned to the others. "Now that we all know Bob is the lover, do you have any questions before I get back to work?"

"Doc, your findings were consistent with what I already believed, but I'd hoped there'd be something which would point to the killer."

"As you know, sometimes I do find something which will give you some clue as to who the killer is, but in this instance, I didn't find it. I do believe the killer wore gloves, possibly surgical gloves similar to what I wear to minimize the transfer of trace evidence from him to her. However, lacking any supporting evidence, I can't include that in my report."

"Doc, you referred to the killer as "him." Can you share your reasoning?" Riggs asked.

"I base my opinion on the two broken ribs, Williams' weight, and the distance from the floor to the noose. It would have taken a pretty strong individual to hold her up that high and still place the noose around her neck. I just can't see a woman doing that, unless it was a very big woman."

"Makes sense to me. Thanks. Doc."

They headed out the door and back to their cars.

"Bob, I'll see you at the restaurant on the northwest corner of 205th and Highway 99 if you're still up for the lunch I promised. John, I'll keep you advised on anything I find out."

"I'll see you at the restaurant," La Moria said, recognizing he might not get the chance to collect on lunch again until the investigation was complete. He also saw it as an opportunity for them to discuss what actions to take next. He knew Riggs was disappointed, but not surprised at Doctor Spears' findings. While the autopsy results had helped so many times before in their investigations, this time it revealed nothing they didn't already know.

Goldsmith waved his acknowledgment to Riggs and La Moria as he climbed into his car.

I wonder what steps they'll take next to learn the identity of the cult members. Whatever they decide to do, I hope they uncover some leads that'll help me solve the murder of Beth Williams.

During the drive to the restaurant, Dispatch advised Riggs to give Pope a call. The return call revealed that no male caseworker or inspector had gone by the foster home run by Rebecca Shelby. Pope advised that she had obtained photos of both Trickey and Ryker. She agreed to make contact with the neighbor, Susan Dixson, to see if she could identify either Trickey or Ryker as the person who visited Shelby on several occasions.

Riggs went over the information just given to him by Pope and the steps already taken in this investigation. *Did I miss something? If so, what? On the surface, the murder of Beth Williams seems to have closed a door, but then, if she was murdered for what she may have known about Kae Carlson and Rebecca Shelby, her murder just might be the key.*

Chapter 16

The restaurant where Riggs agreed to meet La Moria was one he frequented often. He'd become involved in a public relations campaign put on by the restaurant several years ago that had kept him in contact with management and staff.

"I can't believe it! You're finally going to buy me the lunch you've been promising, like since the beginning of time," La Moria said, giving Riggs a friendly punch in the arm.

"Quit whining, it's not becoming. You do remember that I've bought you coffee, lunch, and dinner in the past...many times," said Riggs, pretending to be offended.

"You're right, but I remember it was way, way in the past. In fact, it's so far back that I'd almost forgotten. Besides, you're due for a little ribbing," La Moria joked. It wasn't often that Riggs gave him the opportunity of being on the giving end of harassment.

"Okay, okay, I get the message."

As they walked into the restaurant, Riggs

recognized Penny standing behind the cash register. He'd become fond of Penny over the last several months, a seventeen–year old who worked at the restaurant every day after school. He'd talked to her many times about how she was doing in school, the soccer team she played on, and her plans for the future. Through these conversations, they'd become friends and she'd often seek him out for advice. He knew she'd be graduating at the end of the school year and had advised her to continue on with her education at a local college. She'd assured him she'd start college at her earliest opportunity.

Riggs had taken Toby and the boys to one of Penny's soccer games. His boys couldn't believe a girl could play soccer as well as she did. In fact, Riggs hoped her talent on the soccer field would get her a scholarship to college. It couldn't happen to a nicer kid. She lived with her mother, who had remained single after losing Penny's father in the Desert Storm war. Penny was two at the time and had never had the opportunity to really know her father. She was proud of him because of all the positive things her mother had told her about him. Penny had once told Riggs that her mother had not remarried because she wouldn't be able to find a man of the same caliber as her father.

Penny smiled at Riggs and La Moria as they walked in, heading for the table in the corner where Riggs always sat unless someone else was already there. They had no sooner sat down when

A Birthday to Die For

Penny arrived with a coffee pot and two cups.

"How did you know I wanted a cup of coffee?" La Moria asked her.

"You're a cop and a friend of Riggs, aren't you?" she laughed.

"I'm a cop. We're still working on the friend part," La Moria replied, sneaking a glance at Riggs.

"Well then, it just makes sense that you'll want a cup of coffee, just like he always does."

Riggs couldn't conceal the humor he saw in the verbal exchange between Penny and his partner, which was one of the things he liked about Penny. She was confident, never seeming to be intimidated by others. He also detected a smile tugging at the corners of La Moria's mouth as he enjoyed the verbal exchange with Penny.

"I suppose you'll order the same thing Riggs usually orders too," Penny said, with an 'I–know–you–so–well' look on her face.

"And what would that be, may I ask?" La Moria inquired, obviously enjoying Penny's spunk.

"Fish and chips."

"Fish and chips it is then."

"I knew it. You cops are all alike." She walked away laughing.

Riggs found the little exchange with Penny refreshing, providing a chance to clear their minds for a few minutes, but Kae Carlson's life was hanging in the balance and it was time to get back to the investigation at hand.

"Bob, I've been going over all the steps we've

taken and all the deadends we've encountered, even the information I got from Barb Pope on the way here. She reported that CPS did not send a male individual to inspect the foster home. She's in the process of re–contacting Susan Dixson to show her photos of Trickey and Ryker. Do you have any other ideas we need to look at or what we may have missed? Maybe we need to take another direction in the investigation. What are your thoughts?"

"What Pope told you is interesting. I've also been going over the steps we've already taken and what's left for us to do. Unless Dixson identifies Trickey or Ryker, I can't think of anything we can do. Short of a miracle happening, I don't see any other direction to take. I'm still wondering how Chief Trickey fits into all of this and what hasn't he told us. Maybe Dixson will ID him and we'll get some answers. Not having the opportunity to question him and Ryker about the prostitutes still bothers me."

"I know what you mean, but think about it. If they contact prostitutes for the purpose of abducting them for sacrifice, what are the chances they'd do it on duty? I believe that if...and I think it's a big if, they'd do it off duty, pretending they were vice cops and using their badges to gain the cooperation of the prostitute. There would be no official record of an arrest or even their contact with the prostitute."

As La Moria took in the information, he noticed Riggs was staring past him in the direction of the

A Birthday to Die For

entryway where he knew Penny was standing behind the cash register.

"What's going on?" La Moria asked.

"Bob, a white male in his late teens or early twenties is standing in front of Penny. He has his right hand tucked under the left side of his jacket, which looks a little suspicious. It just might be a robbery. Let's wait and see. Penny's waiting on a customer right now and this guy will be next."

"If it's a robbery and Penny gives us away, there'll be a shooting inside this restaurant and I don't like the idea of my back being towards them," La Moria said, resisting the almost over–powering temptation to turn around.

"Bob, I won't let that happen. I'm going to walk up front and try to signal Penny that we're aware of what's going on, if it is a robbery."

"How the hell do you plan to do that without you giving us away?"

"I don't know, but I'll think of something."

"While you're doing that, I'm going to slide around so I can see what's going on behind me. I hope you don't get our asses shot off."

"I'll try not to," said Riggs, sliding from behind the table and starting towards the entry, contemplating what to do next. He knew Penny was a smart girl and if he did the right thing, she'd pick up on it right away. As he approached, he could see the guy standing in front of Penny, talking to her. He also saw a look of panic on her face.

"Excuse me, young lady, but could you point

207

me in the direction of the men's restroom?" Riggs asked, pretending to ignore the suspect and giving her a quick wink.

"Yes, sir. It's right there," Penny said, pointing down the hall.

Penny immediately knew Riggs was aware that the guy in front of her was planning to rob the restaurant. She pulled the bills from the cash register and handed them over. She didn't see the gun, but he'd told her he had one and would kill her if she alerted anyone before he left the restaurant. *Where's Riggs? What's he planning to do?*

Riggs walked around the corner, rubbing his hands together, pretending to dry them after his visit to in the restroom. He again passed in front of Penny while the robbery suspect was still standing in front of her, continuing back to the table where La Moria was seated but now facing the entry. Penny knew Riggs was going to do something, but what and when had her worried.

"Bob, we have a robbery in progress. I didn't see a gun, but I'm sure he has one."

"How should we handle this?" La Moria asked, his body tense like a tightly wound spring.

"We don't dare do anything while he's still inside the restaurant. If he starts shooting, somebody will be killed and we don't want that to happen. I think we should wait until he leaves and then go for it," Riggs whispered loudly, his eyes still focused on the robbery suspect and Penny. He knew the guy would pull his gun and

A Birthday to Die For

kill Penny if he felt threatened. He couldn't draw down on the suspect unless he had to because no other option presented itself and he was convinced the suspect was going to shoot Penny or someone else.

"Okay, I'll follow your lead," La Moria whispered back.

They both sipped their coffee, speaking back and forth in a low tone as if they were carrying on a serious conversation. Occasionally, one threw a glance in the direction of the entry waiting for the moment when the suspect would step outside and they could spring into action.

"Okay, there he goes, let's go." Riggs slid from behind their table, picking up a bottle of ketchup as he walked towards the front door with La Moria right behind. They both knew without saying so that following a fleeing suspect through the front door was very dangerous. An experienced robbery suspect would be watching the door and would shoot his pursuers.

When they walked by Penny, Riggs told her, "Lock the door behind us and don't let anyone leave until I tell you otherwise."

Riggs was the first to step through the doorway into the parking lot. La Moria followed with his gun drawn, ready to return fire if necessary. To La Moria's surprise, the suspect was intent on fleeing and didn't turn around. Riggs raised his arm and threw the catsup bottle at the fleeing suspect. La Moria was utterly amazed to see the catsup bottle fly through the air and strike the

209

suspect between the shoulder blades with such force that the bottle broke, spewing ketchup everywhere and causing the suspect to fall face down on the asphalt.

As his body hit the pavement, the gun dislodged from his waistband and skidded across the pavement before coming to rest under a parked car. The suspect slid on his face a few feet, skinning his forehead, nose, and chin, creating a bloody mess. Riggs was on top of him in an instant, trying to put the handcuffs on, while the suspect rolled back and forth screaming, "Don't shoot! Don't shoot! I've been shot. I'm dying! I need to go to the hospital!"

"Shut up you dumb son–of–a–bitch. You're not dying and you haven't been shot, at least not yet."

"Yes, I have. I've been shot in the back. Can't you see the blood? I need to go to the hospital now... please."

"Lie still so I can get these cuffs on you. By the way, you're under arrest for armed robbery. You're not going to the hospital, you're going to jail. You're really a piece of work, you know? What an idiot! I'll bet you're a real disappointment to your momma."

"I'm bleeding! I need a doctor. Please take me to a doctor."

"You're not bleeding. It's ketchup, you dummy," Riggs said, trying not to laugh.

"Bob, I'd appreciate it if you'd advise this clown of his constitutional rights. I don't think I

A Birthday to Die For

can do it without laughing and you know this is a serious arrest."

Bob was laughing so hard he had tears running down his cheeks. "I don't know if I can either, but I'll try." He pulled a card from his inside coat pocket and gave him the required Miranda warning.

While La Moria advised the suspect of his rights, Riggs removed the stolen money from the suspect's pants pockets, placing it on the hood of a car along with the recovered gun.

"Bob, my count is $136.85. Would you confirm the count?"

"That's my count," La Moria confirmed, handing the money back to Riggs.

"I'll go call this in and have Penny check her receipts to confirm the restaurant's loss," Riggs said, starting back inside.

"Wait just a damn minute. I want to know why you decided to bean this guy with a ketchup bottle knowing he had a gun."

"Well, it's like this. When I was a kid, I used to imagine I was an Indian warrior and I'd pretend an old hatchet I had was a tomahawk. I spent hours throwing that hatchet at a tree stump. I got pretty darn good at hitting what I aimed at, so I decided because of his age, I'd hit him with the ketchup bottle, maybe scare the hell out of him and capture him without firing a shot. Besides, neither of us could have caught him if he'd started running."

"What if you'd missed and he turned to

shoot?"

"Then you would've killed him."

La Moria rolled his eyes after hearing Riggs' answer. "Thanks partner! Maybe next time you'll let me know beforehand."

"I will if there is a next time. What's the matter, Bob, don't you trust me?"

"I trust you, but do you have any more childhood fantasies you might want to live out that I should know about?"

"None that I can think of at the moment."

"Okay, while you're finishing up with Penny and the management, I'll transport this joker to jail and book him. By the way, you still owe me a lunch. If you think a little robbery is going to get you off the hook, you're sadly mistaken. See you tomorrow. You do know, don't you, that nobody is going to believe this when I tell them?"

When Riggs returned to the restaurant he saw several people milling around the entry, some with their noses pressed to the window as they tried to see what was going on in the parking lot. He knocked on the front door to signal Penny to open it. When she opened the door, he could see in her eyes that she had a hundred questions she wanted to ask, but the answers would have to wait.

Riggs held up his badge to get the attention of the patrons. "I'd like to thank each and every one of you for listening to Penny and staying inside while we apprehended a robbery suspect. You're

A Birthday to Die For

free to leave as soon as you pay Penny for your meals. Have a safe trip home."

"Riggs, how did you do it?" Penny asked, trying to conceal her amazement.

"Remember the ketchup bottle I took with me? I hit him with it and he just gave up."

"You're kidding!"

"You know I wouldn't kid you," Riggs said with an all–telling gleam in his eyes. "I have to put the money into evidence. Do you have your receipts ready?"

Penny hit the keys on her calculator and ripped the tape from it. "Here it is, Riggs, $136.00."

Riggs took the receipt from Penny and was turning towards the door when Jan Ice from the local television station burst into the lobby with her cameraman right behind her.

"Hey Riggs! What have you got for me? I heard there was a robbery and you caught the guy in the parking lot."

Riggs was struck dumb. "Yeah, it happened, but how did you learn about it?"

"Some guy called the TV station from inside this restaurant. He told my editor he couldn't leave because the place had just been robbed and the cops were arresting the suspect in the parking lot."

"Did you get the name of the guy who called and talked to your editor?" Riggs asked, not trusting Ice.

"No, I didn't, sorry."

Riggs shook his head in disbelief. "I've got a

lot of work to do, so I'll turn you over to Penny. Without her cool head, we may have had a shooting in here today. She's a great kid and she'll tell you what you need to know."

"But Riggs, you know my editor always wants the cop's version."

"I know, but not this time. See ya!"

Riggs stuffed the receipt Penny gave him into his pocket and headed for his car. He had locked the recovered money and snub–nosed revolver in the trunk until he could place the items into evidence, along with the receipt.

He thought back to the time Ice had burned him on an investigation. It was a double homicide and he was trying to keep some information confidential for interrogation purposes. He'd asked her not to reveal anything until the suspect had been captured, but she didn't. It was on the six o'clock news. The suspect heard it and fled south to California, car–jacking a vehicle on the way and nearly killing its owner. He wasn't surprised she'd gotten there so fast just now. She was always showing up at his scenes. She was a real pain in the ass with her eagerness to get a story at any cost. Her last name fit her perfectly. She never let sentiment or emotions get in her way when it came to getting a story. Unfortunately, they had disagreed too many times on the accuracy of her words as well as the betrayal. She had a tendency for sensationalism and as far as he was concerned, she was unable to tell the truth, the whole truth, and nothing but

A Birthday to Die For

the truth. If it took a lie or a sad story to get the information she needed, so be it. It wasn't so much what she wrote, but the methods she used and the people she walked over to get the story she wanted. She called him frequently trying to get a lead. He'd caught her following him when he left the office. He knew she wouldn't give up until she found out what his and La Moria's investigation was all about.

The satisfaction he felt as a result of the arrest faded quickly as his thoughts returned to the life or death investigation involving Kae Carlson. This arrest had been another impediment. It was as if a super–power of some kind was creating them. *What's next?* As this thought left his mind, his pager went off, advising him to contact the communications supervisor.

Riggs immediately dialed the number on his pager's display. It was answered by none other than Sandra Reed, the very person who had started him on this roller coaster ride.

"Sandra, what's up?" Riggs asked, feeling he already knew the answer.

"You asked to be notified immediately if there was a report of a church burglary in the Duvall area, didn't you?"

"Yes I did. Do we have one?"

"Yes, but it's not in Duvall, but closer to Fall City a few miles down the road. I've got Boy–Three rolling in that direction. They should be there in the next ten minutes. Are you going to roll on this?"

"Yeah I'm enroute. Alert Boy–Three that I'm responding and to maintain a perimeter around the church until I get there."

"Roger that," Sandra responded, picking up on the excitement in Riggs' voice. She was sure that Riggs' interest in a church burglary was related to the original report she'd taken from Dr. Mitchell regarding the threat to Kae Carlson's life.

Chapter 17

The drive to the church would take about twenty minutes running code two without lights or siren, so Riggs pulled his portable blue light from the floor and activated it as he placed it on the dash. He was driving an unmarked car and even with the blue light flashing, other cars were slow to move to the right. He didn't have a siren and had to rely solely on the blue light and his ability to maneuver between cars. One woman panicked and stopped in the middle of the road until he used his horn to persuade her to move out of the way. A second driver, a young guy probably in his late teens, flipped him off as he passed. Although his speed was impeded by the actions or better said, lack of action by other drivers, he had chosen a route that would save him considerable time.

Riggs was within a mile of the church when he heard the Boy–Three car notify Dispatch, "Boy–Three 10–97," the code for arriving to the detail. "Boy–Three, Boy–Two's also on scene and has set up the perimeter pending the arrival of

Detective Riggs."

When Riggs pulled into the gravel parking lot surrounding the church he spotted Boy–Three's Officer Al Cox stationed at one corner of the church with Boy–Two's Officer Ron Ryals at the back side corner. They had all four sides of the church covered. The church fit the description Turner had given him. It was isolated from a business or residential area, no outside lighting, and trees surrounded the parking lot concealed it from the street running north and south located about one hundred yards to the west. As he pulled up parallel with Cox's car, he heard Cox say, "Glad you're here, Riggs, but why are you rolling on a burglary?"

"Did you see the report on the animal mutilation on the other side of Duvall taken by Officer Bartell?" Riggs asked as he got out of his car.

"Yes, I did. What a cruel thing to do to a horse or any other animal," replied Cox, still puzzled.

"I've been advised by a reliable source that there may be a correlation between animal mutilations and church burglaries, that maybe the animal parts are used for rituals held in the church to practice Satanism and to mock God in his own house," Riggs explained.

"Are you trying to tell me there may be suspects inside that worship Satan and they have the parts cut from that horse with them?"

"That's exactly what I'm telling you. I'm also telling you that if there are people still inside,

A Birthday to Die For

they're extremely dangerous. Do you get the message?"

"I sure as hell do. I'd better let Ryals know what we're up against," Cox advised.

"I agree, so I'll stand by here until you clue Ryals into what's happening, then you and I will go in together while Ryals maintains a lookout for anyone fleeing," Riggs explained as Cox turned in Ryals' direction.

It seemed like only a moment before Cox returned to where Riggs was standing. "Okay, what are we going to do now?"

"What do you know about this church?" Riggs asked.

"I've never been inside, but I've checked the outside exterior on drive–bys looking for any evidence of a break–in or an abandoned stolen car in the parking lot. I do know the church has a silent burglar alarm because one day during a high wind, the alarm was set off and I responded. When the Pastor showed up, he told me about the alarm and turned it off."

"Can we expect the Pastor to show up anytime soon?" Riggs asked, considering what to do if he did.

"He just may, depending on whether or not the alarm company called him as well as the police… meaning us," said Cox. He also recognized the complication it could create if things were to go badly with any suspects inside the church.

"Go alert Ryals to the possibility and advise him to keep the Pastor out of the building and

219

out of our way until we say it's clear," Riggs instructed.

Cox walked to Ryals, then returned. "Ryals says he'll keep the Pastor under control if he shows up. I'm ready any time you are," he said, looking for Riggs to take the lead.

The only lighting available was from their flashlights as they approached the front door. Their attention was immediately focused on the large hole in the door near the doorknob, obviously created by an ax. There were chop marks all over it because it was a solid core door and several attempts had been made to cut through it.

"Well, so much for stealth. Whoever broke in here wasn't trying to be quiet," Riggs commented.

"Hell, they should have been able to hear the noise in the next county," Cox whispered as they slowly pushed the door open and stood outside the doorway, one on each side. They were careful not to shine their light on one another or to hold the flashlight directly in front of their bodies in the event the suspects chose to shoot at the light.

"I'll take the left side, you take the right," Riggs instructed as they quickly moved through the entrance into the church.

Standing just inside on opposite sides, they shone their flashlight beams around the interior while feeling the wall for a light switch. Finding none, they proceeded to opposite sides of the room and started down the aisles between the pews and the wall. The walls were lined with red velvet

A Birthday to Die For

curtains that hung from ceiling to floor. As they moved in synch with one another, they checked between the pews for anyone hiding, then flashed their lights around the room to see if anyone else was in there with them. The room was quite large and their flashlight beams didn't reach the entire distance without creating considerable shadows which made it impossible to expose all areas in which a person might hide.

They were about halfway down the aisles when Riggs glanced towards the floor. He was startled at what he saw near the bottom of the red velvet curtain covering the wall to his left. He turned his flashlight beam towards the ceiling and clicked it off and on to get Cox's attention, then did a sweeping motion with the beam across the ceiling to beckon Cox to his side. With Cox standing next to him, he directed his flashlight beam towards the floor next to the wall covered by the red velvet curtain. Riggs heard Cox gasp as his eyes fell on the toe end of two shoes protruding from under the curtain. Cox quickly moved to the other side of the exposed shoes and waited for Riggs' next move.

Riggs explored the curtain with his flashlight until he found an opening. He clicked his flashlight off and on again bringing Cox's attention to the opening. Cox knew that Riggs would peel the curtain to the right towards him, handing it to him so he could continue to peel it away from the wall and expose the person hiding there.

Holding his flashlight in his left hand, Riggs

reached down and grabbed the curtain near the floor, lifting it rapidly towards Cox who grabbed it and exposed the bearded white male holding a double–bladed ax above his head to allow a downward swing at them. The suspect immediately took a swing at Riggs who was closest to him, missing by only a fraction of an inch. Cox attempted to blind the suspect by shining his flashlight beam into his eyes. He instantly turned towards Cox, swinging the ax back and forth, stumbling forward. While the suspect was facing towards Cox, Riggs jumped on his back, grabbing him around the neck. Riggs had considered shooting the son–of–a–bitch, but needed him alive if he was part of the cult.

Riggs' feet were about two feet from the floor as the suspect lurched in all directions, trying to free himself while Riggs held on to keep himself from flying across the room. Cox dodged as the suspect swung the ax with one hand, while trying to pull Riggs off with the other. His movements were no more affected by Riggs' weight on his back than if he were a pesky fly. The suspect tripped and fell backwards into the pews, forcing Riggs to let go or be injured as they fell. Riggs was on his back when the suspect regained his footing and came at him with the ax raised above his head. Only two pews away, Riggs backpedaled on the floor using his elbows to get out of range of the ax blade as the suspect rushed at him.

Now Cox was on the suspect's back trying to get a neck hold that would bring the guy to his

A Birthday to Die For

knees. Being a little bigger and taller than Riggs, Cox had a better chance of gaining the right hold, but his attempt also came up short when the suspect ran backwards jamming Cox against the wall with such force that he was unable to hold on. As Cox tried to regain his footing, the suspect turned towards him, swinging the ax close enough to slash a hole in Cox's shirt and uniform tie. Seeing this, Riggs jumped onto the seat of a pew and brought his flashlight down in a glancing blow to the suspect's head. With blood running down the side of his face from a torn ear, the suspect shook his head and moved towards Riggs. Cox was back on his feet and used his flashlight to strike the suspect squarely on the back of the head. The suspect's knees buckled and he fell to the floor, dropping the ax which slid under the pews. Without hesitation, both Riggs and Cox jumped on him, holding him against the floor in a nearly unconscious state until they got him handcuffed.

Ryals heard the commotion coming from the inside of the church, but knew he couldn't abandon his post. He was surprised when he saw Cox and Riggs dragging a giant of a man out of the church and place him in the back seat of Cox's patrol car.

"Ryals, come over here and advise this guy of his rights. Also, search his pockets for any identification," Riggs requested as he got out his camera and took photographs of the cut to Cox's shirt and tie. "That was close, Al. He almost

223

gutted you," Riggs commented, watching Cox put his finger through the hole in his shirt.

"You do know we had every right to blow that guy's head off? The ax was a deadly weapon!" Cox complained.

"Yeah, you're right, but I'm hoping I can get some information out of him regarding this other case I'm working. I thought for a minute we were going to have to kill him or be killed ourselves."

"Well, any way you want to look at it, this is a fight we'll always remember. This guy has to be at least six and a half feet tall and about three hundred pounds. I can tell you right now, if you hadn't been there, I would have shot him."

"And justifiably so," Riggs agreed.

"Riggs, I've advised this guy of his rights, but he refuses to say anything. He won't acknowledge his understanding of his rights and he won't ask for an attorney, so what's next?" Ryals asked, looking to Riggs for instructions.

"Did you find a driver's license or other identification on him?"

"Not a thing. His pockets are empty."

"Let me talk to him and see if he'll say anything to me," Riggs said, opening the patrol car door and looking the suspect in the eyes.

"Mister, you're under arrest for burglary and attempted murder. You know you have the right to an attorney before you talk to me. Do you understand that?" Riggs asked as he watched the suspect for any indication that he'd heard what he was being told and understood his rights. He

A Birthday to Die For

saw no response whatever. The suspect kept his eyes forward and didn't even blink.

"What's your name?" Riggs asked, but received no response.

"Can you talk?" Riggs asked, but again, no response.

"Can you hear me?" Riggs shouted. The man did not reply or respond in any way. Cox and Ryals watched as Riggs asked the questions. They neither saw nor heard a response. They also saw no response when Riggs wrote that same question on a piece of paper.

"Why did you ask him whether he could talk or hear?" Ryals asked.

"I had a case one time where an officer shot an individual who had failed to follow his commands. The officer thought he was going after a weapon, but as it turned out, the guy was a deaf–mute. The officer retired after that, never wanting to be in that position again," Riggs explained.

"Did he kill the deaf–mute?" Ryals inquired.

"No, but it was so close the officer was unable to live with the thought of almost killing a handicapped person who could neither hear nor speak. Let's get back to this case," Riggs advised.

"What do you want us to do?" Cox asked.

"Ryals, you finish processing this scene. Take photos of the forced entry, the interior of the church, including the curtains on the walls and any damage caused to the pews during the fight. Also look for any evidence of animal parts, such as testicles, horse ears, a horse tongue. When you're through, place the photos, the ax, and anything else you find into evidence. Let me know if you find the animal parts, which will let me know for sure that this is connected to the cult investigation I'm handling."

"Okay, I'll take care of that."

"Al, since we have this guy in your patrol car, you transport him to jail and book him on burglary and attempted murder charges. Put a note in booking that I'm to be advised before he's released on bail."

"I understand the burglary charge, but why the attempted murder?" Al asked, searching Riggs' face.

"Well, let me ask you this. Did you think he was trying to kill us with the ax?"

"You're damn right he was trying to kill us."

"I feel the same way, so we're going to add attempted murder to the charges."

"Okay, I'll be enroute to the jail with him."

"Al, try and get him to talk on the way. Let me know if he does."

"Will do."

As he pulled out of the church parking lot, Riggs advised Dispatch that he was clear and Boy–Three was transporting the prisoner to jail while Boy–Two completed processing the scene for evidence. *This has been one hell of a day.*

Chapter 18

The surveillance of Kae by Hatch and Decker had been going on for nearly a week without any sighting of a man wearing a knit hat. They'd been on her from the moment she woke up in the morning until she went to bed at night. Time was running out for them and Sgt. Francis was calling them twice a day for updates. They knew it was just a matter of time before she'd pull them back to the drug investigations that were beginning to pile up and needed attention. They'd satisfied themselves regarding Kae's safety during the night because they'd checked out her apartment and the building it was in while she was out with Riggs trying to locate the ceremonial sites. They had discovered that after eight o'clock in the evening, all exterior doors to the building were locked and could only be opened by a resident with a key. They also discovered that the door to Kae's apartment was secured by a single bolt dead lock. She lived on the second floor, so it would be extremely difficult for someone to make entry, forced or otherwise, to harm her.

It was now six in the morning as Hatch and Decker re–established their surveillance. The sun was just starting to peek between the clouds which signaled the potential for rain some time during the day.

"It's my turn to wave the sign today, so I'll move down to the corner while you enjoy this nice dry, warm car," Decker advised as he slid from the front seat into the cool morning air.

"Well, it's your turn today anyway. I did it yesterday and I don't know how much longer we're going to get away with this false advertising. I wonder just how many people have called the phony number on our sign trying to get information on the closeout sale of exotic reptiles," Hatch commented as Decker turned away and started towards the corner.

Hatch kept his eyes glued to the front entry to the apartment building, waiting for Kae to make her appearance and they started their moving surveillance on her. Just what in hell is an exotic reptile? When they put the sign together, they tried to come up with something for sale which would not interest most people, therefore minimizing the number of potential responses, but also recognizing that there were always kooks out there who will buy anything.

It was seven o'clock when Kae walked out of her apartment building. She was wearing brown slacks, a white turtleneck sweater, and a tan hooded jacket as she headed for class. She was

A Birthday to Die For

staying with her routine, walking the same street to Seattle Community College. Hatch kept his eye on her as he popped the trunk lid and Decker threw their sign in the trunk. He stayed put until Decker disappeared around the corner following her at a distance on foot. He then pulled away from the curb and drove to the street that ran parallel with the street Kae and Decker were on. As he drove, he could see both Kae and Decker between the buildings and across the parking lots used by students from the college. Decker carried a small portable radio which kept them in verbal contact with each other. They used a secure channel to avoid being discovered or monitored by someone sharing a standard frequency.

Decker followed Kae onto the campus where she made her regular stop in the cafeteria for hot tea which she drank as she reviewed her notes from the day before. He sat at a table about thirty yards from her, sipping his coffee as he watched Hatch purchase a cup of coffee and move to a table closer to the door. Kae would walk right by him when she left for her classes. The odds were that she wouldn't pay any attention to Hatch as he poured over the textbook in front of him, a prop to help him blend into the college crowd.

It was quarter to eight when Kae left the cafeteria heading for her first class. Hatch got up and followed her as if he was also going to class. Decker hung back, looking the crowd over in hopes of seeing the knit hat or some other action that would pay off. He'd lost sight of Hatch and

229

Kae, so headed in the direction of her first class, the same class they'd followed her to each day of their surveillance.

Decker had just rounded the corner when he heard a loud scream come from the end of the walkway which led to a street running parallel with the perimeter of the campus, typically used by students to park their cars. His attention was immediately drawn toward Hatch who was running towards a black four–door sedan where a man wearing a knit hat was struggling with Kae, attempting to force her into the car.

"Let her go or I'll shoot!" Hatch yelled as he ran towards the car with his automatic in his hand. He could hear Kae screaming as loud as she could. She was crying hysterically. The guy in the knit hat looked in Hatch's direction as he tried once more to push Kae into the car. He knew Hatch would be on him in seconds, so he threw Kae to the pavement and jumped into the right front seat and the sedan sped away, spinning its back tires and leaving behind a cloud of black smoke.

Decker arrived as Hatch was helping Kae up from the pavement. "Are you hurt?" he asked as he re–holstered his gun.

"I'm alright. Who are you?" she asked, wiping the tears from her eyes and brushing off her clothes.

"We're friends of Riggs. He asked us to keep an eye on you. He told us that he'd promised to protect you, so that's why we're here," Decker

A Birthday to Die For

explained as Hatch tried to regain some degree of normal breathing.

"Did you get the license plate number?" Hatch asked Decker.

"No. It didn't have a rear plate, so this was planned."

"How about a description of the guy with the knit hat?"

"The only thing I can add to what we already know is that he's a white male and he has a short–trimmed beard," Decker said, trying to remember every detail of his observations.

"Did you see the driver?" Hatch asked, hoping they'd at least come up with some helpful information.

"No, I couldn't see through the tinted windows."

"Well, we blew it. We've proven the guy exists and that Kae's life is in jeopardy, just like Riggs said. We also know they won't try to abduct her here at the college again since they know we have her under surveillance. Riggs is going to be pissed that we missed this opportunity to catch someone from the cult," Hatch commented, thinking how he wanted to put a round through the back window of the black sedan, but didn't, knowing he couldn't risk the shot with so many students walking around.

"Well, are you going to call Riggs or am I?" Decker asked, looking at Hatch and Kae.

"I'll call him. We need to make sure Kae's in a safe place. Even though they won't try to get to her here again, they may try elsewhere and we won't be around," Hatch said, punching in Riggs' number.

"Riggs, can I help you?"

"Riggs, this is Hatch. I've got some bad news for you."

"What is it?" Riggs asked, fearing that something had happened to Kae before Dr. Mitchell could move her to a safe house.

"They tried to abduct Kae this morning at the college. It was the guy with the knit hat. He was assisted by someone driving the getaway car, a black four–door sedan we believe was a Mercury with no rear plates. Due to the dark–tinted windows, we can't tell you whether the driver was a man or woman. We didn't get close enough to tackle him and we couldn't get a shot off because of all the students in the area."

"Damn! I was sure counting on catching this guy if he really existed," Riggs said, the frustration clearly coming through as he spoke.

"Sorry!"

"Well, thanks anyway. I appreciate what you and Decker have done for me. It's not a complete loss."

"What do you mean?" Hatch asked knowing this was a real letdown for Riggs.

"The way I see it, you and Decker have confirmed there is a guy with a knit hat. Kae's life is in jeopardy, and most of all, you've confirmed the credibility of my suspicions and the need for protective custody."

A Birthday to Die For

"Riggs, we're sorry about this. If there's anything else we can do to help, just let us know." Hatch felt like a failure.

"You guys did the best you could under the circumstances. Don't let it eat at you. On your way to report in with Sgt. Francis, drop Kae off at my office. I need to come up with a plan to keep her alive."

"Will do. See you in a little while."

Riggs motioned La Moria over to his desk where he shared the information he'd received from Hatch and Decker regarding Kae and the guy in the knit hat. He also brought La Moria up to speed on what had transpired at the church the night before.

"You mean to tell me you also were involved in an arrest at a church last night after we made the arrest at the restaurant?"

"Yep! Remember what I told you about Turner telling us about the animal mutilation and its correlation with church burglaries? I alerted Dispatch to notify me if a church burglary was reported in the area of the mutilation. Well, they did and I responded from the restaurant. We arrested the suspect in the church burglary, but he isn't talking. I thought I'd let him spend the night in jail and maybe he'd decide to talk. He's booked under a John Doe, so he isn't going to bail out until his identity is confirmed. I'm also to be notified before he's allowed bail."

"It sounds like you've got the bases covered

regarding the burglary suspect, but it's the pits regarding identity of the guy in the knit hat. We sure could have used that information. It could have blown this case wide open. It just goes to show that you never know which way the cards are going to fall in an investigation," said La Moria. Riggs shook his head in agreement.

"You know what this means, Bob. We've got to make sure the good doctor has hidden Kae away some place safe. I wonder what Dr. Mitchell is going to say about this attempted abduction. Does she think Kae can go into a safe house without causing more psychological damage?"

"We'll find out as soon as Hatch and Decker get here with Kae and we take her to Mitchell's office," said La Moria.

Hatch and Decker had Kae in tow as they entered the office. They both looked like they were carrying the weight of the world on their shoulders as they approached Riggs and La Moria. Not only had they failed, but they also felt embarrassed. Here they were, two of the best undercover cops the department had and they couldn't even catch the guy wearing the knit hat. It didn't matter to them that they'd done everything humanly possible to protect Kae and the other students, the only thing they could think of was that he'd gotten away.

"Come on you guys, it's not that bad. You did everything possible and by the book. You weren't able to use deadly force for two reasons. If you'd

A Birthday to Die For

have killed him, we wouldn't have been able to get the information we needed anyway and you couldn't risk a shot due to the pedestrian traffic in the area. This isn't the first time something like this has happened and it won't be the last. La Moria and I really appreciate what you've done. We'll take Kae off your hands and you two can get back to your own investigations. Just think about all the lives you're saving every time you take one of those drug dealers or suppliers off the street," said Riggs. This time it was La Moria shaking his head in agreement.

The telephone call to Dr. Mitchell was a tough one to make. Riggs knew it would both excite her and scare her, but there was no other choice. He needed to find a safe house for Kae, but he needed the doctor's guidance because Kae wasn't a normal victim or witness. She had multiple personalities and needed the security Dr. Mitchell afforded her.

"Doc, this is Riggs. I need your help."

"What kind of help?"

"This morning the guy in the knit hat tried to abduct Kae. She escaped because the two undercover detectives I had following her came to her rescue. Had they not been there, we would have lost Kae and probably never seen her again. I need to put her in a safe house to ensure her safety. I'd like to bring her to your office and talk about it, so we can decide how we're going to do it. Is that agreeable with you?"

235

"Yes, yes, by all means. Bring her here right now, I'll be here waiting."

The doctor was true to her word. She met them at the front door where she quickly wrapped her arms around Kae and escorted her into the session room.

"Are you alright?" she asked Kae, looking her over for any signs of physical injuries. Riggs watched as the Paula examined Kae, expecting her to respond in her own voice, but instead he heard the voice of Connie.

"I'm alright. The two men with the guns saved my life. They're friends of Detective Riggs. They're really nice. They saved me," she said, then she began to cry.

"I know, I know, all of Detective Riggs' friends are nice. You're one of his friends and you're nice. He kept his promise and protected you, now I'm going to take you to a place where I know you'll be safe. Is that okay with you?" Dr. Mitchell asked, knowing she had to take on the responsibility if she was going to protect Kae not only physically, but psychologically as well.

"Where are you going to take her, Doc?" Riggs asked.

"I've got a place I know will be safe. I'll tell you later. In the meantime, I want you to catch these bastards so this thing will be over," she said, clearly worried.

"I'll do that, Doc. You can count on it," Riggs said, turned towards the door. He stopped, then

A Birthday to Die For

turned around to face her again. "Do you need my protection while you take her to wherever you're taking her?"

"No, I've got it figured out. We'll be safe, don't worry."

"Okay, then. I'll stay in touch."

Chapter 19

When Riggs walked into the office, La Moria could read the concern on his face. He also shared those concerns as it related to Kae's safety and the loss of investigative time with the robbery arrest yesterday. The failure to apprehend the guy in the knit hat was a real setback and not knowing if the church burglary suspect was a deaf–mute or just refusing to talk compounded their frustration. They wouldn't be able to keep Kae Carlson in a safe house forever, so time was running out on her unless some miracle presented itself and soon.

The first stop Riggs made was at the coffee pot where he poured himself a strong cup of black coffee. *What the hell? The stronger the coffee, the better. Maybe it'll wake me up to something I've overlooked and get us back on course.*

Riggs had no sooner pulled up a chair next to La Moria's desk to talk over the case when his pager went off. The number displayed on his pager was familiar to him—it was Paula

239

Mitchell's. The page was alarming since he'd just left her at her office and she'd agreed not to use his pager number unless it was an emergency.

"It's Doctor Mitchell. We have some type of an emergency. She agreed to page me only if there was an emergency and she felt Kae's or her own life was in danger."

La Moria handed his telephone to Riggs, anxious to find out what the emergency was and what they could do about it. He knew Kae was to be taken to a safe house by Dr. Mitchell at Riggs' request. Unless the cult had discovered the location of the safe house, it could only mean that Dr. Mitchell's life was now in jeopardy.

"Doc! This is Riggs, what's going on?"

"Riggs, I just got a call from a man who is demanding to know where Kae is staying. He wouldn't give me his name and the caller ID shows a number for a phone booth in the Tacoma area. He told me if I didn't come up with the information he wanted, he'll kill me."

"Have you already taken Kae to the safe house? Did the voice sound familiar?" Riggs asked, knowing the sacrificial date was near and the cult was frantically trying to locate Kae.

"Yes, I've already got Kae in a safe house. No, I didn't recognize the voice. He spoke very softly, as if he was trying to keep from being heard by people who might be nearby," she said. There was a slight, almost imperceptible tremble in her voice, something Riggs picked up on immediately. He believed it was fear he was hearing, even with

A Birthday to Die For

her attempt to conceal it.

"How do you know it was a phone booth?" Riggs asked, wondering whether or not she would hold up under the additional pressure—the threat to her own life.

"I called the number back. After about a hundred rings, some guy answered the phone and told me I was calling a phone booth in Tacoma."

"Did he tell you where the phone booth was located or whether or not he had seen someone using the phone before he answered it?" Riggs asked, knowing he'd be surprised if she had.

"I feel so dumb! I didn't even think to ask him those questions. Sorry!" Paula said, lowering her voice to almost a whisper.

"Doc, are you going to be okay? Do you want me to come get you?" Riggs inquired, now feeling concern for the doctor's life and wondering how to protect her as well as Kae.

"I'll be alright while I'm in my office. I've asked the business complex security guard to keep an eye on me. I may need some protection when I leave for home, but I'll call you if I do. I may decide to stay in my office until you tell me it's safe to go home."

"Okay, Doc. I'll get back to you as soon as I can," Riggs said, knowing full well he had nothing to go on at this time. How was he going to protect her? *Where is that miracle?*

"Let's go over and check Kae's apartment," Riggs said, handing the phone back to La Moria. "Someone is trying to locate her whereabouts

241

since they failed in their abduction attempt and they've threatened Dr. Mitchell's life. There's no question about it, the cult is getting desperate."

The drive to Kae's apartment was interrupted by a phone call from Pope. She advised that Mrs. Dixson was unable to make a positive ID of either Trickey or Ryker. She did feel there was some resemblance to Trickey, but would not say for sure it was him she saw visiting Shelby.

Kae's apartment was in a three–story brownstone building on the southeast corner of Broadway and James where the residents were mostly students attending Seattle Community College. Kae's apartment was on the second floor, number 202.

They walked up the steep narrow staircase to the second floor, passing a young girl in her late teens or early twenties with waist–length blonde hair, who was coming down. They were forced to press their bodies against the wall to allow her to pass. When she was directly in front of them, she looked them in the eye with an inquiring look which told them they were out of place here and made them feel as old as dirt.

"Well, at least she didn't scream at us or spit on us," La Moria muttered under his breath, as they reached the second floor.

Apartment 202 was the first room on the right at the top of the stairs where they immediately noticed pry marks on the door casing. A slight push on the door caused it to swing inward,

A Birthday to Die For

exposing the interior. The brass plate over the hole which allowed the door to stay shut had been forced from the door frame making the lock unworkable. The room had obviously been ransacked. Drawers were pulled out, papers were strewn on the floor, even the mattress had been pulled from the bed and turned over.

"This certainly confirms what Doctor Mitchell told us. Someone is doing their best to try and locate Kae. I'm sure glad I convinced Doctor Mitchell to put Kae in a safe place."

"Isn't Kae's birthday day after tomorrow?" La Moria asked, looked through the apartment, noting the damage to the door and the mess created by whoever broke in.

"What the hell does this mean?" Riggs shouted at La Moria from the bathroom.

"When you invited me into this investigation, I did a little research on satanic cults myself. I believe the 333+333 means 666, which is an anti–Christ symbol. It's their calling card, a signal to Kae, and that's why it's written on her bathroom mirror," La Moria explained as he looked over Riggs' shoulder, feeling very strongly that he was right in his interpretation.

"Well, it's one hell of a signal and those satanic–worshipping bastards are really getting frantic. They want her in the worst way if they're willing to risk getting caught breaking into her apartment, leaving a message on the mirror, and threatening Doctor Mitchell. They want her for the sacrifice come hell or high water. I think we may have another problem to worry about," Riggs responded.

"What could that be?" La Moria asked.

"Think about it. If they know we're involved and they can't get anything out of the doctor, why not follow us in hopes we'll lead them to Kae's hideout? They're desperate and I believe they'll use whatever means available to find Kae."

"If you're right, then we have to assume they know where we live. If they know that, then we have to believe our families are in danger," La Moria said in a somber tone.

"If we're right with our assumption, then we must take some precautions and bring the girls into it," said Riggs. "Two days ago Toby told me she saw a man walking around our house. At that time I thought it was a meter reader, but now I'm not so sure."

"You know this is going to scare the hell out of them," said La Moria.

"I know, but what choice do we have, especially in your case? Your wife is an administrator with the Catholic Church, which makes her a bigger target than someone else. These bastards practice anti–Christian rituals and they may focus their attention on Robin."

"You've got a point. I can tell you that if any harm comes to Robin or my kids, you won't be able to keep me from killing those evil bastards when we find them."

"The same goes for me. Let's get things done here, then meet with the girls tonight and explain

A Birthday to Die For

the situation. What do you say?"

"I don't think we have a choice. We have to bring them in on what's going on so they can do what's necessary to protect our kids. If we do all this and we keep them from finding Kae, I wonder what they'll do if they can't find her in time to sacrifice her on her twenty–sixth birthday. Will it throw their schedule off? Will they change their minds or will they have another plan?" La Moria wondered aloud in response to what Riggs had just said.

"I'm also wondering if the guilty party who broke into the apartment here left any fingerprints or is that too much to ask for?" said Riggs, looking closely at the surfaces the intruder would have had to touch to empty the drawers and to look at the papers thrown about the room.

"Since we're in Seattle's jurisdiction, let's call them and have them take a burglary report and dust for prints. What do you think?" La Moria suggested as he continued to survey the room and those areas that might hold the intruder's fingerprints.

"Sounds good to me. I'll have Dispatch contact SPD to send a car over," Riggs said.

While they waited for the SPD officer to show up, they talked to the neighbors and inquired whether or not they'd seen the person breaking into Kae's apartment or had any suspicions.

The wait was about ten minutes before an SPD patrol officer showed up to take the report. Riggs gave him the information he needed for his report with an explanation to encourage the officer to dust for fingerprints before leaving and get them over to his office as soon as possible. He also encouraged the officer to interview the young woman in apartment #208 who said she had heard someone run down the stairs. When she looked out her window, she saw a man wearing a dark–colored knit hat get into the front passenger side of a sleek black sedan which pulled away rapidly. She was unable to give any further details.

"Let's go back to the office, check for messages, and do some brain–storming before we go home and drop this on the girls. Things are really starting to heat up," Riggs suggested, pondering whether the black car seen leaving Kae's apartment building was the same vehicle seen parked in front of Beth Williams house at the time of her death. There was no doubt in his mind that it was the same car involved in the attempted abduction of Kae at the college.

La Moria responded with an affirmative nod while mulling over the possible risk to his family and the information he and Riggs had collected. It didn't seem to matter which way he looked at it, the answer was always the same. They had followed up every available lead and each one came to a dead end. Time was running out. Kae was going to die.

They made a quick stop at the nearest coffee shop before heading to the office. Suddenly, La Moria told Riggs, "Go around the block, I need to check

A Birthday to Die For

out something."

"What did you see?" Riggs asked. Oh no, not another distraction.

"I think I just spotted a Ford pickup truck involved in a homicide I've been investigating," La Moria answered, not taking his eyes off the parking lot for the Steaks & Spirits Bar & Grill.

"How's it involved in your investigation?" Riggs asked.

"My suspect is Lawrence Mayes, who killed his girlfriend about ten days ago. He was last seen fleeing the scene in an old white Ford truck, similar to the one I see in the parking lot over there. Unfortunately, I'm not sure that's the truck and he's described only as a white male, approximately six feet tall, which fits a large portion of the population here in Seattle."

"What are the chances we can tie him into my case? Maybe he's killed a prostitute? Maybe he likes to watch women as they're sacrificed with a knife being plunged into their chest?" Riggs asked, realizing the time he'd lose in the pursuit of the devil worshippers.

"Not a chance. This guy likes to shoot women in the face with a 45–caliber automatic," La Moria answered, knowing Riggs was concerned about the loss of time in his own investigation, but he also knew he may not have another chance to arrest this asshole for the murder of his girlfriend.

"What do you want to do?" Riggs asked, knowing that if this was the right truck, La Moria

247

wouldn't be able to pass up the opportunity to arrest Mayes.

"Let's pull in beside the truck and I'll run the plate. If it comes back to Mayes, we'll have to come up with some way to identify Mayes and get him to come out of the bar," La Moria instructed as they pulled into the parking lot. A quick check of the license plate number with Dispatch confirmed the truck was owned by Mayes.

"Okay, we know it's Mayes' truck, what do you want to do now?" Riggs asked, wondering what plan La Moria was cooking up in his mind.

"You know how you're always telling me that cops are the best actors in the world because of all the different faces we have to wear? Remember that scam you pulled on the robbery suspect to get him to come out of his apartment last year? Well, I think one of us should go inside the bar and pretend we backed into that truck and caused damage, just like you did. We'll ask the bar keep to ask the owner to come forward to exchange insurance information, then we'll get him to come outside to look at the damage and we'll arrest him. What do you think?"

"Sounds like a plan. Who goes in?" Riggs inquired with a smile.

"Well, it's my case, so I'll go in this time and put on the show. When I walk out with the guy, stick your gun in his ear right away. He knows he's wanted for murder and if he realizes this is all a con, he might start shooting. Since I'll be walking in front of him, I'd like you to not let that

248

A Birthday to Die For

happen."

"I hear you. I'll make sure he doesn't have time to pull a gun. Have some faith, Bob, I've got your back."

"I've got the faith," La Moria said, as he headed into the bar.

The bar was dimly lit. As La Moria walked in, he could see two men seated at the bar with their hands wrapped around their drinks. There was a couple in their mid–twenties seated at a corner booth and an older couple seated at the table in front of the dance floor. A hockey game was playing on the television hanging from the ceiling at the far end of the bar. The bar–keep was polishing an empty glass with a white towel.

"Bar–keep, can I get you to do me a favor?" La Moria said, glancing at the two men seated at the bar, wondering if one of them was Mayes.

"Sure, what can I do for you?"

"I just backed into a white pickup truck in your parking lot. I've caused some damage and I'd like to give my name to its owner and have him look at it."

"Anyone in here own a white pickup truck parked in the lot outside?" the bar–keep asked, wiping the bar top with his towel.

The man seated right next to La Moria answered, "Yeah, I do."

"Sir, I've caused some damage to the right side of your truck. I'd like you to take a look at it. I'll give you the name and number of my insurance

249

company," La Moria explained.

"Don't worry about it. It's already got so much damage to it that a little more won't make any difference."

"But sir, I'm not sure you'll be able to drive it. You may need a rental car. I'd sure like you to take a look and see if you think it's drivable," La Moria said, surprised at the owner's lack of concern. He was now convinced that the owner was Mayes, his murder suspect.

"I said, don't worry about it."

"Bar–keep, can I get your name as a witness? Since this gentleman doesn't want to take a look at the damage, I want a witness that I offered to exchange information."

"Damn it! I told you I didn't care, but if you're that paranoid, I'll take a look at the damage," Mayes said, pushing his drink to the other side of the bar as he stood up.

"Thank you. I know I sound paranoid, but I don't want any trouble with the cops. Just follow me out and I'll show you the damage." Leading the way, La Moria exited the bar into the parking lot. The sun was shining bright as they walked out of the building and they were both blinded from the glare.

"Police! Don't move or I'll blow your head off," Riggs said, pushing the barrel of his gun against Mayes' right temple.

Hearing Riggs' order, La Moria immediately turned around to frisk Mayes for a weapon and found a .45 caliber automatic stuffed in the

A Birthday to Die For

waistband of his pants in the back.

"I'll bet this is the same gun you used to blow your girlfriend away," La Moria commented, stuffing the gun under his own waistband as he handcuffed Mayes.

While placing Mayes in Riggs' car, La Moria advised him of his right to an attorney. When asked if he had anything to say, Mayes replied, "Only through my attorney, you dirty, stinking, lying, bastard."

"Yeah, you're right. You just never know what we're going to do to catch a lowlife like you," said La Moria, slamming the car door, cutting off the flow of profanity coming from Mayes' mouth.

After completing the paperwork to impound Mayes' pickup truck, they headed for the jail to book Mayes on a count of murder before heading home to alert their wives to the possible risk. While La Moria handled the booking of his murder suspect, Riggs decided to take a look in on his church burglar and see if he was ready to talk.

Approaching the booking desk, he asked the booking officer to have the suspect brought to the interview room, but was immediately advised, "Detective Riggs, your suspect committed suicide last night. You should have been notified."

"Well, I wasn't. How did he do it?"

"You're going to find this hard to believe, but he actually chewed into his wrist until he severed an artery with his teeth. He was found this

251

morning when we did our morning head count, lying in a pool of his own blood."

"Did you ever get the guy's true identity?" Riggs asked, wondering how anyone could do that to himself.

"We've run his fingerprints through every local, state, federal, and international print system available and come up with nothing. Maybe the Medical Examiner will have better luck than we've had. Your man is currently being held in the morgue as a John Doe."

"Thanks for the information," said Riggs, realizing another opportunity to possibly tie someone directly to the cult had disappeared.

When La Moria learned of the suicide, he couldn't believe it was another dead end. "This investigation is really getting hairy. We need to get our families to safety so we can get our focus back where it should be without worrying what might happen to them," La Moria said as they headed for the elevator leading to the county garage and their cars.

Once again, Riggs' pager went off advising him to contact Detective Pope. Barb Pope's page was unexpected. She had covered almost all the bases a Missing Persons detective could as it related to finding the whereabouts of Shelby, but what the hell, maybe she worked a miracle.

"What's up, Barb?" Riggs asked, leaning against his car with his cell phone pressed to his ear, watching La Moria who was anxiously waiting to hear what Pope had for them.

A Birthday to Die For

"Riggs, I got a call from SPD Missing Persons. They received a call from Jim Perry, the editor and supervisor of your close friend, Jan Ice."

"Okay, why should that be of interest to me?"

"This Perry guy wants to file a missing persons report with SPD, but due to their departmental policy, they won't take the report until she's been missing for at least seventy–two hours," Barb explained.

"Okay, so why did they call you?" Riggs asked, trying to guess the reason.

"After you and La Moria made the arrest of the robbery suspect at the restaurant, Jan Ice showed up, didn't she?"

"Yes, she did, but what does that have to do with SPD calling you?"

"After you cleared the scene at the restaurant, did you respond to a burglary at a church?" Barb asked, as she also tried to put two and two together.

"Yes, I did. We arrested the suspect, but I just learned that he killed himself in jail last night."

"Well, according to this Perry guy, Jan Ice split from her cameraman after her interviews at the restaurant and she heard over her police scanner that you were responding to a church burglary."

"Is Perry telling us she followed me to the church?" Riggs asked.

"He's only guessing, but she did ask her cameraman why you would be responding to a burglary when you're a homicide detective."

253

"I can understand why it would get her attention, but it still doesn't explain why Perry called SPD."

"Ice didn't report to work today and no one at the station has heard from her since then. She doesn't answer her home phone or cell phone. The cameraman says she was obsessed with finding out what you and La Moria were working on."

"The pieces are starting to fall into place, Barb. I think she followed me to the church and she was intercepted by members of the cult. I believe that's why we didn't find a ritual being performed. She frightened them away from the church, but they decided to take her anyway, thinking she might have information which would lead them to Kae."

"If you're right, Riggs, she'll soon be a dead person, if she's not already."

"Barb, I think you might be right. I tried to warn her, but I knew she wasn't listening to me. It was always the story that drove her."

"What do you want me to do?" Barb asked, feeling the chance of finding Ice alive was slim to none.

"Let's take the missing persons report. There's enough unusual circumstances to justify our taking the report. These same circumstances also indicate the possibility of foul play being involved in her disappearance. Check her credit card history for the last three days. Maybe she's used it or whoever abducted her did."

"Okay, I'll get right on it. While I'm doing that,

A Birthday to Die For

what are you and La Moria going to be doing?"

"We're going to protect our families any way we can. Think about it, Barb. We've found one of our witnesses hanging from a chandelier in her own home, Kae was almost abducted, there was an animal mutilation, a church burglary we feel was related to the mutilation, as well as a interrupted satanic ritual, the burglary suspect kills himself, and now Jan Ice has disappeared. The way La Moria and I see it, the cult is frantic and they may zero in on our families."

"Seeing it the way you guys are, I feel the same way. Go protect your families and I'll carry on. If there's anything I can do to help, just let me know."

"Thanks, Barb, we'll let you know if we think of anything." Riggs terminated the call and filled La Moria in on what the conversation was all about.

Chapter 20

When Riggs pulled into their driveway, Toby knew immediately that something was wrong. He never came home during a shift unless she called him.

"Jerry, what's wrong?" Toby asked, the worry apparent on her face.

"You know that investigation I've been working on? Well, La Moria and I feel that you, Robin, and the kids might be at risk. We're investigating a satanic cult that's trying to locate a young woman we have hidden away. They may follow me, La Moria, or both of us in an attempt to locate her. They may have already done that, so they know where we live and they may try to do something to you or the kids to either get me to back off the investigation or to reveal the location of the young woman."

"What are you telling me? Do you mean these people would harm our boys?" Toby pressed her hands against her cheeks. "Oh god, I think they may have already found us."

"What do you mean?" asked Riggs, fear for his family suddenly running through his body.

"I've noticed a black sedan driving by the house and I think it followed me to the store the other day. I'm not sure it was really following me, but it got the boys' attention. They wondered if it might be a new neighbor. They told me they've seen it several times. In fact, they told me it was parked just outside the chain–link fence at the school's baseball diamond. The driver never got out of the car, so they thought whoever was in the car was just watching the game. I never thought anything of it until you told me this."

"Do you know what make of car it was?" Riggs asked, hoping against hope it wasn't a Mercury.

"The boys told me it was a Mercury."

"That ties the knot, the getaway car in the attempted abduction of our girl at the college is a Mercury and I have every reason to believe this is the same car," said Riggs. Tears welled up in her eyes and she started to shake.

"Toby, honey, calm down. This is not a time to panic. We don't know for sure whether they've followed us or not, but we must assume that the black Mercury belongs to a cult member. We need to take some precautions in the event we're right and the car is associated with the cult. I want you to take the kids to Justine's house out at the lake. I want you to stay there until I get to the bottom of all this. Make sure you keep the doors locked and I want you to keep the 32–caliber automatic I gave you close at all times. If anyone breaks into

A Birthday to Die For

the house, you shoot them, do you understand?"

"Yes, I understand, but you better not let anything happen to our kids. Do you understand?"

"I certainly do! Also, make sure Justine is in the house with you at all times. Agreed?"

"Agreed!"

"I've got to get back to work if I'm going to make sure nothing happens to you or the kids. I'll have a patrol car drive by your sister's house every once in a while to make sure everything's okay."

"Go...and don't you come back until you know we're safe," she said, pushing him towards the door.

It was like an old homecoming when La Moria walked through the church office towards Robin's desk. He knew everyone that Robin worked with and they'd all had been to their home on numerous occasions for parties or some function for the church.

Robin looked up when Bob walked in. She could tell from the look on his face that it was something serious. "What's wrong, Honey?"

"I need to give you a heads–up on an investigation I'm working on with Riggs. It involves a satanic cult that may choose to harm you or the children to learn the whereabouts of a young woman we've got hidden. They want to sacrifice her to the devil. We're particularly worried about you. We're afraid they might zero in on you because of your job with the church.

259

Everything they do is anti–Christ, which may make you a bigger target for them. We're not sure, but we want to be safe and take whatever precautions we can."

"Are you telling me there are real people who want to sacrifice a girl and if they can't find her to carry out their sinful deed, they may come after me or the kids?"

"The way I see it, it's a possibility. It's something we can't afford to ignore. I want you to take the kids either to your sister's or your mother's as soon as they get out of school. Tell them what our concerns are and have them keep the kids indoors. I'd like you to stay with them wherever you decide to take them until I tell you it's safe to go back home. Will you do that?"

"Of course I'll do that. What are you going to be doing in the meantime?"

"Riggs and I have a plan. If it works, we'll have this all wrapped up in a very short period of time."

"What's your plan?"

"I can't tell you right now. Just trust me!"

"Does Toby know?" Robin asked.

"Yeah, Riggs is talking to her right now."

"Bob, you be careful. I don't want anything to happen to you."

"I'll take care of myself as always. Don't worry about me, just take care of the kids," he said. He turned to leave, but stopped when his cell phone rang.

"La Moria," he answered.

A Birthday to Die For

"Bob, this is Riggs, I think the cult has already found my home and they've been following Toby and the boys. They've seen a black Mercury driving by the house, following them to the store, and parked at the school. I think you'd better ask Robin if she's noticed anything suspicious around your house or the church."

"I'll take care of it," said La Moria. He walked back to Robin's desk. "Let's go outside and talk," he said, taking hold of her hand.

Robin immediately knew something was wrong and the phone call to Bob was probably from Riggs. She couldn't explain it, but she suddenly felt vulnerable, a feeling she'd never felt before—at least not since she was a child. "What's wrong?" she asked, searching for some reassurance in her husband's face.

"The cult has found Riggs' home. He's moved Toby and their boys to her sister's house at the lake. Her sister and brother–in–law will be with her until this investigation is over. Since we have every reason to believe Riggs and his family have been compromised, we have to assume we have been too. Have you seen anything which would make you feel you've been watched or followed?"

"I don't know for sure since so many things happen here at the church," Robin said, searching her memory for anything out of the ordinary.

"Have you seen any strange cars following you or people in or around the church who were acting in a suspicious manner?"

"We have street people coming in here all the

261

time. We watch them real close to make sure they're here to worship and not to steal items from the church. If we see some way to help them, then of course, we do. Sometimes we have candles stolen. We've suspected satanic cult worshippers, but we've never been able to confirm it."

"Robin, that's interesting, but it's not helping. I need to know if you've seen any suspicious individuals, other than a typical street person in the church."

"There was a man a day or so ago who didn't take his hat off, kneel, or make the sign of the cross when he walked in. This was brought to my attention and I went to investigate. I stood at the corner of the sanctuary in the front so I could watch what he was doing. He stared back at me for a few minutes before he got up and left."

"What did he look like?" Bob asked, feeling he already knew the answer.

"He was a white male with a beard neatly shaven around his upper lip and chin. I could see he had dark–colored hair which protruded from under the knitted ski hat he wore. It was either dark blue or black and matched the color of the clothes he was wearing."

"You got a pretty good look at him. Do you think you could help with a sketch of his face?"

"The shadows kept me from seeing that much detail, but I can try if you want me to," she offered.

"I don't know that we've got the time, so we'll just go with what we've got. You still did real

A Birthday to Die For

good," he said, giving her a hug.

"Well, what did you expect with me being married to a cop all these years? There's one more thing I remember that may be related to this threat."

"What's that?" Bob asked, his concern for his family increasing at a rapid rate.

"You know that rhododendron plant under Terri's bedroom window? It had a branch broken off and I found a footprint in the dirt beneath it. I didn't think anything of it until now."

"Did you ask the boys about it?"

"I didn't bother because they wouldn't have admitted it anyway."

"Robin, I don't think we can ignore the guy you saw in the church or the footprint. I believe we've been compromised as well. It was a guy wearing a knit hat who tried to abduct our girl. I think the man you saw was one and the same guy. We need to get our children and take them to your sister's or your mother's. There needs to be someone with you and the kids all the time. When you decide which house you're going to, call Dispatch and let them know. I'll alert them to the problem so they'll have a patrol car drop by and check on you every once in awhile."

"Okay, but first I've got to alert the parish priest and get permission to leave," Robin advised before returning to her office. She looked at the paperwork on her desk, which now seemed unimportant. The protection of her twin boys and daughter was paramount in her mind.

263

Chapter 21

In the office, Riggs found a note from Captain Osborn and a copy of the aged–enhanced photograph of Kae's foster mother, Rebecca Shelby. The note from Osborn read, "My flight crew picked up an image of one person moving around within the ceremonial site perimeter just outside the City of Granite Falls last night. Come see me as soon as possible."

"Here, take a look at these," Riggs said, as he handed the note and photograph to La Moria.

"Maybe this is the miracle we've been hoping for. Let's go see Osborn and see what he has to say."

A smile appeared on their faces as they practically ran to their car and headed for the Captain Osborn's office. It had been too long since they received any information which could offer up a lead that they felt almost euphoric; however both had been down this road before in other investigations and knew they shouldn't get their hopes up. A thought raced through Riggs'

265

mind that the individual spotted by the flight crew may have had a legitimate and legal right to be there, so it might just be a coincidence that he happened to be in the area of the ceremonial site.

"What do you think? Do you think there's a chance that this guy the flight crew spotted might have a good reason for being there?" La Moria asked, even though he was thinking No way! A person having a legitimate reason for being there would have done so in the daylight.

Riggs just looked at him and raised his brow. He knew La Moria had already answered his own question. He'd asked himself the same thing.

Captain Osborn was seated at his desk when Riggs and La Moria walked in. He saw a look of excitement on their faces, realizing how important the sighting by the flight crew was to their investigation.

"Have a seat, boys," he said, motioning them to the chairs in front of his desk. While they were taking their seats, Riggs couldn't help but smile when he saw Osborn clearing all the rubber bands off his desk. The Captain must have had trouble getting the bug juice off his tie after his last visit.

"I don't really know much about these supernatural Satan–worshipping idiots or what or why they do the things they do, but I do know on the nights of a full moon, weird things begin to happen," Captain Osborn explained, watching

A Birthday to Die For

Riggs and La Moria for a reaction.

"We won't argue with you on that point," Riggs said, watching the Captain's eyes and waiting to hear what else he had to say.

"We all know the full moon brings out the animals that play havoc with everything and any person around them," La Moria added, impressed with the Captain's willingness to use his imagination.

"Since we're in agreement, I've got some ideas regarding your investigation. I believe the person spotted by my flight crew was checking out the area to make sure it was okay for another ceremony. I also believe the full moon, which is expected tomorrow night, and the fact that it's your victim's birthday, that a ceremony will be held at that location. What do you think?" asked Osborn, now feeling the excitement of the chase.

"I hadn't given any thought to the full moon, but I'd already come to the conclusion that a ceremony was going to be held there," Riggs said, looking at La Moria for confirmation.

"I agree with both of you. I think we should run with it. If we plan things right, we just might catch these weirdos during their ceremony, something I know we'd all really enjoy," La Moria said, his eyes reflecting the pleasure he was experiencing just thinking about capturing the cult members during the ceremony.

"Okay, Riggs, what's your strategy going to be? If my flight crew is going to be involved, I need to know how and when so I can get it organized

267

with the crew."

"This is the way I want to work it, if you two agree. We know from the information I've been able to get from Kae's personalities that the ceremonies are held late at night, which should give us enough time to get into position and stake out the ceremonial site. Captain, with your permission, we can use some of the SWAT equipment, such as night goggles and portable radios with secure channels to move into position. I'd also like the flight crew to be overhead with their infra–red imaging device working to alert us to the number of people on the ground and their positions as it relates to our location. I'd also like them to video what they see through the infra–red imaging device."

"Okay, Riggs, you've got the use of the SWAT equipment. How are you going to get to the location without giving yourselves away? How about backup?" Captain Osborn asked, being aware of the risk involved in this type of operation.

"We'll coordinate the drop off and backup with Sgt. Goldsmith of the Snohomish County Sheriff's Department. We'll have him drop us off just as the sun is going down. We'll also have him create a staging area where officers from his department can wait until we need them," Riggs explained.

"That's a lot of resources from Sno County. Will Goldsmith be able to pull it off?" Captain Osborn asked.

"I don't believe he'll have any problem. If

A Birthday to Die For

we're right on this, he'll solve the murder of Beth Williams. What do you think, Bob?"

"Sounds good to me."

"Okay you two, sounds like you have a plan. I'll brief the flight crew. I'll have them in the air tomorrow night. They'll contact you via your portable radios on the secure channel," Captain Osborn said, wishing he could be in the field with them.

Riggs could feel his excitement build while Captain Osborn retrieved the night vision goggles and portable radios with the secure channels from the SWAT storage room. When they were handed to La Moria, Riggs could see he was feeling the same way. What they were about to do would be a challenge, but not unusual for a County cop. The thought of a City cop crawling over the terrain through brambles and dirt brought a smile to his face. *It's this type of police work that caused me to go with the Sheriff's Department rather than the city.*

"What are you smiling about?" La Moria asked, as he caught his devilish grin.

"Just thinking about how our brothers with the city would handle what we're about to do," Riggs laughed.

"Oh, they'd do it and do a good job, but it would still be fun to watch," La Moria agreed.

"Yeah, wouldn't it?"

"Okay, you two, quit picking on the city. They've saved our bacon more than once and you know it," Captain Osborn advised.

269

"You're right, Captain. They like to remind us of that every time we get together, so the thought of seeing them get a little sweaty and dirty would be entertaining to us," Riggs said, knowing the cops of both agencies got a lot of pleasure harassing each other, but all in good fun.

Riggs and La Moria were still laughing as they got back in their car and headed back to the office. The city cops' territory consisted of asphalt, cement, and nicely trimmed lawns, not the great outdoors.

In the office, Riggs made a quick phone call to Sgt. John Goldsmith, who listened to their plan and agreed to have marked police cars available to respond from a nearby staging area selected by him. He also agreed to meet Riggs and La Moria at his office the following morning at o'dark thirty and he would them drive them to the drop off location.

"Thanks, John. With any luck, we'll catch the cult members, we'll keep Kae from being sacrificed, and we'll solve the murder of Beth Williams at the same time. La Moria and I will see you in the morning."

La Moria listened as Riggs made the arrangements to meet with Goldsmith. He could see Riggs was in deep thought, probably going over in his mind all that needed to be done before tomorrow's adventure and the dangers ahead. *Had he forgotten about Dr. Mitchell?* "Haven't you forgotten something, Riggs?"

A Birthday to Die For

"What did I forget?" Riggs asked, looking puzzled.

"The good doctor. Do we need to meet with her before calling it a day and make sure she's safe?" La Moria asked.

"You're right! I'm damn glad you remembered. I was caught up in my planning for tomorrow," Riggs said, somewhat embarrassed at his memory lapse.

"I know, that's why I reminded you."

Riggs glanced at his watch as he picked up the telephone and dialed Dr. Mitchell's number.

"Doctor Mitchell. May I help you?"

"Doc, this is Riggs. Are you okay? How are things going?"

"I'm fine for now. I'm not going to take any chances. I'm going to stay here in my office. The Security Guard has been keeping a very close eye on me. I hope you get to the bottom of everything pretty quick because I don't want to take up permanent residence here."

"I hear what you're saying, Doc. I'm doing everything I can to put this investigation to bed so you and Kae can get back to a normal life. By the way, are you sure Kae is still safe?"

"She's safe and that's all I can tell you in case they have my telephone bugged."

"Good thinking, Doc. You're starting to think like a cop."

"Frightening, isn't it?" she quipped.

* * *

271

During his drive home, Riggs kept his mind occupied trying to remember everything Detective Turner had told him. *There will be guards around the site armed with automatic weapons who will kill any intruders, anyone who gets too close. The danger is obvious, but we need to arrest the High Priest, so the danger is a given. He's the one person who runs the cult's operations and actually performs the sacrificial ceremony. He's the real killer.*

It was dark when Riggs and La Moria met at their office and gathered up their equipment for the adventure upon which they were about to embark—night vision goggles, a bulletproof vest, maps of the terrain, a compass, dark–colored jump suits, jump boots, flashlights, extra flashlight batteries, drinking water, and extra ammo for their handguns.

"What about a carbine rifle?" La Moria asked.

"I don't think we need it. If we're discovered and start taking fire, we'll call in Goldsmith's troops. In the meantime, let's check with the Sheriff and get his blessing."

When they walked into the Sheriff's office, they were surprised to see Captain Osborn seated behind the Sheriff's desk.

"What's going on, Captain? Are you the Acting Sheriff today?" Riggs asked, wondering if this would be another obstacle for him to overcome.

"I knew you boys would need the Sheriff's

A Birthday to Die For

assistance in getting the Snohomish County Sheriff on board, so I took care of that for you last night. I briefed the Sheriff on your plan and he cleared it with the Snohomish County Sheriff, who has deputized both of you. You'll be working under their authority on this one."

When they drove into the Snohomish County garage, Goldsmith was standing beside his car dressed in a dark–colored jumpsuit and boots.

"I know my responsibility is to coordinate the response of my officers, but shit happens and I just want to be prepared. Besides, why should you two have all the fun?"

"We know what you mean and appreciate all your help," Riggs commented as he and La Moria crawled into Goldsmith's car.

"Okay, let's go over our plan. Do you see any scenario that will get us into trouble that we can't get out of?" Riggs asked, trying to consider all the unknowns and prepare himself for action.

"I can't think of anything we haven't already discussed, but as John has so elegantly verbalized, shit happens," La Moria replied.

"Since we can't come up with any scenario we aren't prepared for, let's go with the plan we've already agreed upon. John, you'll drop us off a quarter mile west of the power line road. Bob and I will navigate our way from there through the forest and find a high spot near the ceremonial site that will allow us to observe the approach to the site and the ceremony. The flight crew will be overhead to warn us if necessary should a guard get too close. If the cult members flee, we'll alert you, John, so you can have your troops move in and hold them until Bob or I get there to make the arrest. If anything else happens, we'll just have to play it by ear."

The plan was on schedule as Goldsmith pulled to the side of the road. The glow of the sun was still visible on the horizon as they waited for cars to pass out of sight before crawling out of Goldsmith's car. Riggs and La Moria quickly moved into the forest as Goldsmith pulled away.

Chapter 22

Riggs and La Moria pushed their way under tree branches and through the underbrush. The dust from the nearby road had settled on the leaves and boughs of the pine trees, creating a dust cloud each time they brushed against a limb or caused any movement to the vegetation around them. The terrain was all uphill, the elevation increasing with each step, and their breathing was becoming labored with the climb.

"Who said this was going to be easy?" La Moria mumbled as sweat rolled down his neck.

"If I'd told you this was going to be easy, I must have been hallucinating. I hope we have enough energy left when we get to the top to make it into the valley to set up our surveillance," said Riggs, gasping between his words.

They were now on their hands and knees, crawling up the hillside, grasping low branches, rocks, and undergrowth to pull themselves along. It seemed like they'd only been on the climb for a short while, but a check of their watches showed they'd been climbing for more than an hour and they were already feeling exhausted.

"Boy, are we ever out of shape," Riggs exclaimed, stopping momentarily to catch his breath.

"Sure glad the city boys aren't watching," La Moria huffed, wiping his forehead, which smeared the caked dirt on his face.

"You're one scary–looking dude, Bob. Lucky we're going to be operating in the dark when we make the arrest or our suspects will have heart attacks thinking they're being attacked by aborigines."

La Moria smirked at him. "You don't look so good yourself," he said, appreciating the humor.

They'd been forced to break their own trail as they moved up the mountainside, but now they were following a well–worn animal trail so the going was easier, but Riggs had an uneasy feeling about it. Visibility was only a few feet in front of them. The full moon lighted the trail ahead and created ghostly images in the shadows, causing the hair on the back of their necks to stand up as they stopped to evaluate what they were seeing and determine if it was a threat.

"Well, according to the compass, we're still going in the right direction, but this map isn't telling me anything I can fully understand. Why don't you take a look at it?" Riggs asked, handing it to La Moria.

Taking the map, La Moria leaned over to conceal the glow of his flashlight as he tried to

A Birthday to Die For

interpret the map.

"The way I read this, we'd better be on the lookout for a canyon up ahead. See these squiggly lines and this different coloration? I think it means we have a canyon or some major change in the terrain, but I'm just guessing."

Riggs shrugged. "Your guess is better than mine. If we don't watch where we're going, we could find ourselves in big trouble."

La Moria handed Riggs the map and on up the hillside they went, moving cautiously, fearful that their next step might take into the abyss. Both realized any injury could be fatal to their efforts to gain the high ground for surveillance purposes and the eventual arrest of the High Priest and his followers.

"Let's stop and put on the night goggles. Maybe we can see better and avoid killing ourselves," Riggs suggested, pulling his goggles from his backpack.

"It's about time… I'm having a lot of trouble even finding something to grab onto to pull myself up the hill. The moonlight is good, but it doesn't help us see into the shadows," said La Moria.

Both let out a sigh of relief after they donned the goggles and adjusted the straps to hold them in place. They immediately noticed visibility was good for at least fifteen to twenty feet ahead, sometimes farther, without obstructions being in the way.

"Damn, look out!" Riggs cried out, falling backwards into La Moria.

Frank Atchley

"What the...?" La Moria asked, trying to calm himself after Riggs slammed into him.

"See that bush? It's right on the edge of a major drop off. I damn near stepped off the edge!" Riggs took several deep breaths in an attempt to recover from his fright and let his heart rate settle down a little. "My damn number was nearly up!"

"Couldn't you see it with the goggles?" La Moria asked, staring into the darkness.

"I was looking at the bush I was grabbing for. It was just luck that I looked down before stepping around it," Riggs explained, still feeling like his heart was in his throat.

La Moria crawled past Riggs to the ledge. Looking over, he saw a ravine about seventy–five to a hundred feet deep.

"Well, I'm guessing this is what the map was trying to tell us. We sure as hell aren't any Daniel Boones or Davy Crocketts," La Moria mumbled, backing away from the edge. "It would be pretty embarrassing if we fell into a hole and were reported missing by Goldsmith. We probably wouldn't be found until our bodies rotted and the coyotes scavenged our bones."

"Never heard you so pessimistic before," Riggs said, but agreed with the possibility.

"Now that we know what the map was trying to tell us, let's take another look at it and avoid anything resembling the same markings," Riggs suggested. He leaned over to conceal the glow of his flashlight and they both peered at the map.

La Moria traced along a trail marking with

278

A Birthday to Die For

his finger. "It looks like this trail is just a short distance west of where we are. Let's go in this direction."

"Okay, I'll lead," Riggs answered, moving to the opposite side of the bush on the ravine ledge. As they adjusted to the visibility the goggles allowed, they proceeded on and up, realizing time was getting short and they'd have to hustle to get into position.

Reaching the ridge of the valley was exhilarating. It looked like a big black hole as they stood on the ridge, peering into the darkness. Even with the night vision goggles, they were unable to see the valley floor.

"Man, it's dark down there. The nice thing is, the walk is all downhill from here and with any luck we should find a high spot for our surveillance before the suspects start arriving," Riggs said as they started down towards the ceremonial site.

"You know, Riggs, we've been walking, climbing, and crawling for what seems like an eternity. It sure is nice to be on the downhill side," La Moria said, his breathing returning to normal.

"I'm with you. I feel like we've been doing this for days. Every bone in my body aches," Riggs shot back.

"Mine too," La Moria replied, tapping the face of his wristwatch. "Maybe we should consider joining a gym so we can get some exercise after we finish this investigation. What do you think?"

"Do you think you could handle the humiliation

when they see your body?" Riggs asked.

"Speak for yourself. You're no Arnold Schwarzenegger," La Moria chuckled, wanting to get in the last word.

The banter back and forth stopped as they drew close to the ceremonial site. They navigated their way through the brush looking for an appropriate high spot to set up their surveillance. The presence of a cult scout was unlikely, but they didn't want to take any chances. They reduced all communication between them to soft whispers and hand signals.

"This is the spot," Riggs whispered, stopping at the top of a small hill about a hundred yards from the ceremonial site.

"Looks good to me. This should allow us to see the cars approach. My only concern is whether or not we're too close. I wonder how large of a perimeter the outer guards will set up. I'd hate for one of them to step on us and all hell break loose before we're ready," La Moria said as his eyes surveyed the area.

"Good point, but if we're much farther away, we'll have a hell of a time reaching the site in time to make the arrest if something happens and they start to run," said Riggs, pointing out the obstacles in their path.

"I can't argue with that. I think it's worth taking the chance and staying here. We'll be able to see their approach. If we have to make any adjustment and with any margin of luck, we'll do it then," La Moria nodded his head in

A Birthday to Die For

agreement.

It was ten–thirty. Darkness covered the valley like a heavy blanket, with moonlight breaking through clouds moving above. It was quiet, too quiet, as they sat motionless waiting for the arrival of the cult members and the High Priest. Every once in a while the stillness was interrupted by a night breeze brushing through the trees, dropping a pine cone to ground or the echo of an owl in the distance—sounds which were unfamiliar at first, commanding their attention until they could identify the source.

"You know, Riggs, I've never given any thought to it before, but the screech of an owl when it's as dark as hell and you're waiting for devil worshippers to arrive is a real scary sound. Made me feel like I was going to piss my pants."

Almost an hour passed before their attention was drawn to the ridge line of the valley in the direction of the dirt road the cult members would have to travel to get to the ceremonial site. A glow appeared just beyond the ridge line and crest of the hill, but soon they saw the first set of headlights come into view. They counted eight cars crest the hill and drop down into the valley, moving towards them, then immediately cutting their lights.

"It sure looks like we called this one right," Riggs whispered.

"How long are we going to wait before we make our move?" La Moria asked.

"Let's get the helicopter into position with

their infra–red imager working so we know how many people we're dealing with. I'd like them to get the actual ceremony on tape before we move in for the arrest," Riggs advised, putting the ear piece in his ear and turning on the portable radio he'd packed in. La Moria followed Riggs' actions before turning on his own portable radio and calling for the helicopter crew to answer on the secure channel.

"This is Guardian One, do you copy?"

"This is Detective La Moria. We copy you loud and clear."

"Guardian One back to La Moria. We're in position at about twelve hundred feet altitude and two hundred yards downwind from your location. Can you hear our rotors?"

"I can hear them, but they sound like you're off in the distance, not real close. I don't believe the rotor noise I'm hearing will alert them to our presence. Can you pick up our heat source on your Infra–red Imagery at the altitude you're flying and the distance you are from us?"

"We see you two clear as a bell and we've turned on the video recorder. By the way, we've been here for awhile and we've been watching another heat source which seems to be stalking you two."

Riggs heart raced. "Have you identified the heat source?" Riggs asked, interrupting the conversation between La Moria and the flight crew.

"We sure have," the flight crewman replied.

A Birthday to Die For

Some laughter was heard in the cockpit.

"Okay you flying clowns, what is it?" La Moria asked.

"Well, from our viewpoint, you two are about to become supper for a full–grown cougar. It's sniffing your trail about twenty–five yards due west of you."

"Glad you see the humor in this. You assholes better remember who we're after and not spend your time up there watching to see if that cougar is going to have us for dinner," Riggs said with real concern in his voice.

"Lighten up, Riggs, we know what we're supposed to do, but you have to admit this is a pretty funny predicament you've gotten yourselves into."

Riggs didn't acknowledge the last radio transmission, but had to agree with the flight crew. This was one hell of a predicament—one that could get him and La Moria killed if the cougar decided to attack or did something to attract the guard's attention towards them. He could feel it. *Something bad is going to happen.*

"Tell you what. While you keep an eye on the ceremonial site, I'll keep an eye on our back trail in the event that damn cougar pokes his head through the bushes licking his chops," La Moria suggested, turning and peering into the bushes for some sign of movement.

Riggs had to suppress an urge to laugh as he listened to La Moria. *Here's a man I've been in battle with before, but this is the first time*

I've detected any degree of fear in him. They'd faced armed suspects and had been involved in shootings in the past, but this was the first time they had to concern themselves with the possibility of being attacked by a wild animal, a scary thought any way you looked at it.

The silence of the night was interrupted by the chatter of cult members as they approached the ceremonial site. Riggs and La Moria listened, straining to make out the words that might give them a clue about the purpose of the ceremony, but the distance was just too far. They could hear rustling in the underbrush nearby and guessed it was either the perimeter guard taking up his position or maybe it was the cougar. In either case, they found themselves hugging the ground beneath them to avoid detection.

La Moria nudged Riggs and pointed to the ceremonial site where torches were being lighted. They watched as other members arrived. Some were already wearing their red robes, while others could be seen putting robes on over their clothing and pulling the hoods over their heads. A tall individual moved among them. The members bowed to him as he approached. He was obviously a person of authority, maybe the High Priest.

As they watched, the tall individual they now believed to be the High Priest moved to the makeshift altar. They watched as he raised his hands, then they heard the chanting begin. They listened to the chanting, trying to make out the words until their attention was drawn to the

A Birthday to Die For

opposite side of the clearing. There they saw an individual dressed in a full length white gown or robe being supported between individuals wearing red robes with hoods over their heads.

"Wish we were closer so we could see whether we're dealing with men or women, although I don't see that it makes any difference," La Moria whispered.

"Are they holding the person in the white robe up or are they trying to keep them from running?" Riggs whispered, knowing La Moria had no better idea than he did.

"I don't know, but it looks like their holding them up, almost as if that person has been drugged. See how their head has dropped to one side like it's resting on their shoulder? I've seen unconscious people before and when we tried to move them, their head would either fall forward or off to the side like what we're seeing now," La Moria said, keeping his eyes glued to the scene and what was happening.

"The only logical answer to what we're seeing is the person in the white robe is about to be sacrificed," Riggs deduced. "We're going to have to make our move before that happens. Thank God we have Kae in a safe place."

"Riggs to Guardian One, are you getting all this on video tape?"

"We're getting most of it, but the interior of the ceremonial site is obstructed in many places by the tree branches."

"Get as much as you can. It looks like they're

285

going to sacrifice a person unless we stop them."

Riggs and La Moria began to crawl towards the ceremonial circle until they heard the rustle of underbrush and the footsteps of the perimeter guard. They froze in position, trying not to move a muscle or to even breathe, hoping to remain undetected. Fortunately, luck was on their side. They stopped their forward movement in a shallow ditch, which helped to conceal them. The guard was within ten feet of their location. They could smell the smoke from his cigarette. They could feel the sweat on the back of their necks when the cold breeze hit them while they waited for the guard to move away.

Suddenly, the wait was interrupted by movement in the brush behind them and all hell broke loose. A quick look over their shoulders through the green glow of the night vision goggles revealed the head of the cougar, its eyes a bright solid color and its mouth wide open exposing its fangs and a pinkish glow of its tongue—a message that couldn't be any more clear unless it raised its paws in prayer to thank God for the meal it was about to receive.

Their fear of being the cougar's supper disappeared as rapidly when the guard fired his automatic rifle in response to the noise in the brush. He sprayed a barrage of bullets in the direction of the noise and directly over their heads. They could feel the swish of the bullets passing within inches of their bodies and getting closer. The flame from the rifle barrel lit up

A Birthday to Die For

the terrain around them with each shot, nearly blinding them because of the night vision goggles. Simultaneously, they knew they had to move and take out the guard.

"Police! Drop the gun!" Riggs shouted as he pulled his weapon and pointed it at the guard's chest.

La Moria moved to the side, pointing his gun at the guard's chest. "Drop the gun or we'll kill you."

The guard twisted his body, spraying a hail of bullets in a sweeping motion as he tried to shoot both Riggs and La Moria. His movement was answered with what sounded like one shot, but was actually two. Both Riggs and La Moria returned fire, striking the guard in the center of his chest, the impact of the bullets picking him off the ground and throwing him backwards. The automatic rifle was still hanging by the sling draped over his right shoulder as his body convulsed one or two times before it went still.

Riggs ran to the guard, pulled the sling from his shoulder, and handed the automatic rifle to La Moria. He checked the guard's neck for a pulse, but found none. "He's dead. Let's get the others. Keep your eyes open for the other guard. He's probably nearby, maybe hot–footing it this direction."

Pandemonium had broken out. People in red robes were running in all directions as Riggs and La Moria ran into the ceremonial site. The flight crew had the shooting of the guard and the fleeing of the cult members on tape. Recognizing that Riggs and La Moria had their hands full, Guardian One radioed Goldsmith to move his troops in and arrest all of the cult members as they ran from the clearing.

"I'll get this side," La Moria yelled at Riggs, chasing fleeing robed figures in the direction of their parked cars.

"I'll go this way," Riggs yelled back, heading in the direction where the High Priest was last seen near the sacrificial altar. As he drew near he could see the outline of a body dressed in a white robe on the table. A closer look revealed that it was a white female with a ceremonial dagger protruding from her chest. Blood had seeped out of the stab wound and saturated the white cloth of the robe. He instinctively checked her for a pulse, hoping for some sign of life, but she was dead. *If it hadn't been for the cougar, we might have prevented this from happening. So where in the hell did that demonic bastard go? I've got to find him.*

Riggs glanced in every direction trying to spot the High Priest when he heard gunshots behind him. It sounded as if they were near the vicinity of the parked cars in the direction La Moria had taken. He'd heard the first gunshot, which was immediately answered by a dozen or more. He wondered if La Moria was okay. He knew La Moria wouldn't allow himself to be surprised by the other guard, but still he had to fight back the impulse to run in that direction and possibly lose

A Birthday to Die For

the opportunity to apprehend the High Priest. He tried to raise La Moria on his portable radio to insure he was okay and if the High Priest was in his vicinity. Getting no response and still exploring the terrain for any evidence of what direction the High Priest might be trying to escape, he tried Goldsmith. Again, the attempt met with no response.

"Riggs to Guardian One."

"Guardian One back."

"Did you see where those gunshots came from?"

"Riggs, we don't know exactly what happened, but the shots came from the vicinity of the parked cars where Goldsmith and his people are trying to arrest anyone who's not a cop."

"Do you see La Moria?" Riggs asked, now worried about his partner.

"There's a lot of hot spots down there, but we're unable to determine exactly who's who. We assume everyone holding a gun in their hand is a cop, but then again, we can't be sure."

Riggs fought back the urge to run towards the fracas as he stared at the dead woman in front of him. There was no doubt in his mind. It was Rebecca Shelby—the woman who had disappeared more than ten years ago, the woman they had searched for since Day One of their investigation. *Was she sacrificed because they hadn't found Kae or was it to eliminate her as a witness? I've got to find her killer, but if I leave her before I'm certain of his whereabouts, he could come back and remove the dagger or destroy other pertinent evidence.*

La Moria had run in the direction of the parked cars as he pursued two individuals dressed in red robes. Just as he was about to tackle them, a shot rang out striking the dirt embankment just to his right. His survival instincts kicked in immediately as he dove for the ditch that ran parallel with the dirt road, drawing his automatic at the same time. He searched the darkness with his eyes for the second guard, but with negative results. He thought about using his flashlight, but realized he'd immediately become a visible target, so he waited for the sound of movement from across the road or maybe even a second shot which would expose the whereabouts of the second guard. He heard Riggs through the ear piece trying to raise him, but to respond would have revealed his location, a mistake he wouldn't make, so he ignored the call. The two individuals he was pursuing had disappeared into the darkness. He hoped they'd been captured by Goldsmith and his officers; however, everything had once again become quiet again. He guessed Goldsmith and his officers had taken cover and were also waiting for something which would reveal the whereabouts of the shooter. He knew Riggs was fighting back the impulse to come to his rescue, but also knew he wouldn't risk losing the High Priest.

A Birthday to Die For

* * *

Goldsmith was crouched down behind the parked cars with his men. They'd captured all the individuals in red robes and escorted them to patrol cars where they were being held under guard by two officers who'd been assigned that duty. He wanted the guard who had them pinned down. He knew it would be only a matter of time before the shooter made a mistake and revealed himself. The silence was suddenly broken by pounding from inside the trunk of the car and another gunshot rang out. It had obviously come from the guard. The flash from his gun barrel revealed his location, drawing a hail of bullets fired by the officers concealed behind the parked cars.

"You guys stay in your positions until we know the guy has been hit and is out of commission. Loomer, move back toward the patrol cars and bring one down here. We'll use the spotlight to see if we can locate the shooter before we all leave our cover," Goldsmith ordered. Officer Loomer immediately crawled away, out of the shooter's line of fire.

"Sgt. Goldsmith, what about the pounding in the trunk?" one of the officers asked.

"We'll check it out after we know the shooter has been neutralized," said Goldsmith, looking towards the patrol cars, anxiously awaiting Loomer's return.

Loomer rolled up to the parked cars with the

291

lights out to avoid silhouetting Goldsmith and the other officers. As he pulled between the concealed officers and the possible location of the guard, he turned the spotlight on, shining it towards the guard's last known location. No shots were fired and seeing nothing, Goldsmith ordered, "Spread out. Let's find this guy."

Guns held at the ready and flashlights on, under Goldsmith's direction the officers moved towards the spot they believed the guard would be found. As they walked around a large boulder, they found him lying on his back with his face shot off. His automatic rifle was laying about three feet from the tip of the fingers of his right hand.

"Holy cow! I wonder how many times he was struck when we returned fire?" Goldsmith heard one of the officers say.

"A lot," Goldsmith replied, suddenly aware that La Moria was standing beside him.

"John, we now have at least two dead here with both guards being dispatched to the hereafter and who knows what Riggs has run into," La Moria reported.

"I know, and we still don't know who or what we have in the trunk of one of the suspect vehicles," Goldsmith advised as they moved back in the direction of the parked cars.

The pounding inside the trunk of the black Mercury sounded frantic and desperate as La Moria and Goldsmith approached.

"Loomer, get inside this car and pop the

A Birthday to Die For

trunk," Goldsmith ordered as he and La Moria took a positions on each side near the rear of the car.

The trunk lid popped open and revealed the occupant to be none other than Jan Ice, the TV news reporter. Her mouth was covered with gray duct tape, which also secured her wrists and ankles. Her right eye had been blackened by a blow to the head and she had a large scratch running from the corner of her left eye, across her left cheek, down to the edge of her mouth.

La Moria and Goldsmith lifted her out of the trunk, pulled the tape from over her mouth, and cut the tape from her wrists and ankles.

"Are you alright, Jan?" La Moria asked as Goldsmith looked on.

After taking a few deep breaths, she answered, "You sure took your time letting me out. I want to talk to that rotten son–of–a–bitch."

"You means Riggs?" asked La Moria, even though he knew that's exactly who she meant. "He's down the hill a ways trying to apprehend the High Priest of this social club," La Moria advised, barely suppressing a grin.

"I know what you two are investigating. It's a satanic cult. They were going to kill me! Do you know that?" she screamed at La Moria.

"It doesn't surprise me, but Riggs tried to warn you. John, will you keep an eye on her while I go see if I can help Riggs?"

Riggs was still standing over Rebecca Shelby's

body on the ceremonial altar when La Moria walked up.

"I'll be damned! We finally found her. By the way, we found Jan Ice tied up in the trunk of a black Mercury owned by one of the suspects."

"You what?" Riggs asked.

"Yeah, and is she ever upset with you."

"Why me? I told her to stay away. Well, we can let Pope know she's no longer missing and that we've also found Shelby," said Riggs.

"Yeah, we sure have. She's been missing for over ten years and she finally shows up with a dagger in her chest. Since they couldn't find Kae, I guess they sacrificed her foster mother instead. Makes you wonder, doesn't it?" La Moria responded.

"Guardian One to Riggs. You have a lone individual running in the opposite direction from your location. We believe it's the person you've identified as the High Priest."

The light of the torches enabled Riggs to see a trail the High Priest would have taken. "Bob, stay here and protect the crime scene," he yelled over his shoulder as he started off at a full run.

He brought the portable radio to his mouth. "Guardian One, keep this subject on your screen and tell me which direction he's going. The trail I'm on leads out of these trees and opens up, so you should be able to maneuver if you have to touch down."

"Guardian One copy. Keep following the trail you're on. He's about seventy–five yards in front

A Birthday to Die For

of you. He's running towards a river and if he submerges himself in the water, his heat source will disappear and we'll lose him."

"Don't let that happen."

Riggs was breathing heavily as he tried to pick up speed and close the distance between himself and the High Priest.

"Riggs, you're closing in, but we don't think you're going to overtake him before he gets to the river. What do you want us to do?"

"If it looks like he'll make the river before I catch him, do whatever you can to force him to the ground. Be careful, he may have a gun."

"We copy. We'll do whatever we can."

Riggs could see Guardian One dropping in altitude and becoming visible to those on the ground. He could see the spotlight attached to the bottom of the helicopter come on and light up the trail ahead. He could see the High Priest as he tried to avoid the beam of the spotlight, zigzagging back and forth across the trail, ducking behind bushes, but still moving towards the river.

Riggs was closing in, now within thirty yards. He knew the river was closer than that and he had to get to him before he jumped into the cold water and disappeared downstream. He tried to increase his speed, but his legs felt like rubber and his chest was about to explode. He could see the dark outline of the High Priest's body as he got closer, but knew he wouldn't get to him before he reached the river.

"Guardian One, force him to the ground,"

295

Riggs shouted into his radio between gasps of air. He watched Guardian One touch down on the trail ahead of the High Priest, who turned to run back the way he'd come, but saw Riggs coming at full speed. He turned back towards the river again, but the helicopter blocked his path. When he tried to run around it, the pilot lifted a few inches off the ground and moved to cut off his escape route. The pilot was using the loud speaker, ordering the High Priest to lay face down on the ground, hands behind his neck. The High Priest attempted one more dash to freedom, but was struck on his back just below his shoulder blades by the helicopter's skids, knocking him to the ground and giving Riggs the opportunity to jump on him.

Riggs pulled his gun just before making a flying leap and landing on the High Priest, pushing his face into the dirt and pressing the barrel of his gun against the back of the Priest's head. With his knee on the back of the Priest's neck, Riggs knew with absolute certainty that he was firmly under his control. "Okay asshole, give me an excuse and I'll kill you."

Guardian One's pilot maintained a low hover overhead with the spotlight trained on Riggs and the suspect. "Riggs, shake your head if you've got everything under control," the pilot said over the loud speaker.

Riggs heard the pilot's request and nodded his head affirmatively. The pilot saw Riggs' nod and knew he had the suspect under control, but

A Birthday to Die For

he'd also remembered what Captain Osborn had told them about what this bastard had done to a thirteen year–old girl. He wasn't about to let him escape from Riggs' grasp. He also remembered that the members of this cult were extremely dangerous and would do anything to avoid detection or to escape, something that wasn't going to happen if he had anything to do with it. The flight crew watched as Riggs followed the book and professionally restrained the suspect.

"Bring your left hand up and place it on the back of your neck," Riggs ordered, his voice raspy with fatigue and anger as he kept the gun barrel pressed against the back of the Priest's head.

His tone and the pressure of the gun barrel left no doubt in the suspect's mind. He knew Riggs meant what he'd said—that he'd kill him if he failed to follow orders. He knew if he did the wrong thing, the consequences would be death.

Riggs snapped the handcuff on the suspect's left wrist, then ordered, "Now bring your right hand up and place it on the back of your neck."

As soon as Riggs had the cuffs on both wrists, he patted him down for hidden weapons. Finding none, he pulled the man to his feet and turned him around.

He experienced a sickening feeling in his gut when he pulled the hood from the suspect's head. Bile surged up into his throat as he glared at the High Priest—a man who killed innocent babies. Anger and surprise surged through his veins like molten lava and he had an uncontrollable urge to smash his fist into the face of the man dressed in his fine robe—Detective Sergeant Dennis Ryker, Chief Trickey's assistant.

The flight crew could tell something was wrong. They watched Riggs double up his fist and hold it in front of the suspect's face. They knew Riggs was a laid–back, methodical investigator, one who used his brains to solve a case, but someone you should never piss off. It wasn't his style to beat up a prisoner.

"Guardian One to Riggs. Is everything under control?" the pilot asked, watching the arrest unfold.

"Yeah, it's under control," Riggs growled. "It's so under control, I ought to just shoot the S.O.B." *This man is a disgrace to the human race, let alone law enforcement.*

Riggs threw his flashlight on the ground and grabbed the handcuffs of his suspect. The pilot rotated the helicopter into a better position as he hovered overhead in an attempt to get a better look at the face of the High Priest. "We can't really see his face. Who is he?"

Riggs grabbed the back of Ryker's collar and pushed him towards the helicopter to give the flight crew a better look. Ryker tried to pull away as he felt the wind from the rotor blades, shying away from the hate pouring out of Riggs.

Riggs pushed Ryker into the spotlight, letting him wonder if the plan was to push him into the rotor blades. "Meet Dennis Ryker, a police detective and number one asshole." The silence

A Birthday to Die For

from the flight crew was almost deafening.

"Son–of–a–bitch, a dirty cop," the pilot hissed. "Why don't we just let him disappear into the river, like forever, never to walk the face of the earth again?"

A quick look at his crew and the expressions on their faces showed they shared his feelings. They too felt the shame associated with the knowledge of a fellow cop being dirty. It was hard for them to fathom a cop worshipping the Devil and killing babies.

"You know, Riggs, this guy doesn't deserve to live. In fact, we'd be doing the world a favor if we tied a rock to his feet and threw him into the river he was trying so hard to reach. It would be a fitting death for a rat, a worthless human being like himself."

Riggs couldn't argue with their feelings, but knew they wouldn't do it, even if given the chance. He knew they shared his feelings about the job and their responsibilities. They'd gladly see this bastard go to prison on a capital charge and face the death penalty.

Riggs turned Ryker in the direction of the ceremonial circle and pushed him along as the pilot maneuvered the helicopter just overhead.

"We'll be right on top of you. If you try to run, asshole, I'll take your head off with my rotor blades," the pilot shouted over the outside speaker mounted on one of the skids. Riggs smiled. It was a warning the pilot wanted Ryker to hear and worry about.

Riggs headed back to the site keeping his hands on the cuffs behind Ryker's back, pushing them upward to force his cooperation. The march allowed Riggs' feelings to run the gamut from the satisfaction of catching him and preventing the sacrifice of Kae on her birthday to the disappointment that he was unable to prevent the Rebecca Shelby's death. He was still searching for an explanation that would explain her execution. Knowing she had also come from a foster–home, he wondered if she too had been raped at a young age and forced to produce a baby that died on a sacrificial altar at the hands of a High Priest. He also wondered if Ryker was the male individual Dixson had seen visiting her. He realized the answers to these questions would go to the grave with her because no one in the cult would ever tell.

Ryker hadn't said anything the whole time. As he was pushed along the trail, he waited for Riggs to show some sign of weakness, but the pressure on his arms showed no evidence it would happen. He weighed in his mind whether or not he'd have a chance to escape, but knew if he tried, he'd die. He had violated the trust of the brotherhood by disgracing the profession. He knew the officers would be looking for a way to balance the books and restore the image. He also knew each officer was taking this personally, as a reflection on themselves, so if he gave them any excuse to enhance his departure from this earth, they'd take it. The only thing keeping him

A Birthday to Die For

alive to this point was the profession itself. He knew the officers wanted him dead, but they wouldn't allow themselves to act on the impulse. They wouldn't kill him unless he gave them some provocation, such as a threatening move or an attempt to escape, actions he wouldn't give them. He thought about the embarrassment of going to trial, but in the back of his mind he wondered if a jury would really believe that a Detective Sergeant could do the things he'd be accused of doing.

La Moria and Goldsmith were standing in the ceremonial circle near Rebecca Shelby's body, staring at the dagger protruding from her chest when Riggs returned.

"I see you caught the demonic bastard," La Moria said, looking at Ryker's face. "I'll be damned. I wouldn't have been at all surprised if it had been Trickey Dickey himself, instead of his favorite assistant."

"I know what you mean. Surprises never cease in this job," Riggs said, increasing his grip on Ryker.

"I thought this guy was acting strange when we were in Trickey's office. I thought it was because he and Trickey had something going on between them, maybe some kind of sexual relationship," La Moria said, trying to evoke a response from Ryker. "Maybe you were having an affair with Rebecca and she knew too much about you, so that's why you decided to put her under the knife, so to speak. Am I right?"

301

As La Moria spat out his theories, they watched Ryker wince as each one was thrown at him.

"I think his future sex life will be at the pleasure of the meanest son–of–a–bitch in prison. It'll give him a whole new definition for the word 'asshole'," Riggs said.

"He can bet his life on that," La Moria said, smiling at Ryker.

"I knew he was an asshole the first time I laid eyes on him. Turns out I was right. He's a weirdo pervert who's going to get the death penalty. If I'm given the chance, I wouldn't mind watching as they stick the needle in his arm. In fact, I wouldn't mind putting the needle to him myself," said La Moria.

"Tell me, Ryker, did you kiss Trickey's ass just so you could be in a position to cover your tracks? As his assistant, you'd be on top of any information coming in that would be a threat to you and the other sick perverts in your club. I suppose it was you who convinced him there was no such thing as devil worshippers, right?" La Moria said, his intense glare never leaving Ryker's face.

Riggs watched for Ryker's response to La Moria's questions. He didn't really expect Ryker to answer, but hoped he would. Ryker was a coward and would stay quiet rather than risk saying anything that could be construed as a confession and a sure ticket to the death chamber.

Ryker knew they had the goods on him, but he was convinced a jury would find it difficult to

A Birthday to Die For

believe a police officer could be a High Priest of a satanic cult and would never find him guilty. There was an even stronger possibility his trial would end in a hung jury. In either case, he'd be free. The odds were in his favor and there was no way he was going to do or say anything that would change those odds.

The more Riggs watched Ryker for a reaction or to show some sign of remorse, he realized it was a fruitless cause. The son–of–a–bitch was too calm and too confident. *Why? Does he really believe he can avoid prison and the death penalty? Maybe it was time to shake this bastard up a little.*

"Ryker, you prick, I want you to know that your pretty boy and crying routines aren't going to fly in court. I'm going to make sure you don't get away with anything. In fact, when you're booked into jail, we're going to make sure every inmate you come in contact with knows you're a dirty cop."

La Moria picked up on what Riggs said and added to it. "We're also going to make sure they know you're a baby killer. Based on your own experience as a cop, you know they'll be out to get you. The way I see it, you're not going to get much sleep from now on."

"They'll be waiting and looking for the right time to stick a shiv into your heart and Satan be damned," Riggs added.

"Think about it. I know I'll be waiting to hear the news of your death." La Moria said, wanting to have the last word.

303

Riggs turned to Goldsmith. "John, he's all yours now. I'm through with him. There's no doubt in my mind we can tie him to the murder of Beth Williams. A search warrant for his home, his car, and his office will do that for us," Riggs said, noticing the color had left Ryker's face. He was as pale as a ghost. He pushed Ryker towards Goldsmith with such force that he almost fell.

"You guys know a jury will never convict me, especially when they learn how you pushed me around and threatened my life," Ryker said, trying to show some bravado as he recovered his balance.

"Shut your mouth. You have no idea what's in store for you, but we can guarantee that it isn't going to be pleasant. You're going to believe you're in hell before you actually get there," Riggs said.

"Since we've got my investigation of Williams' death and you've got the ritual sites in your investigations, let's discuss what evidence we're looking for regarding both of our investigations. I'm going to put the affidavit together for the warrant, so I need to know what to list and why," Goldsmith asked. Riggs did a quick mental list to identify what he wanted included in the search warrant before responding to Goldsmith.

"John, there should be some DNA evidence somewhere in his car, home, or maybe the locker at his office, maybe the rubber gloves he was wearing when he strangled Williams. There may also be trace evidence that will tie him to Pope's missing prostitutes.

A Birthday to Die For

"I agree and I've already thought of that, but what about your investigations?" Goldsmith asked.

"We're looking for blood, bodily fluids, hair, anything else we can think of. We know he's responsible for the death of Rebecca Shelby. Hell, he was standing over her at the time of her death. He wasn't wearing gloves, so we should be able to get his fingerprints off the dagger. There was also a lot of blood from the dagger wound to Shelby's chest which could have splashed on his robe. There's the rope used to hang Williams from her chandelier, maybe we can find some matching rope in his house, car, or work place. Those are just a few things I can think of at the moment. Maybe you and La Moria will think of things I've overlooked."

"Bob, can you think of anything else we should include in the warrant?" Goldsmith asked, continuing to jot down the things Riggs had already mentioned.

"In your affidavit, explain that the gloves he might have been wearing at the time he strangled Williams may have skin transfers from Williams to the gloves or she may have slobbered spit while being strangled," La Moria said, searching his mind for anything else they may have forgotten or overlooked.

"Okay, I've got all that. I'll describe it in my affidavit and list it on the search warrant for Ryker's car, house, office, and locker. By the way, do you two have extra side–arms to carry? I need

305

to collect your guns because of the guard you blew away. You'll get them back after the inquest hearing. I'll have to collect the guns from my own guys as well because of the second guard," Goldsmith explained.

"We knew that was coming. Yes, we have extra sidearms back at the office. We can use those relics the department originally issued to us," Riggs responded, handing his gun to Goldsmith. He then turned to La Moria, who had taken his gun from its holster and given it to Goldsmith.

"You'll find one round fired from each gun," La Moria advised. Turning to Ryker, he added. "I wish the rounds could have been used on you, maybe a silver bullet to your Satan–worshipping heart."

"I'm going to put your guns into evidence until the Inquest Jury declares the shooting justifiable. I've also alerted my Sheriff to the shooting of both guards. He contacted your Sheriff and the two of you will be assigned to administrative duties until the inquest is concluded. You're to report to your office in the morning."

"I expected that assignment, but that was quick. How did we make out on the arrest of the other cult members?" Riggs asked, wondering if Dan Fowler was one of those arrested. He felt Fowler was an accessory to the murder of both Williams and Shelby. He also had a feeling in the pit of his stomach that Kae was still at risk as long as Fowler was still at large because he might try to eliminate Kae as a witness because

A Birthday to Die For

her testimony could put him and the other cult members away for a long time. Since their first and only meeting, he hadn't been able to shake the feeling that Fowler was somehow involved in the disappearance of Rebecca Shelby.

"I don't know if it's just a coincidence, but if you count the dead guards, Ryker, and the number of people arrested by my troops, we've accounted for thirteen cult members present at the ceremony. When they were arrested, each was advised of their constitutional right to an attorney. It should come as no surprise, but each declined to give a statement. I'll be referring them to the prosecutor for charges, all for murder. Hopefully, Ryker will be charged with at least two counts of murder, as well as kidnapping since the reporter was found in the trunk of his car. One murder count for Rebecca Shelby and one for Beth Williams, providing we find the evidence to tie him to her death," Goldsmith explained as he placed Riggs' and La Moria's guns into evidence bags.

"I'm curious—who were the other members arrested?" Riggs asked, as remembering that Turner told him that cult members come from every walk of life.

"I don't have their names, but before they were advised of their rights, they did identify their occupations. I'll get their names from my officers after they book them. I do know we've arrested a doctor, two nurses, an assistant fire chief, an assistant city manager, the owner of a pizza place, and two longshoreman."

307

"Do you know if Dan Fowler was one of those arrested?" Riggs asked, looking at La Moria.

"I don't believe so. None of those arrested matches Fowler's description. It looks like he's still on the loose and a threat to Kae's safety," Goldsmith advised. He saw the disappointment on their faces.

"How about search warrants?" La Moria inquired as he shook his head in disbelief at hearing who the cult members were and Fowler not being one of them.

"Yeah, we'll get search warrants for their cars, homes, and work locations. We'll do whatever we can to close down their activities in our counties and put these people away for a long time. In the meantime, the M.E. is on her way to take possession of the three bodies. She'll probably do the autopsies in the morning. If your sheriff will let you attend, I'll see you there." Goldsmith radioed to ask the approximate time of arrival for the Medical Examiner.

The wait for the Medical Examiner was interrupted by a cell phone call from Loomer to Goldsmith. Loomer was trying to keep Jan Ice calm until they arranged transportation to police headquarters for her, then a ride to her office, if that's where she chose to go.

"Riggs, you've got to do something about this reporter. She's driving Loomer crazy. She's threatening Loomer and everyone else she lays eyes on. As far as my troops are concerned, she's

A Birthday to Die For

a real bitch."

"I'm not surprised she's got a temper, but how in hell is she threatening your officers?" Riggs asked, noticed the puzzled look on La Moria's face.

"She's threatening to sue them for false imprisonment, harassment, and what have you. She's even threatened to sue them for rape unless they allow her to talk to you before they take her to Headquarters."

"Okay, have Loomer bring her down here. I'd like her to take a look at Ryker anyway...and maybe a look at Shelby with the dagger in her chest. That might just bring her back to reality and put things into perspective for her."

It was about two minutes when Loomer showed up with Jan Ice in tow. Her mouth was going a mile a minute with every swear word you could imagine.

"Okay, Jan, calm down. I hear you want to talk to me," said Riggs.

"Riggs, you lousy son–of–a–bitch. You nearly got me killed!"

"How did I do that?"

"You should have told me you were investigating a satanic cult."

"Jan, your history kept me from telling you everything. You would have blabbed everything and the very person whose life we're trying to save would have been killed. You made your own bed."

"Do you know what those evil red–hooded bastards did to me?"

"Not in detail, so why don't you tell me?"

309

"They stopped me just before I got to the church. They pulled a car in front of me and one behind me. They ripped my door open. One of them grabbed me by my hair and pulled me out of my car. My head hit the doorframe. They kept asking me where Kae Carlson was and when I told them I didn't know Kae Carlson, the guy who pulled me out of the car punched me in the face with his fist. They put tape over my mouth and wrapped it around my wrist and ankles, then shoved me into the trunk."

"Well, Jan, I did tell you that what we were working on was dangerous and to stay away, didn't I? If you hadn't followed me, none of this would have happened to you."

Jan socked him in the chest and let loose with another outburst of profanity. "Damn you, Riggs! They were going to kill me. They pushed my company car into the river. I heard them say it looked like an accident and whoever discovered it would think my body floated down the river."

"Jan, I know they would have killed you. See that woman lying on that makeshift table over there? Well, that's their sacrificial altar where they killed her. You do see the dagger sticking in her chest, don't you? You see, they probably planned to do the same thing to you." She gasped in horror. Riggs watched the blood drain from her face. "Damn it, Jan, don't you pass out on me. I don't want to have to give you mouth–to–mouth," Riggs said, shaking her shoulders to get her attention.

A Birthday to Die For

"Okay, okay, I'll be alright," she said, sucking in a deep breath.

"That's better. You okay?" Riggs asked, more gently this time.

"What did you mean you wouldn't give me mouth–to–mouth if I needed it?"

"If I did that, I'm afraid you might start thinking we're friends and I don't want that to happen. It would ruin our relationship."

"Riggs, you're a real asshole," she said, smiling.

"I know...and you're not the only one who thinks that."

"Now that exchange was funny," La Moria said as he saw Goldsmith trying to conceal a laugh.

"Okay, John, will you have Officer Loomer take Jan back to his car and drive her to your Headquarters? It looks like she might need to stop by the hospital, so have him take her there first, if she wants to go."

"It'll be taken care of," Goldsmith agreed, no longer able to conceal his chuckles.

A short time later, Medical Examiner Robin Spears arrived with her assistant in tow.

"Riggs and La Moria ... I might have known. Why is it I'm always finding you two at the scene of every murder that happens here in Snohomish County? It seems like my workload has increased significantly since you two started prowling around. You know this has got to stop," she said with a sly grin.

311

"I know, Doc, but we just can't help ourselves," Riggs answered, following her to view the bodies of the two guards and Rebecca Shelby.

Riggs and La Moria watched as she examined each body and listened as they explained the sequence of events.

"Sounds like you boys were really lucky. If this one guard had fired a few inches lower, I'd be examining your bodies too," Spears quipped in a serious, but professional tone.

Spears' comment was sobering to both Riggs and La Moria. They knew they had to kill the guard, but after hearing the doctor's words, a chill rushed over them.

"We were lucky this time," Riggs commented. La Moria nodded his head in agreement.

"Doc, we'd like to attend your autopsies, but since we're responsible for the death of one of the guards, we'll stay away. We wouldn't want the Inquest Jury to get the wrong idea."

With that, Riggs and La Moria headed towards the helicopter which had landed in a nearby clearing, waiting to transport them back to their own jurisdiction. The flight crew had a hundred questions they wanted to ask, but they held them. They could see Riggs and La Moria were deep in thought as they flew back to the hangar and a waiting car. Everyone knew they were trying to deal with the fact that they'd killed a man who had given them no choice, but they'd taken a life nevertheless.

Chapter 23

They were still several feet away from the waiting car when Riggs stopped cold in his tracks and grabbed La Moria's arm. "Bob, we still have a loose end to tie up before we can be absolutely sure that Kae is safe."

"You mean Fowler, don't you?" La Moria said, remembering their first contact with him. They both felt Fowler had something to hide, which explained his reluctance to admit that he was a reference for Shelby on her foster mother application or that he'd been her neighbor at one time.

"Yeah, we've got to make sure he's no longer a threat. Maybe we can add him to the arrest tally. I know he's involved, I just don't know to what extent. He could be the one who killed Williams. In any case, we've got to make sure. What do you think?" Riggs asked, knowing full well that La Moria was thinking the same thing.

"Let's do it, but first we need to stop by the office and pick up some firepower before we see

Fowler in Pierce County. I don't know if those old revolvers will work or not, but what choice do we have? I haven't shot anything but an automatic for years," said La Moria, looking forward to another face–to–face with Fowler.

In the office, they retrieved their department–issued Colt 357 caliber revolvers from their lockers. They unwrapped the protective cloth, replaced the old cartridges, spun the cylinders, and strapped the holsters to their belts.

"I think we're ready," La Moria said, waiting for Riggs' response.

"Before we go, let's give Chief Trickey a call. Since this might involve a little more than just a talk, we should have someone with jurisdiction on site with us. Besides, it'll be interesting to see how Trickey handles himself. I'm still not real sure about whether or not he's also involved. He could have been Shelby's visitor. Remember, it was his investigation where she came to the rescue and took his suspects' children into custody. This could be a real touchy situation. Since we really don't know which way either he or Fowler will jump, we need to protect each other's back more than usual," Riggs explained.

"I hear you loud and clear," La Moria said, not liking the odds, but agreeing it was a good plan.

Riggs made a quick call to the Pierce County Sheriff's Dispatch and after talking to the supervisor in charge, got the home phone number for Chief Trickey.

A Birthday to Die For

"Hello Chief, this is Detective Riggs. We're heading into your county enroute to talk to Dan Fowler. Remember, he was one of the references for Rebecca Shelby to become a foster mother? We've arrested the cult members tonight and we believe Fowler is involved, so we'd like to tie up this loose end. We'd like you to be present during our contact and interview of Fowler. Can you meet us at his address?"

"Is there any particular reason I should be there? Why can't I just send a patrolman there to assist you?" Chief Trickey asked.

"Well, it's like this. I've got information which is real important to you. I'll give you the information when we see you at Fowler's. I don't want to discuss it over the telephone," explained Riggs, wondering why the Chief was so hesitant. It was as if the phone line had gone dead as Riggs waited for an answer.

"Okay, I'll meet you there. What's the address?"

Riggs took a deep breath before he gave the address to Trickey.

"It will take me at least an hour to get there," Trickey advised.

"Why didn't you tell him about Ryker?" La Moria asked, still trying to understand the logic of keeping it a secret.

"We still don't know for sure the extent of the conspiracy and those involved with the cult. If, by chance, Trickey is actually involved, he'll want to know what we have. At the very least, I've

315

left him with the idea that we have information important to him, so important we won't give it to him over the phone. Now tell me, do you know anyone whose curiosity would allow them to pass up that kind of opportunity?" A grin formed on Riggs' face.

"Putting it that way, I can't think of anyone," La Moria answered, appreciating Riggs' play on words. "You know, Riggs, as long as we've worked together, it still surprises me just how devious you can be."

"You shouldn't be surprised, I learned it from you. Why do you think I watch and listen to you so much?"

"You're so full of shit," La Moria responded. "You come by your deviousness all by yourself."

"We'd better get to Fowler's before Trickey, just in case he warns him we're coming and he's in the wind like a rabbit," Riggs said. They headed for their car, still laughing at who was the most devious.

When they pulled to the curb in front of Fowler's house, Trickey had not yet arrived. The house was dark in the front, but through the front window they could detect a glimmer of light emanating from the rear of the house.

"Shall we take a look or wait for Trickey?" La Moria asked, anxious to get things rolling. They'd been without sleep for about thirty hours and they were both feeling fatigued.

"Let's wait for Trickey. We need to see how

A Birthday to Die For

he reacts under these circumstances. We may not learn anything, but on the other hand, we could learn a whole lot. If he's involved with the cult too, he just might reveal something we can use. What do you think?" Riggs asked, feeling as tired as La Moria looked and wanting to bring an end to this investigation as soon as possible.

"I think you're right. We do need to know."

While they kept a visual on the front of the house, Trickey pulled up. He showed some good sense when he cut his headlights and rolled to a stop behind them. He disabled his dome light before getting out of his car and closed the door softly to avoid alerting Fowler of their presence, actions noted by both Riggs and La Moria.

"Okay you two, what information do you have that's so damn important you couldn't tell me over the phone? I can understand your interest in Fowler, but what's that got to do with me?" Trickey asked, a frown covering his face, his agitation quite apparent.

"Well, it's this way, Chief. We arrested thirteen members of the cult tonight, including your assistant, Dennis Ryker. Turns out he's the high priest and responsible for the murder of Rebecca Shelby. We know this for sure and we believe he's responsible for the murder of the social worker, Williams. We also believe Fowler has inside knowledge and is an accessory to the murders.

"To top all this off, we're not real sure about you. Along with the fact that Ryker was your assistant, Fowler and the social worker were references for Shelby to become a foster mother, who then introduced our victim, Kae Carlson, into the cult and that's why we're more than a little suspicious of you. We have reason to believe you were seeing Rebecca Shelby, maybe you and she were having an affair. Given these circumstances, well, we just felt the need to talk to you in person. I'm sure you can understand our reasons," Riggs explained, looking directly into Trickey's eyes, waiting for his reaction.

La Moria watched the Chief's facial expression change from anger to panic. A frown wrinkled his forehead like that of an old man. He thought he detected some perspiration too, but it was hard to tell in the dark. Just as Trickey started to say something, they heard the distinguishable crack of a gunshot and they hit the ground behind their cars.

"It came from Fowler's house. I thought I saw gun flash before we hit the ground. It's got to be Fowler," La Moria shouted to Riggs and Trickey.

Riggs and La Moria looked at each other, wondering what to do next. They could see that Trickey held an automatic in his hand. He peeked over the hood of his car towards the front of Fowler's house. They could read what was going through each other's mind. *Is Trickey a threat and are we at risk being on the same side of the cars as he is, or is he someone to be trusted?*

"Fowler, this is Detective Riggs. We want to talk to you. Put your gun down and come out with

A Birthday to Die For

your hands on top of your head," he shouted at the man he assumed was Fowler standing in the shadows just to the right side of the front porch.

"I'm not coming out. You're going to have to kill me this time, Riggs. I knew you'd be back. I'm ready for you this time."

"Fowler, I have Chief Trickey of the Pierce County Sheriff's Department with me. This is his jurisdiction and if you don't want to come out and talk, he'll call in his Special Weapons Assault Team. You'll probably be killed. Is that what you want?" Riggs asked, watching the Chief's reaction and waiting for Fowler's response.

"Fowler, my name is Trickey. I'm Chief of Detectives with the Pierce County Sheriff's Department. I want you to come out with your hands on top of your head. I don't want to have to call out the SWAT Unit to take you into custody. I don't want you to get hurt. Do you hear what I'm saying?"

"I hear you, but I'm not coming out, so you can all go straight to hell," Fowler yelled back and at the same time shot in Trickey's direction, striking the front windshield of Trickey's car. Shattered glass flew in every direction. Trickey reacted instantly and fired a volley of shots in the direction of Fowler's voice.

"Fowler, give yourself up!" Riggs shouted.

There was no answer from Fowler. The night became still with lights coming on in the neighboring houses.

"Come on, Fowler, answer up," Trickey

hollered, looking at Riggs and La Moria, realizing he had possibly killed Fowler.

"Fowler, answer me. Have you been hit?" Trickey shouted over the sirens he could hear in the distance. Someone had obviously called the police.

"Chief, La Moria will stay behind the cars and watch for any movement by Fowler while you and I approach from both sides of the porch at an angle so we don't shoot each other. We'll see if you hit Fowler and if so, if he's still alive," Riggs told Trickey in a low tone, knowing full well why he wanted La Moria to cover them. He was still unsure about Trickey.

"Okay, let's move out now," Trickey said, moving around the back of his car in the direction of the porch.

Riggs started his approach from the opposite side, but his movement was guarded. Fowler could be waiting for them to make a mistake or maybe Trickey would turn on him. He wondered if Trickey had returned fire at Fowler to eliminate him as a witness—a question he concluded would never be answered if Fowler was dead. They had Fowler pinned down, why didn't Trickey wait for the SWAT team? Did he just react to being shot at? If he had, it was understandable. Most cops would have done the same thing, but given the other circumstances, it was questionable.

The approach was slow, but without incident. The beam of Riggs' flashlight fell upon Fowler's body. He had fallen to the floor of the porch with

A Birthday to Die For

his back against the front of the house. There was a large splatter of blood on the wall and holes in the siding. It looked as if the bullets fired by Trickey had struck the siding with some passing through Fowler's body first. There was no movement by Fowler and a closer look revealed no movement of the chest to indicate he was still breathing. The blood was pooling on the porch, surrounding his buttocks and running parallel with his left leg towards the edge of the porch.

Riggs quickly moved to Fowler's body to check his carotid artery. Nothing, no evidence of a heartbeat or the pumping of blood was detected. He could hear no breathing... nothing. La Moria was now beside Riggs. He also checked Fowler's carotid artery and came to the same conclusion as Riggs, Fowler was dead.

"Chief, Fowler is dead. You need to call your boss and the homicide unit. We'll stick around and give statements to your Investigators, but before we do, tell us about your relationship with Rebecca," said Riggs, keeping a close eye on Trickey, who looked like he was about to vomit.

Struggling to speak, Trickey said, "Riggs, I swear I did not have anything to do with the cult. Yes, I did visit Becky and I was quite fond of her. I stopped dropping by to see her after my promotion to chief and that's all I'm going to tell you."

"Well, I suppose that's all I'm going to get out of you, but let me tell you this. All this information will be given to the King County and Snohomish

321

County Prosecutors for their consideration as to whether or not you were involved in a conspiracy regarding the cult and murder of Rebecca Shelby. They may even decide to take you before a grand jury."

"Why would you do that?" Trickey asked, searching Riggs' face for some sign of compassion.

"Because it's my duty and because I don't know if you're telling me the truth. Call your people and we'll give them our statements as it relates to the shooting of Fowler."

"Okay!" Trickey answered, turning away and raising his cell phone to his ear.

While Trickey was on his cell phone, a black and white patrol car pulled up with the emergency lights still flashing. Right behind the patrol car, a black four–door sedan pulled up and a male individual about six feet tall got out of it. Riggs watched as he approached the patrol officer and flashed a badge. The individual then walked over to Trickey and flashed his badge again. They exchanged a few words, then Trickey pointed in their direction.

"You Riggs?" the individual asked.

"Yeah, that's me and this is my partner, La Moria. Who are you and what can we do for you?"

"I'm Special Agent Larry Kent with the Drug Enforcement Administration. I need to know why you were investigating Fowler."

A Birthday to Die For

"What's the DEA's interest in Fowler?" Riggs inquired, looking sideways at La Moria and back at Special Agent Kent. Kent looked like a typical Fed, tall, with thinning gray hair, wearing a black, double–breasted suit, white tie, and spit–polished shoes—hardly the dress for an uncover agent. The white tie was a little too much, something you'd expect to see in an old Mafia movie.

"Can we talk in my car? What I'm about to tell you, I don't want the world to know," Kent said, opening both the front and rear doors on the right side of his vehicle.

Riggs crawled into the right front seat while La Moria took the rear seat. The inside was spotless, as if a suspect of any crime had never sat in the back seat, which didn't surprise either Riggs or La Moria. Their opinion of federal officers lacked a great deal of respect. Their experience with the Feds was that they usually presented a superior attitude, which almost always pissed off the local officers, including them. It was generally felt that if you took the calculators away from them, they couldn't solve anything.

"Okay, we're here. Tell us why you're interested in Fowler, then we'll tell you why we were investigating him." Riggs waited for Kent to respond.

"Well, it's like this. DEA has had Fowler under surveillance for maybe nine or ten years. We also had him tagged in NCIC and FBI records for us to be alerted if another jurisdiction ran a records check on him, which occurred tonight,

323

which is why I'm here now. My information says the records check was made by Chief Trickey, but he told me you two were conducting the investigation."

"We now know why you're here, but you still haven't told us anything important as to why you had him under surveillance in the first place," La Moria said, looking over the back of the front seat, trying to see Kent's facial expressions.

"Fowler has been trafficking drugs up and down the Interstate Five corridor from Mexico to Vancouver, British Columbia for years. He's led us to several drug pushers and suppliers. We've been pretty successful in arresting some of these people without them knowing how we got onto them. What we'd really hoped to accomplish was the break–up and arrest of the Martinez Cartel out of Sonora, Mexico. Some of the information we uncovered while following Fowler was funneled to Interpol and the governments of Mexico and Colombia. The information was to assist them in identifying members of the cartels working in their countries. Now, with Fowler dead, this arm of the investigation comes to a screeching halt."

"I find this very interesting, but what does it have to do with our investigation?" Riggs asked, knowing Fowler's life may have been spared had DEA alerted them beforehand, something DEA and other federal agents usually weren't willing to do. *They always want to keep everything to themselves until it blows up in their faces.*

"I'm not really sure what I've got to offer you

A Birthday to Die For

since I don't really know about your investigation, however, if Fowler was involved, I may be able to fill in some of the gaps, at least as it relates to Fowler. First, you need to tell me about your investigation," Kent explained, noticing some hesitation by Riggs and La Moria.

Riggs and La Moria told Agent Kent about Kae and the fact that she was introduced to a satanic cult by her foster mother, Rebecca Shelby.

Agent Kent listened to the long story regarding their efforts to identify cult members and save the life of Kae Carlson. As soon as he heard the name "Rebecca Shelby," he knew he could provide some information that would be of help to them. Their investigation had led to the arrest of thirteen cult members, but left unexplained the true involvement of Dan Fowler and the whereabouts of Rebecca Shelby for the last twelve to thirteen years.

"I know where Rebecca Shelby has been all those years," Agent Kent said, noticing the surprised look on the faces of Riggs and La Moria.

"Okay, I'll bite. Where was she?" Riggs asked.

"About ten years ago we watched as Fowler was arrested by a Pierce County Detective by the name of Trickey, for possession of marijuana. We didn't want to blow our cover, so we didn't notify Trickey that we had observed his arrest of Fowler or that we had Fowler under surveillance. We did check with the Pierce County Jail a few

325

days later, only to discover that Trickey had not booked Fowler or filed a report on the arrest. We didn't know his reason for not booking Fowler or filing a report, so we assumed he'd made a deal with Fowler to serve as a snitch and turn information for the Sheriff's Department." Kent paused, observing Riggs' impatience as he waited for information he felt was pertinent to his investigation.

"Go on, we're listening," Riggs urged, wanting desperately to clear up the question of Shelby's whereabouts for the last several years.

"Okay, okay, I'm getting to Shelby, just hang on. A little over nine years ago, Fowler traveled to Sonora, Mexico, taking a woman with him. The woman was identified at the border crossing as being Rebecca Shelby. Our counterpart on the other side of the border followed Fowler to the home of the Martinez Family where they last observed the Shelby woman. She did not return to the United States with Fowler, who re–entered the next morning. We didn't see this woman again until about three months ago. We followed Fowler to Sonora where he picked up the Shelby woman and brought her back into the States and to the home of a Beth Williams. We did not see Shelby again. We had thought about contacting her at the home of Beth Williams, but feared alerting Fowler and blowing our surveillance."

"You do realize both Shelby and Williams are dead, with the common denominator being Fowler, don't you?" La Moria asked.

326

A Birthday to Die For

"Yes, I see it now, but our focus was on closing down the Martinez Cartel and the number of lives we could save through the identification of the dealers and pushers Fowler would lead us to. We did not know or have reason to suspect his involvement with a satanic cult," Kent admitted, dropping his gaze. He could feel the stares of Riggs and La Moria as he wondered if he could have handled his surveillance and investigation any differently and prevented the deaths of both Williams and Shelby.

"Is there anything else you can tell us which may be relevant to our investigation while you had Fowler under surveillance?" Riggs asked.

"Not that I can think of at this time. If I remember anything, I'll get back to you right away," Kent answered, extending his hand and shaking the hands of both men before they left his car.

"Thanks for the information. You've certainly cleared up the mystery of what happened to Shelby and why we were unable to find her. We know how and where to get hold of you if we have any further questions," said Riggs. He watched Kent drive away.

"You know, Riggs, I'm not sure I would have handled it any different than Agent Kent under the same circumstances. He's feeling responsible for Shelby's death because he didn't do anything, but then again, how would he have known he needed to do something? This was one of those times when you're damned if you do and damned if you don't," La Moria stated, knowing Riggs shared the same opinion.

"You've got that right, partner. Let's get our statements done and give them to the homicide guys, then get the hell out of here and get some sleep. What do you say?" Riggs asked, looking at La Moria, who looked like he could curl up on the hood of the car and go to sleep right there.

"If you think you're going to get an argument from me, you're wrong. I'm ready to get out of here now. I've got my statement done and I'm ready to go," La Moria mumbled, walking towards Trickey and his homicide investigators.

"Thanks for your statements," Trickey said, placing their statements inside his car, but failing to look them in the eye.

"Chief, we have one more question if you'd care to answer it. Why didn't you book Fowler or file a report when you arrested him for possession of marijuana?" Riggs asked as La Moria looked on.

"With hindsight, I now know I should have, but Ryker talked me out of it. He told me he was going to develop Fowler as a confidential informant, that he believed Fowler was an inside man on some of the local drug operations we had in the county. I believed him. It was my mistake," Trickey admitted, obviously embarrassed and unconvinced that either Riggs or La Moria believed anything he said.

"Thanks for the information, Chief. Good luck on your inquest and with the prosecutors," said

A Birthday to Die For

Riggs. He and La Moria turned and walked away, both anxious to get back home to their families and assure them they were safe.

Chapter 24

Riggs dropped La Moria off at his car in the county garage before turning towards home. The night had passed and the streets were starting to fill with commuters. These people had no idea what had happened over the last thirty–plus hours. They were only worried about getting to work on time, then the end of their shift so they could go home to their families. They knew nothing of the deaths of the two guards, Williams, Shelby, or Fowler, nor did they know that the life of Kae Carlson had been saved.

Riggs thought of Kae as he turned onto Fourth Avenue heading towards the freeway and how frightened she had been for such a long time. Her worries were now over and she needed to know it. She shouldn't have to go through another day of fear, expecting the cult to come for her.

Riggs dialed Dr. Mitchell's number as he drove in the direction of her office.

"Dr. Mitchell. May I help you?"

"Doc, this is Riggs. I'd like to talk to you and

Kae in your office. How long before you can have her there?"

"Thirty minutes. Is this important?" Her question was abrupt.

"I think so. See you in thirty minutes," Riggs shot back, fighting to stay awake.

During the drive to Mitchell's office, Riggs felt good about the meeting he was about to have with the doctor and Kae. He wondered where Paula had been hiding her. Kae had lived in fear for such a long time, through her teen years and into her mid–twenties, always believing the cult would kill her on her twenty–sixth birthday. He looked forward to telling her that the threat was gone and that she could live without fearing the cult any longer. He wondered how she would take the news as he parked his car in front of the doctor's office.

Dr. Mitchell met Riggs at the front door. He could see Kae close behind her, looking over her shoulder. They both appeared anxious and worried.

"Good Lord, what's happened to you?" Paula asked, staring at the dirt on Riggs' unshaven face and the filthy jumpsuit he was wearing.

"Sorry! In my excitement to see you two this morning and deliver the news, I guess I forgot how bad I look. I've been up all night and just didn't have a chance to clean up," Riggs explained, trying to wipe some of the dirt from his face.

"What's the news?" Paula asked, pulling Kae closer to her.

A Birthday to Die For

"Kae, you no longer have to be afraid of the cult and what they'll do to you. Last night, we arrested the High Priest and the other cult members. They're all sitting in jail as we speak. You may have to testify in court at a later date and if that happens, I'll be right there beside you. Are you willing to do that?"

Riggs looked into Kae's eyes as tears started to flow. For the very first time, she smiled. She turned to Paula and threw her arms around her neck, hugging her. The doctor was also crying and laughing at the same time. It was beautiful sight, a scene that made police work rewarding.

Suddenly, he was receiving the same hug that Dr. Mitchell had received and a light kiss on the cheek. "Thank you. Thank you, Detective. I owe you so much," said Kae.

The voice Riggs heard was new. It was different than the voices used by Kae's different personalities. He looked at Paula, who had the biggest smile he had ever seen before. It was almost like she wanted to jump up and down with excitement.

"Kae, is it really you?" Riggs asked, watching Paula, who was shaking her head in the affirmative.

"Yes, it is. I'm so happy!" Kae answered.

Kae's answer sent a warm feeling through his body. He couldn't remember any other time he had a feeling of such accomplishment, something he hoped to experience again sometime.

"Thank you! Thank you! I'm so glad it's over.

If you hadn't agreed to investigate this, I don't know what would have happened. You're a very special person, Detective Riggs, and I'm glad I met you. I can tell Kae feels the same way. I know I can now communicate directly with Kae and we'll be able to get her life back to normal. She now has a chance, thanks to you."

Riggs turned towards the door with a huge smile on his face. As he opened the door, he couldn't help himself. He needed to know where Kae had been staying."Doc, do you mind telling me where you had Kae hidden?"

"She was with my cousin. She lives in those new condos a short distance from the Pike Place Market. The security there is better than Fort Knox."

"I commend you, Doc. If I ever need another safe house, I'll ask your advice."

"You're kidding, of course... aren't you?"

"Doc, you just never know."

As Riggs opened the door and stepped into another day, Kae heard him say, "By the way, Kae, Happy Birthday!"